The Papers of Tony Veitch

The Papers of
Tony Veitch

William McIlvanney

HODDER AND STOUGHTON
LONDON SYDNEY AUCKLAND TORONTO

For Hilda,
who knows why.

British Library Cataloguing in Publication Data
McIlvanney, William
    The papers of Tony Veitch.
    I. Title
    823'.914[F]   PR6063.A237

    ISBN 0 340 22907 1

Hodder and Stoughton Editorial Office: 47 Bedford Square, London WC1B 3DP.

1

It was Glasgow on a Friday night, the city of the stare. Getting off the train in Central Station, Mickey Ballater had a sense not only of having come north but of having gone back into his own past. Coming out on to the concourse, he paused briefly like an expert reminding himself of the fauna special to this area.

Yet there was nothing he couldn't have seen anywhere else. He was caught momentarily in the difficulty of isolating the sense of the place. Cities may all say essentially the same thing but the intonations are different. He was trying to re-attune himself to Glasgow's.

There were a few knots of people looking up at the series of windows where train departures were posted. They looked as if they were trying to threaten their own destination into appearing. On the benches across from him two women surrounded by plastic shopping-bags looked comfortably at home. Nearby a wino with a huge orange beard that suggested he was trying to grow his own bedclothes was in heated debate with a Guinness poster.

'They'll no serve ye, sir.' The speaker was a small man who had stopped to watch the wino. The small man was in his sixties but his face was as playful as a pup. 'I spent an hour last week tryin' tae get a drink there.' He glanced at Mickey before moving on. 'Hope springs eternal in the human chest.'

It was the moment when Mickey arrived in Glasgow, in a city that was about proximity not anonymity, a place that in spite of its wide vistas and areas of dereliction often seemed as spacious as a rush-hour bus. He understood again the expectancy that overtook him every time he arrived. You never knew where the next invasion of your privateness was coming from.

He remembered, too, why he found Birmingham easier. This place was full of enthusiastic amateurs, Sunday punchers. You were as likely to get yours from a bus-conductor or a quiet man in a queue, especially at night. He remembered the words of a song about Glasgow that he liked:

Going to start a revolution with a powder-keg of booze,
The next or next one that I take is going to light the fuse –
Two drinks from jail, I'm two drinks from jail.

Still, it was good to be home, if only for a short trip, and knowing you would be leaving holding a lot more money than you came with. But there was no sign of Paddy Collins.

He crossed to the "Royal Scot Bar" in the station and went through the glass doors. The orange plastic hollows that were some designer's abstract idea of seats held three or four separate people looking vaguely dispossessed of themselves, in transit between incarnations. The place had the gritty untidiness of belonging to no one, a litter bin for wasted time.

But the conversation at the bar, where he remembered to ask for a pint of 'heavy' instead of 'bitter', suggested that this was a local for some. The barmaids might be the explanation for that. One was young and pretty, made up as colourfully as a butterfly. The other was older. She had been pretty. Now she was better than that. She looked mid to late thirties and as if she hadn't wasted the time. She had eyes that suggested you might find Ali Baba's cave behind them, if you knew the password, and had managed to arrive before the Forty Thieves.

Savouring the beer, he wondered about Paddy. He should have been here. It was a bad beginning to the trip. He couldn't imagine that there had been any complications because the whole thing seemed about as risky as mugging a baby in a pram.

A man with spectacles at the bar had got himself drunk enough to imagine that he was on a private line to the

6

barmaid with the eyes. He had found Svengali at the bottom of his glass and was staring at her in a way no woman could resist.

'That's the truth,' he was saying. 'I'm telling you. You've got the most beautiful eyes I've ever seen.'

She looked mistily past him as she dunked a pint-dish up and down on the automatic cleaner. He might as well have been sneezing.

'I'm telling you. The most beautiful eyes I've ever seen.'

She glanced at him.

'Gonny give me the name of your optician? I'll send my man.'

Mickey decided this was long enough. He finished the pint and lifted his travelling-bag. He went downstairs to the lavatory and grudged paying his money at the turnstile. Everything costs nowadays. Inside the cubicle, he unzipped the bag, ferreted in it for the loosely sheathed blade that had black tape for a handle. He put it in the long inside pocket of his jacket. He flushed the toilet.

As he came out, he watched a man who looked like an oil-worker tickling his heavy growth with one of the small, fitted electric razors. It must have been like sandpapering roughcast. He checked his bag into the left luggage and walked out into Gordon Street.

The weight of the knife felt good, as he didn't like going anywhere strange unless he had the message with him. From his other inside pocket he took a piece of paper and checked the address. The best way was to go up West Nile Street and keep going.

It was a pleasant evening. He walked up past Empire House, enjoying the place. He passed two men talking. One was on about his wife's attitude to drink. 'It wid put tits on an adder,' he said.

The entry was pretty scabby. The Italian name he was looking for was three stairs up. He pressed the bell and it made the electric razor sound tuneful. Nothing happened. He pressed it a long time and paused, listening. He heard high-heeled shoes on an uncarpeted hall. The door opened

7

slightly. Her face was preoccupied, as if all of her hadn't arrived back from where she had been.

'You like to come back later, please?'

The accent was Italian all right.

'No,' he said and pushed open the door.

'You just wait a minute, you.'

But he was already inside. Flummoxed, she had tried to hold the door and the pink dressing-gown had opened briefly. He saw that she was wearing only a black suspender-belt, stockings and stiletto-heeled shoes. Whoever was in the bedroom was a shoe-man. He closed the door.

'Friend of Paddy Collins,' he said. 'If you're busy, get unbusy.'

He walked along the hall into a sitting-room-cum-dining-room that had started out with good intentions. There was a wickerwork chair with a red cushion, a moquette chair and settee. There was a white circular table with white chairs. But the room was untidy and dusty. There were unwashed cups on the table, a heel of dried bread.

She had followed him in, re-tying the belt of her dressing-gown. She looked troubled.

'I can't do that,' she said, and didn't believe her own words.

'Oh yes, you can.'

In the doorway a man appeared. He had pulled on his trousers and his belly wobbled over the waistband. His bare feet looked vulnerable. His face had the petulance of somebody used to good service and disappointed.

'Come on,' he said. 'What's going on here?'

'Put yer clothes on,' Mickey said.

'Listen. I paid good money.'

'Ye don't want tae go home with a sore face. Yer wife'll wonder where ye got it.'

'Listen—'

'I've listened all I'm gonny listen. On yer bike. Like now. Unless ye want tae take yer face home in a hanky.'

8

Mickey sat down in the wickerwork chair. The man went back through to the bedroom. The woman made to go after him but glanced at Mickey. He nodded her towards the moquette chair. She sat down. She wasn't bad for a scrubber, Mickey thought, going fat a bit but not quite shapeless yet. The shoes helped her legs, which would have been too heavy otherwise. She took a packet of cigarettes from the coffee-table beside her chair, offered Mickey one. He shook his head. She lit up and they listened to the man getting ready in the bedroom.

He appeared again in the doorway. He looked a lot more impressive in his suit. He seemed to have put on indignation with his clothes.

He said, 'I think—'

'Good for you,' Mickey said. 'Keep doin' that. Now piss off.'

The man went out. Mickey waited till the door closed before he spoke.

'So you're Gina.'

She nodded nervously.

'I'm Mickey Ballater.'

Her eyes widened and she crossed her legs. The dressing-gown fell away and he let his eyes rest on her thigh.

'Where's Paddy Collins? He was supposed to meet me.'

She shrugged and looked at the ceiling. Mickey got up and walked across to her. Leaning over her carefully, he slapped her face very hard. She started to cry. He walked back and sat in his chair. He looked round the room while she composed herself.

'Where's Paddy Collins?'

'He is in the hospital.'

'How?'

'He has been stabbed.'

'How do you know?'

'His brother-of-law is here yesterday. Very angry. He tells me Paddy is stabbed. Serious. He thinks he will die.'

It didn't take long for the images of Paddy Collins that occurred to Mickey to convert from regret to energy, like

9

old photographs thrown on a fire. If Paddy Collins died, the pay-off would be better for himself if he could find Tony Veitch. But there were problems.

'His brother-in-law, Cam Colvin? You're sure it was him?'

'Mr Colvin.'

'That's all we need. How did he know about you?'

'My address is in Paddy's clothes.'

'That's handy. What did you tell him?'

'How Paddy is lookin' for Tony Veitch.'

'It looks as if he found him. What else?'

'Nothin' else. I know nothin' else.'

Mickey found the Scottish inflections in her Italian accent attractive. He began to notice her again.

'Did you tell him about me?'

She shook her head.

'You're sure?'

'Paddy said silence. Or.'

She made a throat-cutting gesture. Mickey almost laughed. It sounded like Paddy all right, good at frightening women and still following the script of an old Edward G. Robinson film.

'What else did Paddy tell you?'

'To do the things he says and be all right.'

That sounded convincing too. Paddy hadn't told Mickey much that mattered either. All he could remember was that Veitch knew Hook Hawkins' brother. And it looked as if Paddy was going to get even better at keeping a secret.

'Where *is* Tony Veitch?'

'Nobody knows still.'

'Come on. Cam Colvin must have been at the hospital.'

'He is in a com- Combo?'

'Jesus Christ. Hidin' in a band?'

'Como. Comma?'

Mickey stared at her.

'Coma. You mean Paddy's in a coma?'

'He doesn't speak.'

'But *you* know Tony Veitch.'

'Not since the trouble with Paddy. Since two weeks nobody can find him.'

'Ach!' Ballater's eyes strafed the ceiling. He pointed at her. 'Listen. Ah didny come up here for the view. Anything you know ye better tell me.'

'Only you are to be my husband for Tony.'

He watched her carefully. She didn't look hard, more like an amateur still slightly surprised to be getting paid for it. When Paddy had set her up for Veitch, the second stage of the ploy with himself appearing as a husband who had to be bought off must have taken her by surprise. She probably couldn't help.

But time was short. If Veitch had done Paddy, buying a box of matches could be a foolishly long-term investment for him, unless he wanted to leave it in his will. Mickey would have to move fast but carefully. He knew this place well enough to know that he didn't know it well enough any more. He remembered another couple of lines of the song:

They're nice until they think that God has gone a bit too far
And you've got the macho chorus swelling out of every bar.

You don't skip through minefields. He needed a bomb-detector. It came to him as a small inspiration that the obvious one was Cam Colvin himself.

'What hospital is Paddy in?' he asked suddenly.

'Victoria Infirmary.'

A baby started to cry. He watched her stubbing out the cigarette, careful of her nails. She got up and he heard her feet on the floor of the hall, then those private noises a mother makes to a child, as if she knows the whole world's against it but she's telling it a secret that will see it through.

He went out of the room and found the phone in the empty bedroom, where the light was still on and the bed was mussed. The voice in the Victoria Infirmary told him that the relatives of Mr Collins were with him. He reckoned he still had a little time.

11

When he came back into the sitting-room she was standing uncertainly at the fire. She turned as he crossed towards her. She contracted slightly as if he was going to hit her. He pulled the belt of her dressing-gown and slipped the garment off to fall on the floor. He pointed towards the bedroom. As she stilted awkwardly ahead of him, he watched her flesh quiver.

'Ye're supposed to be ma wife,' he said. 'We might as well have the honeymoon.'

2

The phone-call seemed just a casual interruption, but then one stone can start an avalanche.

'And then,' Ena had been saying. 'What do you think? The car conked out completely. Just died on me. In the middle of the Clyde Tunnel. And where was Jack? On a case, of course. In Morecambe!'

Laidlaw had heard the story before. He had once suggested to Ena that presumably everyone had heard it, with the possible exception of the North Vietnamese. His rancour came from understanding the bizarre meaning the story had come to assume for Ena: the failure of the internal combustion engine equals marital neglect.

'I'm sorry,' he said. 'I should've been running after it. I just forgot.'

The remark was accepted by the others as being funny as a dirty joke at a funeral. Laidlaw could feel his sense of isolation grow aggressive. He was saved by the phone.

'I'll get that,' he said.

He was careful to moderate the pace of his departure, in case he burned the carpet. The phone was in the hall.

'Hello?'

'Is that Detective Inspector Jack Laidlaw?'

'That's right.'

'Is this *the* Detective Inspector Jack Laidlaw? Doyen of the Crime Squad? Protector of the Poor? The Punters' Choice?'

Laidlaw recognised first the style and then the voice. It was Eddie Devlin of the *Glasgow Herald*.

'Christ, Eddie,' he said. 'Your copy's getting worse. Could you not get your sub-editor to come on the phone with you?'

'It's all this giving the public what it wants. Listen, Jack.

There's somebody in Casualty at the Royal who wants you to go in and see him.'

'Tonight? Did they say whether I was to bring Maltesers or black grapes? What is this, Eddie?'

'No. Straight up, Jack. I got a tip from one of the porters. Old bloke brought in. Chin like a brillo-pad. Smelling like a grape harvest. Just about conscious. But he kept asking for Jack Laidlaw. Must see Jack Laidlaw. Porter in there is one of my tipsters. You know? Well, he's heard me mention you before. So he thinks he better let me know. But I wouldn't think there's anything there for me. He's probably just got the d.t.'s. No offence, Jack. I mean, you're not Errol Flynn. But you've probably got the edge on spiders and pink elephants.'

'Any wounds?' Laidlaw said.

'Didn't seem to be. But I didn't get too much information. He's a trier, this. But he's not too hot on the verbals.'

'When did you get this call, Eddie?'

'Got it at the pub here. Five minutes ago. I thought I'd better let you know before I leave. I want to look in at the Vicky. The Paddy Collins thing. I might get some famous last words. Anyway, it's up to you, Jack.'

'Thanks, Eddie. I owe you one.'

'Aye. When the revolution comes, I'd like a press-card. Cheers, Jack.'

'Cheers.'

Laidlaw put down the phone. The sound of Eddie's voice had been an injection through the ear. Things were happening in the city. But he had guests. Well, Ena had guests. He tried to be fair and decided they wouldn't miss him. His absence would probably be a relief.

Any weekend that Laidlaw wasn't working was pre-arranged for him. Familiar with the anti-social hours policemen kept, Ena had learned to try and compensate. If Laidlaw insisted on treating the calendar the way an alcoholic treats liquor—big benders of absence, brief domestic drying-outs—she was determined to ensure that his off-duty time was spent exclusively with her.

14

She deployed baby-sitters like chessmen—check, mate. She counteracted his thirst for the streets of Glasgow with events carefully bottled like home-made wine, each neatly labelled in advance. 'Friday—Frank and Sally coming.' 'Saturday—Mike and Aileen's party.' 'Saturday—Al Pacino film at La Scala. Baby-sitter arranged.'

Tonight was 'Friday—Donald and Ria.' It wasn't one of her best vintages, a mild cabbagey flavour that never got you high but which might, Laidlaw suspected, rot the social taste-buds over a prolonged period so that you couldn't tell a bromide from the elixir of life. He tried not to have anything against Donald and Ria. It was just that the four of them together gave him the feeling of being involved in field-work on group sedation.

Besides, maybe it was someone who had done him a favour. Maybe it was someone who was dying. Nobody was dying in the room he had left. Maybe four or so of them were dead. But nobody was dying.

He was wearing a red polo-neck and black slacks. Reaching into the cupboard in the hall, he took out his denim jacket and put it on. He might as well announce his intention to the committee. They'd veto it, of course, but he'd made his decision. He felt guilty but that was a familiar feeling.

3

From Simshill in Cathcart, where Laidlaw lived, to the Royal Infirmary in Cathedral Street was a short trip but a big distance. Fortunately, the architecture changed in stages, like decompression chambers, so that you didn't get the bends.

One half of the first gate was open yet and he drove in. A lot of cars were in the parking area but there was plenty of room. Locking the car, he was struck again by the size of the place, three huge linked units, each with its own imposing dome. It seemed to him a castle of black stone. It made illness appear not a leveller but an accolade that admitted you to a Gothic aristocracy.

Across the courtyard was the single-storey Casualty Department like a gatehouse where they examined your credentials. He went in. It was after eleven.

The hallway was the parking place for the blue leather invalid-chairs, maybe thirty of them. On one of them a boy of twenty or so was sitting. But he wasn't an invalid. He looked ill enough to chew railings. The slight skinning on his right cheek only accentuated his appearance of hardness. He was nursing a light jacket the shoulders of which were black with blood, like the patch on a Wimpey reefer. He was waiting for someone.

'Hey, you,' he said as Laidlaw came in. 'Gonny give us a fag?'

Laidlaw looked over curiously. He recognised drink but not drunkenness and the residual aggression from a fight not lost, the adrenalin spin-off that could be captioned 'Who's next?' Laidlaw turned towards the doorway to Casualty.

'Hey, you! Big man. Ah'm talkin' to you. Gi'es a fag!'

Laidlaw went over.

'Here, son,' he said. 'So far you've only managed mild abrasions. Is this you trying for intensive care?'

The boy looked momentarily blank at the medical references but the tone was esperanto.

The boy said, 'Come on. Ah asked a wee favour.'

'So don't make it sound like a threat.'

Laidlaw gave him a cigarette.

'You put the tipped end in your mouth. Then you light the other bit.'

The boy was smiling. Laidlaw turned to the casualty room. It is a single, long, arched place, both basic and ornate, like a Victorian nissen hut. Laidlaw entered it like a time-warp.

The first things he noticed were a couple of ghosts of his youth, two constables whose faces were fresh-laid eggs. Near them stood a group wearing doctors' white coats. Laidlaw hoped they were students. All of them, policemen and doctors, looked young enough to have been given their uniforms for Christmas. Suddenly, Laidlaw was Rip Van Winkle.

He checked the treatment room on the right. While two nurses looked on, a doctor was remonstrating with a boy who was stripped to the waist. From hairline to belt, the boy was blood. The red made the place look like a dressing-room for one of the more preposterous Elizabethan tragedies, say *Titus Andronicus*.

'No problem!' the boy was saying.

Physically, he seemed to be right. Laidlaw could see a long cut on the back of his neck and nothing else. He was obviously enjoying that taste of the heroic your own spilled blood can give you. Probably the worst thing they could do for him would be to wash him clean. Then he would have to settle for himself again. Laidlaw didn't know him but perhaps he would.

Starting opposite the treatment room is a row of cubicles. They presented Laidlaw, as he went, with a succession of tableaux that might have come from a contemporary

17

mystery play. A girl whose eyes were still in shock was holding a bloodstained bedspread, waiting for someone or something. There was a young man with a left eye like a piece of bad fruit. He was protesting hysterically about injustice while a doctor attended him. A woman was crying while her arm was being bandaged. 'He gives me some awfu' kickings,' she was saying. A middle-aged man was explaining to a nurse, 'It's a kinda shifting pain,' while two young policemen looked on. Laidlaw recognised a familiar art, that of postponing arrest by young policemen through the contraction of sudden, mysterious maladies.

Cubicle E, the one Laidlaw knew to be used for delousing, was empty but showed signs of recent use. He recognised nobody, except perhaps the two plain-clothesmen who had just come in. He didn't know them as individuals but he knew that style of moving on tramlines of professional preoccupation. They merged with the rest of the scene as subtly as Mormons.

Looking back along the room, Laidlaw found nothing specific to him, only the city processing its Friday night pain. The place was a confessional. You came here to admit to frailty, brittle bones, thin skin, frangible organs—the pathetic, haphazard machinery we make bear the weight of our pretensions.

Most of all, you came to admit to blood. It was everywhere here, on the people, the swabs, the floor, the coats of the doctors. Like a betrayal, it leaked out of the spurious certainties we make of our natures. Like honesty, it was difficult to look at.

Laidlaw felt here more strongly what he had against that other room he had just come from, where Ena and Donald and Ria were still sitting. It told lies. This one tried to do the same, no doubt, but it at least was compelled to unavoidable admissions of its common humanity. That other room was simply exclusive. It was based on inaccurate assumptions about what people are like. Laidlaw remembered that one of the things he hated most was élitism. We share in everyone else or forego ourselves.

18

'Hullo there, captain.'

He was an elderly man, slightly cut at the edge of his eye and more than slightly drunk. Laidlaw had noticed him wandering along the room accosting people vaguely, an ancient mariner short of a wedding guest.

'You a doctor then, sir? It's ma eye here. Played at headers wi' the pavement. Ye know? Pavement beat me wan–nothin'. Ah would've won if ah hadny been drunk.'

Laidlaw smiled and shrugged.

'Sorry,' he said. 'I'm a stranger here myself.'

The man went on past the partition at the end of the room. Beyond that lay the legendary Room 9, resuscitation room at the Royal, a place that has seen a lot of what there is to see in the way of physical calamity. The man was ushered out again at once by a doctor who directed him back along the casualty room.

'Excuse me,' Laidlaw said. 'I'm looking for someone.'

Laidlaw showed his identification-card. The doctor looked at it, his tongue resting on his front teeth, and nodded, showing nothing. He couldn't have been older than late twenties, bespectacled and shaggy-haired, but already he looked the type who might raise his eyebrows at an earthquake. His coat was speckled brown with the statutory bloodstains.

'A heavy night,' Laidlaw suggested.

'No. This is a quiet one. Although a couple of R.T.A.'s and an M.I. through here.' He nodded towards Room 9. 'So who are you looking for?'

'I don't know,' Laidlaw said.

The doctor didn't show surprise or amusement or interest. He just waited. He was checking the progress of the elderly man along the room. Laidlaw knew that an R.T.A. was a Road Traffic Accident. He thought he'd better not ask about the M.I. The doctor didn't look in the mood to stand in for a medical dictionary.

'I've been told somebody was brought in here asking for me. Asking for Jack Laidlaw. An old bloke. Unshaven. Probably well bevvied.'

19

The elderly man had found the haven of a nurse. The doctor's eyes came to rest on the floor. He looked up at Laidlaw, as if measuring him for an improbable connection.

'You mean the old wino?'

'I might.'

'Yes. That *was* the name, I think. Kept repeating it. I thought maybe it was his own. Could get nothing else out of him. Having trouble with his airways. They had him in E. God, he was filthy. Didn't know whether to dialyse or cauterise. A walking Bubonic.'

'So what happened?'

'He just got worse. Seemed to use the last of himself just getting here. Cleaned him up. They had him in the Lavage Room. Alcohol and Belair were about all they got, I think.'

'So what's wrong?'

The doctor shook his head.

'How about everything?' His eyes were moving around the room again. 'The nearest they got to a diagnosis was imminent death. The respiratory problem was getting worse. Rather than intubate him here, they took him straight to Intensive Care. He's just gone.'

'Where's that?'

'Surgical block. That's—'

'I know.'

'But they'll probably not welcome you.'

'They don't have to,' Laidlaw said.

On the way out, he threw a cigarette to the young man on the invalid chair. Placate the gods.

4

It was cool outside. Laidlaw took his bearings. The middle unit of the main building, the one in darkness, was administration. The unit on the right, nearest the gate, was medical. He went left.

Crossing the courtyard, he took the doctor's point. It probably was a quiet night. It was all comparative. Laidlaw himself had a simple shock-absorber he used to enable him to cope with some of the things he had to look at. He remembered Glaister's *Medical Jurisprudence and Toxicology*—a quiet name for the most harrowing book he had ever looked through. Talking reasonably about horrifyingly exotic deaths, reproducing good photographs of decapitation, strangulation, genital mutilation, its depiction of accidental and compelled brutality made the Marquis de Sade look like the tourist he was. Once you knew that's where we live, you had to accept the need to face what you would rather not see.

Laidlaw accepted. He climbed the curving stair to the first floor. The blue board with white lettering said 'Intensive Care Unit'. He went through the swing doors and found himself in a short, wide corridor, faced with another set of swing doors.

Immediately, a woman looked out from a side-room. Her face became a prohibitive notice, the professional's annoyance at the clumsy intrusion of the layman. Laidlaw felt as if he had a camera round his neck. She came out, pointing herself towards him like a gun.

'Yes?'

'Excuse me. I believe you've just had someone brought in. He was asking to see me. My name is Laidlaw. Detective Inspector Laidlaw.' He showed her his card.

21

'Yes?'

'I wondered if I could see him.'

She gave a short, monosyllabic laugh, like the barking of a distant guard-dog and as indicative of humour. She shook her head in officialese and offered that stern, condescending look that's supposed to make the hordes of the uninformed flee for the longboats.

'Are you serious?'

'Trying to be,' Laidlaw said.

'This is an Intensive Care Unit.'

'I didn't think it was a café. And I'm in a hurry.'

She stared at Laidlaw, presumably reassessing him: not just your average idiot—Nuisance Grade One. In such cases it may prove necessary to provide a façade of minimal facts, preferably incomprehensible.

'We're preparing to use a ventilator. Dialysis may be required.'

'Is he conscious?'

'Not coherently.'

'But conscious.'

'For the moment.'

'Well,' Laidlaw said. 'He wants to see me. It must be important to him. It's what he wants and I assume he still has rights. So. If you don't want me to go in, you'd better find a way to stop me.'

He walked past her. She caught up with him before he reached the double doors.

'Wait here, please,' she said and went in.

In a few moments she came back out and collected a hospital gown from a pile of freshly laundered ones neatly stacked on a shelf. She enjoyed watching Laidlaw trying to work out how it went. Having seen the right films, he managed to decide that it was worn back to front. She didn't offer to help with the tie-strings, so he followed her with his hands behind his back, feeling he was infringing the Duke of Edinburgh's copyright.

Once beyond the second double doors, she said, 'Wait here, please.'

The room was dim. Down the right-hand side there was a row of glass-partitioned cubicles, from some of which came muted sounds. You got the sense that life was lived on tiptoe here. A couple of nurses moved almost soundlessly around, vestal virgins of this inner sanctum.

The god appeared to be technology. Across a television monitor ran three recurring serrated lines. In the middle of the room, like an altarpiece, was the only patient Laidlaw could see. He lay terrifyingly still, plugged into a ventilating machine, an aerated corpse. Watching him, Laidlaw understood something he had heard somewhere, that if such patients aren't oiled and turned every two hours, they develop bedsores.

From where he stood now, Laidlaw saw the people in Casualty as extras with delusions of grandeur. Their declarations of their nature seemed outrageously crude. Their stridency was apprentice stuff. This man bore witness to all of us without melodrama. He was honed to the act of breathing. He made no further claims, his humility was absolute. Pull a plug and he died.

Some sounds were coming from the first cubicle on the right. Laidlaw assumed that was where his man must be. Sure enough, the sister who had treated him like bacteria was now beckoning him into the cubicle.

Coming round the partition with some trepidation, he experienced the shock you feel when you see death engaged with someone you know. All the past confident moments count for nothing. You realise that you want death always to be anonymous. Otherwise, it's got a fix on you.

He saw the confirmation of a suspicion that had already been forming. It was Eck Adamson. And if he wasn't dying, Laidlaw was immortal.

A doctor came between Laidlaw and the bed. He was Indian, young and delicately handsome. His voice was a startlingly pleasant contrast to the gutturals of Glasgow, soft with the consonants and original with the intonations, a sari in Townhead.

'Now you may see your friend, if you wish. We are about

23

to put him on a ventilating machine. The thing which is the most essential at the moment will be to stabilise the breathing. If you can get through to him, you must see if you can learn what has happened.'

Laidlaw nodded. The first thing that struck him was that this was the cleanest context in which he had ever seen Eck. They made you nice for dying. Only the several days' growth hinted at the kind of life Eck had come from; that and the eyes. Always jumpy, they had now gone completely over the top, darting crazily, as if Eck knew finally that the world was out to mug him. The doctor and nurses were waiting to relieve him of himself.

'Eck,' Laidlaw said. 'It's Jack Laidlaw.'

As he repeated it, Eck's eyes passed him several times but kept coming back until they hovered on him, still mobile, but at least moving within the orbit of Laidlaw's presence. They didn't settle on his face but seemed to take in different parts of him, as if Eck was piecing Laidlaw together like a jigsaw. Eck was trying to speak.

'Right,' Laidlaw heard.

'Right,' he replied.

'Right.'

'Right.'

Eck's head jerked in distress.

'Write it doon,' Laidlaw thought he was saying.

Laidlaw found an envelope in his pocket and took out a pen.

'What happened to you, Eck?'

But he might as well have tried to talk to a teleprinter. Eck was receiving no messages. On the last of himself he was sending out information. His pain was obvious. The way he dragged the words out past it suggested they were very important to him. Listening, Laidlaw wondered why.

Eck was incoherent. He spoke like someone after a stroke, afflicted with that slow-motion glottal drunkenness that compounds the grief of physical trauma by rendering its expression of itself idiot. Out of the distorted mouthings,

24

like a record played too slow, Laidlaw thought he could decipher one repeated statement. He wrote, more out of respect for the disintegrating identity he had known than because of any significance he saw in the words, 'The wine he gave me wisny wine.'

He could catch nothing else. It was like eavesdropping on a riot. Eck's desperate distress intensified and the doctor stepped forward.

'The gentleman can wait in my room,' he said.

A nurse led Laidlaw to the end of the ward and showed him into a small place partitioned off from the rest. There was just enough room to lie down in. Laidlaw sat on the single bed.

He looked at the back of his envelope, the last will and testament of Eck Adamson. He remembered reading about a cleaner who had worked in a lawyer's office. On her deathbed she had regurgitated swathes of legal Latin. Eck was getting close.

It was maybe fitting that what looked like being Eck's last piece of information should come across like Linear B. As a tout, he had never been too useful. But Laidlaw had always liked him and once, in the Bryson case, he had helped Laidlaw more than he could know.

Things had gone quiet beyond the partition and the doctor appeared. He shook his head.

'I am sorry,' he said with that formal timing a foreign language can give.

Laidlaw put the envelope in his pocket.

'He was your friend?'

Laidlaw thought about it.

'Maybe I was about as close as he got. What did he die of?'

'I can't tell at the moment. Who is he?'

'Alexander Adamson. He was a vagrant. In the winter he slept in doss-houses. Summer, wherever he could. I don't know of any relatives. What an epitaph.'

Laidlaw remembered one night finding Eck sleeping across a pavement grille outside Central Station. He was using the heat that came up from the kitchen of the Central

25

Hotel. These were the obsequies to that bleak life, a few sentences between strangers.

'It wasn't bad for him at the end,' the doctor said. 'He died quietly.'

Laidlaw nodded. Like a leaf.

'I want a fiscal post mortem.'

'Of course. It is procedure.'

'Today? I would like it today.'

'We shall have to see.'

'Yes. We will.'

On his way out to the car, Laidlaw looked in at Casualty again. The boy with the bloodstained jacket was gone. A nurse showed him Eck's things in a brown envelope: an empty tin with traces of shag, a stopped watch, seven single pounds and a grubby piece of paper. Unfolding the paper, Laidlaw read a handwritten statement in biro.

The Puritan Fallacy is that there can be virtue by default. You do the right thing because you don't know any worse. That is society's Woolworth substitute for morality. True morality begins in choice: the greater the choice, the greater the morality. Only those can be truly good who have prospected their capacity for evil. Idealism is the censorship of reality.

Ranged neatly beneath that statement were an address in Pollokshields, the names Lynsey Farren and Paddy Collins, the words 'The Crib' and the number 9464946 in black biro.

Laidlaw's first responses were practical. He noted that the handwriting was the same throughout and then that the written paragraph was in blue ink. It suggested to him that the bit of hand-woven philosophy had just happened to be on the piece of paper when the same person had added the other information. For the use of Eck?

Certainly the first part had surely not been meant for Eck. Beyond perhaps an instinctively Pascalian response to the two-thirty, Eck had never evinced any interest in philosophy. But neither did the addresses seem to fit.

26

Pollokshields, where the money grows, was hardly Eck's territory. The number was meaningless to Laidlaw. Only 'The Crib' made any kind of sense.

Then, like humanity supplanting professionalism, a slight chill came over Laidlaw as he held the piece of paper. Trying to locate where the feeling came from, he read over the paragraph again. Perhaps it was just that he sensed a dangerously distorted version of that Calvinist self-righteousness that forms like an icicle in the hearts of a lot of Scots. He wondered who had given Eck this strange message.

Looking up, he had his gloom partly dissipated by the pleasant round face of the nurse, who was preoccupied in doing practical things. She reminded him he'd better do the same.

'Excuse me,' he said. 'I need this. You want me to sign for it?'

5

Licensing laws can be fun. Without them, the arcane joy of after hours' drinking would never have been known—that sense of membership of a very temporary club. There is a Yukon cabin romanticism to it, while real time slobbers like a toothless wolf at the locked door.

It was that kind of atmosphere in "The Crib", a strangely named pub not really suitable for children, where on a good night Behemoth would have been no better than even money.

It was half-past midnight. Outside, the streets of the Saracen, a tough district north of the city centre, were quiet. Inside, five people had formed an impromptu pentagram and summoned forth an instant celebration of themselves.

One of them was the regular barman, Charlie, who had moved here from a pub in the Calton. He was in his fifties and wise beyond his years. Although he had spent most of his life among violent men, his bulky body's hardest fights had been with beer barrels.

The secret of his unmarked face's longevity was a delicate sense of hierarchy. Like a Glasgow Debrett, he knew the precise mode of address for any situation. There was the further safeguard of working for a man whose name could be worn like a livery made of armour. Being associated with John Rhodes of the Calton was a bit like having Securicor as a taxi-service.

It was an advantage Charlie never abused. Even now, in the security of the locked pub, he measured his participation carefully, knowing how enjoyment leaves you open. He had drunk a couple of moderate whiskies and joined quietly in the chorus of one of the songs.

It wasn't that he knew his place so much as he knew where it wasn't, which was hospital. This was Dave McMaster's event. Charlie was content to listen to yet another of Dave's stories.

'So they're along at the Barras, right? One of them's dressed up as Santa Claus. A hundred-weight of cotton wool an' Army surplus wellies. The ither yin's got the toays, things like dinky cars an' half-chewed bubblegum. Santa lures them in an' his hander takes the money. All day they're at it, an' all the time they're nippin' intae the pub tae get mair central heating. Well. By about shuttin' time they're in again. Divvyin' up. Only the helper's doin' a two-tae-me, wan-tae-you job on Santa. Santa gets slightly annoyed. Wallop! Can ye imagine it? A present from S. Claus. Then he's tattooing his ribs wi' the wellies. Swearin' enough to set his beard on fire. Funniest bit wis when the bouncer threw him out. Santa's lyin' on the pavement an' the bouncer's shouting, "Ye're barred, Santa! Ye're barred." The barring of Santa Claus.'

Charlie shared the laughter but not the abandonment that went with it in the others. Charlie wasn't just participating in the evening, he was understanding it. The other three were paying court to Dave.

The girl was his. Every time he talked, her eyes ate him whole. She laughed at his jokes as if laughing was a contest. With her polite accent, her fancy clothes and her blonde sophistication, she belonged in "The Crib" like a virgin in a brothel. But then there had to be more to her than first impressions suggested. She had been around Dave for a month now. Whatever was turning her on to him, it couldn't be his suave manners.

Dave McMaster was a new version of an old type. Charlie had seen it many times, the tearaway with ambitions to have a reputation that went further than his friends, to promote violence from a hobby to a career.

In a fight between two young rival Possil teams one night, Dave had gone berserk with a bayonet, scattering more than six of them. Charlie could imagine how he must

29

have wakened up next morning to a reputation as demand·ing as a heroin-addiction. He had progressed from there but Charlie still had his doubts about him. Dave had come on fast. He was now right-hand man to Hook Hawkins, who among other things minded four pubs roughly in the Saracen area for John Rhodes, including "The Crib". Dave was ambitious. What Charlie wondered was whether his am-bition wasn't too heavy for him.

None of the others seemed to be sharing Charlie's doubts. They were as critical as a fan-club. Besides the girl, there was Macey, a small-time break-in man, and a boy called Sammy that Charlie didn't know. Probably Macey was trying to get his reputation to go further than it could on its own by giving it a tow from Dave's.

Sammy was a tourist, somebody Macey had introduced. He looked like a cousin from the country. His eyes were shining with appreciation of Dave's toughness. He was probably the kind of gruesome simpleton who would have bought a ticket for a road accident. He desperately wanted to be one of them but he couldn't help himself. He was so square you could have laid him out and used him for a table.

He had tried to tell a funny story and it came out roughly like someone describing a golf-ball hollow by hollow. But he could sing, a light, sweet voice that didn't deserve him. It had occurred to Charlie that Sammy should have stayed home in bed and just sent tapes.

'It's true,' Dave was saying. 'When they went to see him, he had a turning-lathe in the bedroom. Didny even know what it was for. Just stole it in case it might be valuable. First time he knew whit it was was when he heard the charge.'

Their laughter didn't measure the funniness of what was being said, just the authority with which Dave had said it. He had a confidence which could make an atmosphere where anything he said grew funny, although transplanted into a retelling it might wither into nothing. They were still laughing when the knock came at the street door.

Dave made a face into the pause.

'Check it, Charlie,' he said. 'Unless it's somebody special, they're bombed out.'

Charlie went through and opened the door, keeping it on the chain.

Through the gap, he saw Cam Colvin. There were two people behind him but Charlie couldn't see who they were. He didn't have to. Cam Colvin was enough. Charlie wished John Rhodes were here.

'Mr Colvin. Can ah help ye?'

'You can help yourself by opening the door. Unless you want your pub to be open-plan.'

Charlie knew his duties, and they didn't include standing up to Cam Colvin. Dave had said only to let him in if it was somebody special. Cam qualified. Charlie slid the chain.

Behind Cam, Mickey Ballater and Panda Paterson came in. Mickey had been out of Glasgow for a while, was less well known than he had been, but Charlie had a long memory. Panda was named after his deceptively comforting appearance, a hulking heaviness topped by a roundly innocent face. He might be a teddy-bear but the claws were real.

Charlie's face showed none of his surprise at their presence. Neither of them was a Colvin man. Charlie, aware of the imminence of Paddy Collins' death, could only suppose that they had turned up at the Vicky to prove their goodwill to Cam, like a retrospective alibi. But surely Ballater didn't come up from England just to do that. Both of them had known Paddy Collins but that didn't explain why they were here. Charlie didn't like it. He had a fairly precise knowledge of which people belonged with which and strange groupings always upset him. They usually meant trouble. He locked the door and followed them through and went behind the bar.

Cam Colvin stopped a little way from where the others were sitting. They saw a medium-sized man in a Crombie coat. All his clothes looked expensive but just a bit behind current fashions, as if he had been reading 'The Tailor and

31

Cutter' in a dentist's waiting-room. His hair was slightly long but carefully cut. Charlie wondered if they knew what they were looking at.

In the shifting league-table of professional Glaswegian hard men, established informally by those who know, in pub conversations and awesome anecdotes, Cam Colvin was currently at the top. The qualities most commonly cited as justifying his place there, like goals for and goals against, were his extreme viciousness and his absolute caution. He had a name for acting with brutal exactitude, like a paranoid computer.

For him to threaten his way into a pub minded by John Rhodes didn't indicate carelessness. It meant there was something very serious on his mind.

'Cam,' Dave said. 'Charlie, get the man a drink. What's it to be?'

Charlie didn't move. He knew who was giving the orders.

'I'm looking for Hook.'

'He's not in the night, Cam. What's it about?'

'I didn't say I was looking for you. I'll explain it to him. Where is he?'

The voice was light and flat and it made the talking clock sound effusive.

'Not a clue,' Dave said. 'Ah don't think he's at home the night. Can ah give him a message?'

Cam walked past Dave through to the other room. He came back into the doorway.

'Put on the lights,' he said to Charlie.

Charlie did. While Cam was gone, Panda Paterson was studying the girl as if she was on the menu.

'What's *your* name?' he asked her.

'None of yer business,' Sammy said.

The sound of his voice shocked even him. It had happened by a kind of spontaneous combustion, an accident of the atmosphere. He had become so involved in his awareness of this place, which he had heard of, in the presence of Dave and the others that he had spoken somehow from his sense of them rather than himself. He was left looking round

32

glumly as if trying to find whose voice had come out of his mouth. Panda was studying him like a culture.

'Her name's Lynsey,' Dave said. 'An' she's mine.'

Panda looked at him.

'Ye're goin' wi' a male chauvinist pig, hen,' he said. 'You're Dave McMaster.'

'Ah know who ah am. Who are you?'

Dave's brash ignorance was one of the things about him that worried Charlie. Some day he was going to drown himself playing at Canutes.

'Ah'll have a pint of heavy,' Panda said.

Charlie was filling it out as Cam Colvin came back through. His face showed nothing. He looked at Dave.

'Tell Hook I want to see 'im,' he said. 'Macey. You can bring me word. Where and when. But don't be slow. Tell Hook that.'

Panda Paterson took his pint from the bar. He crossed as if to join the others and began to pour the pint very carefully over Sammy's head. Charlie suspected Panda was staging an exhibition for Cam's benefit. Mickey Ballater's face was impenetrable.

It was a long, long time happening. It was an act of astonishing cruelty, far more sadistic than striking him would have been. The slower that gentle decanting was, the more fully it demonstrated Sammy's abjectness. The others watched him pass from shock to a strangled anger to a smothered attempt to get up, to a terrible understanding of himself. He closed his eyes and became as still as a corpse. By the time Panda Paterson almost solicitously shook out the last dregs, Sammy's shame was in poster colours. The others could hardly bear to look. Panda laid the glass gently on the table, as empty as Sammy's sense of himself.

Cam Colvin had been looking on disinterestedly, seemingly preoccupied with something else.

'Tell Hook,' he said and went out, followed by the other two.

Dave didn't let the silence settle.

'Get him a cloth!' he said contemptuously.

33

It wasn't clear where the contempt was aimed. While nobody else moved, Charlie brought a dishcloth and wiped Sammy the way a mother would.

'Tae hell wi' it, son,' Charlie said. 'Nothin' wis the right thing to do. Ah would've done the same maself. That wis a catchweights contest. You could never be as big a bastard as he could. That's pure bastard. When he wis wee, he wis showin' old women *half-way* across the road. Leave it to John.'

The humanity of Charlie's voice began to thaw the room. The girl said, 'Phoo.' Macey touched Sammy on the shoulder.

'Forget it, kid,' he said, which was like throwing a strip of elastoplast to a napalm victim. 'So what was that about?'

'Trouble,' Dave McMaster said. 'For somebody.'

6

Ena had an old script ready for him getting back. It was the one where she was Rome and he was Attila the Hun. His share of the lasagna lay vandalised with absence, congealed in its own grease. The guests were gone, Ena hinting at a flowering of deep communication he had missed. With his last look at Eck's dead face still fresh in his mind, he had trouble remembering his lines.

She said the bit about his social poise. This time he was as suave as King Kong. She was so genteel she should be sewn on to a sampler. He was a monument to selfishness. Faced with concern like hers, everybody could die of frost-bite. He had certainly done his utmost to make Donald and Ria hate him. With enemies like them, who needed friends?

The vaudeville of mechanical insult over, Ena went to bed and Laidlaw half-filled a glass with Antiquary and topped it up with water. He went to the phone, hoping he would be lucky enough to get somebody he knew and got on with—not the easiest trick, he thought ruefully. He was lucky. The Duty Fiscal was Robbie Evans.

'Yes, Jack. What news from the front?'

Laidlaw told him about Eck.

'You suspect more than natural causes?'

'It just seems possible.'

'Like what?'

'Poison?'

'How could you tell? Isn't that what he's been doing to himself for years?'

'Just as long as he did it to himself. There'll be a fiscal p.m. anyway. I would just like to make sure it happens as soon as possible. Like this morning. He looked as if he might have

35

been a fair time dying. If somebody did do him, any clues are going to be cold. I'd like to try for them before they get deep-frozen.'

'We'll see to that. Ruined your night, did it?'

'Aye. It didn't help Eck's a lot either.'

'You can phone for word tomorrow, Jack.'

'Thanks.'

He sipped some of his Antiquary and went up to check the children. After he had seen bad things, that was a compulsion with him. He remembered an occasion years ago when he was still in uniform, not in Glasgow, and he had been the one to arrive first at the scene of a murder. The victim was a homosexual who had been tortured by two young men he had picked up in a lavatory and taken to his flat. One of the young men was an apprentice butcher and for a finale, after the homosexual was strangled, he had cut him from groin to breast-bone and gutted him like a chicken. The butcher had said later, 'He wisny normal.'

At that time, Moya had just been born and Laidlaw had found himself checking up on her so often it felt like sentry-duty. Big bad world, I've got my eye on you.

Tonight they were fine. Moya, at eleven, slept almost smiling, as if she had a secret. It looked like a sensuous one. Her body was softening these days and her face withdrawing into thoughtfulness. The good problems were coming. At ten, Sandra looked younger than her age, still seemed to have ambitions to make it as a boy. In the box-room Jackie lay in his usual elaborate abandon, like an accident. He was seven. They were fine.

He came downstairs and took a header into his drink, filled out another. He wondered about reading something. But everything seemed a bit far from Eck lying dead in the Royal. He thought about Eck. He felt a small need to tell someone who might care. Everybody's dying should matter to somebody. The more people who cared, the closer you came to some kind of humanist salvation. There was no other he could believe in.

He remembered that since he had worked with Brian

Harkness they had talked to Eck a few times. Brian had met Eck on the Bryson case.

Laidlaw went to the phone. It was early morning already but he rang. It took a lot of ringing before Brian's father answered. Brian wasn't home. Laidlaw apologised. Brian's father was a nice man who had met Laidlaw several times and who seemed to exempt him from his general dislike of policemen. He took the word about the death and said he would tell Brian the earlier time at which Laidlaw wanted to meet him. But he didn't know Eck.

Laidlaw put down the phone and took Eck's piece of paper from his hip pocket. Holding the paper, he remembered the money. For Eck to have seven pounds was as unusual as a win on the football pools. That number had to be a telephone number, three digits for the district. He dialled it. He let it ring fifteen times. There was no answer.

That not very surprising fact took Laidlaw's depression further down. If the intensive care unit had seemed like rock bottom, this was potholing. The silence at the other end of the line had felt absolute, as if he had been trying to telephone God. That recurrent ambush of despair about how little we care for one another trapped him again and wiped out any sense of achievement he could imagine.

Everybody mattered or nobody did. He remembered as a teenager wrestling with lofty matters as if he was the first person ever to think of them, what he thought of as his wherefore-are-we-put-upon-this-earth phase, when he sometimes wandered around with a head like a billboard containing its caption of the day: Is There A God? What Is The Meaning Of Life? He could smile at it now but it was a rueful smile.

The truth was that some of the impossibilities he had come up against then still haunted him. He could recall giving up any belief in an overall meaning to living because any such meaning would have to be indivisible, unequivocally total, giving significance impartially to every drifting feather, every piece of paper blowing along a street.

Eck was like one of those pieces of paper. You couldn't

say the meaning of things was elsewhere and Eck was irrelevant. That was a betrayal. All we have is one another and if we're orphans all we can honourably do is adopt one another, defy the meaninglessness of our lives by mutual concern. It's the only nobility we have.

Laidlaw tried to reinstate his energy by declaring war, over his whisky, on all brutalisers of others, all non-carers. Yet the very thought embarrassed. He would have been such a compromised champion, a failure opposing failures. He admitted to himself that he wanted at this moment to phone Jan at the Burleigh Hotel and felt a double guilt. There was the guilt of being tempted to use Jan to soothe him now when he gave her so little of his life. There was the guilt of betraying Ena. The compromise of his own life, so hurting to others, appalled him.

But he couldn't think of anybody else who would care about Eck enough to find out what had happened to him. Laidlaw had better try. Pathetically, it seemed to him, he could only think of small things to do. He would check the address and the names. He would phone that bloody number till somebody answered. He would get a post-mortem tomorrow.

At least tomorrow he could tell Brian, somebody who would know who was dead. It would swell the mourners' roll by one. But the thought still left him with an angry sadness.

7

Harkness woke up into a problem of his own. It had become his constant companion lately, the ante-room to every day. When was he going to get married? Finding an answer was complicated by the second question which always came attached to the first, like a Siamese twin: who was it he was going to marry?

Wearily, he went through his early morning programme of thoughts, what he did instead of press-ups. He was fed up scuffling around. He wanted to get married. He fancied Morag. He fancied Mary. He didn't want to give up Morag. He didn't want to give up Mary. He wanted to get married. He was fed up scuffling around.

His present situation confirmed it. He was lying on a couch in his underpants with a blanket over him. The couch was an insomnia-machine. It was cunningly constructed so that one arm clamped your head at a right angle to your body while the other etched a moquette pattern on your calves. His feet stuck out beyond the blanket and the big toe of his right foot, turned black when he stubbed his foot playing mid-field for the Crime Squad, seemed to accuse him of pretending to be younger than he was. He was twenty-seven already. His toenail looked like falling off. What next?

He had worked out where he was. At first he had thought it might be a girl's place. He had gone to the disco at 'Joanna's' last night. (What was he trying to do, find a third possibility?) But then he recognised the inimitable decor of Milligan's poky flat, a kind of waiting-room baroque.

The walls were dun and featureless, the furniture was arranged with all the homeyness of a second-hand saleroom and clothes were littered everywhere. It wasn't a room so much as a suitcase with doors.

39

There was the spatter of something hitting a frying-pan in the tiny kitchen and then Milligan's voice cheerfully kicking 'My Way' to death.

Harkness smiled. When he had worked under Detective Inspector Milligan in North Division before going to the Crime Squad he had become familiar with the infectious breeziness of Milligan, as if the world was a parade arranged for his benefit. Thinking of the tension of Laidlaw's nature, Harkness thought he could understand why his present superior and his past one disliked each other. Their natures were a mutual contradiction.

Milligan padded through, wearing a dark blue towelling Marks and Spencer's bathrobe. It looked old enough to have been bought in their Penny Bazaar. He was laying the table. Always slow to come to the surface, Harkness thought he should at least show willing. He opened his mouth to speak and it came out distorted by a yawn, something like 'Narrgh'.

'Can I quote you on that?' Milligan said. 'You were well on last night. What did you do? Fall into a vat?'

'Drowning my problems.'

'What problems? Your only problem is you don't have enough.'

Seeing Milligan bursting out of his acres of towelling, his rumpled hair going grey, his big face looking as if it had taken as much of life's pounding as Beachy Head, Harkness felt suitably naive in the matter of problems. He was looking at a broken marriage, a stalemated career and a quality of survival that would have whistled through an air-raid.

'I keep thinking I have,' he said modestly and got up. His feet were frozen. 'Thanks for taking me in last night.'

'I thought you might have an extra bird with you. Like a carry-out.'

Going through to the bathroom, Harkness washed himself and used Milligan's only remaining blade, which was like shaving with a hacksaw. When he was dressed, he asked if he could use the phone.

'If they haven't cut it off.'

40

He phoned his father to see if there were any messages. It annoyed him that he hadn't been there to talk to Laidlaw about Eck. He assured his father he would be in plenty of time to meet Laidlaw. He thought of phoning Simshill but, seeing five-to-eight on his watch, he let it go.

Breakfast was a penance. The ham and eggs were doubtless good but he had only been able to clean his teeth with his forefinger and the crap still in his mouth made everything taste like feathers. Milligan's ferocious brightness didn't help.

'I think I'll get married,' Harkness said more or less to himself across Milligan's monologue.

'Why not do something more sensible? Like playing Russian Roulette.'

'You don't recommend it?'

'I hope you're not proposing. Just because I'm good at making breakfast. Actually, I'm spoken for. Wife and me are thinking of patching it up. True. I was with her for two or three hours last week and I didn't feel like hitting her once. It must be love. She still hasn't filed for a divorce, you know. It's a sin. Once I've been there, I spoil them for everybody else.'

'When's this happening?'

'Give it time. She'll surrender. The kids are driving her daft. Use the house like an adventure playground. They need a father's firm foot. Be a pity to leave my wee, snug bachelor-pad, mind you.'

'You could force yourself.'

'This could be the last time you get to crash down here. And that's only the beginning. I'm going to show these bastards how a real polisman operates. I'll embarrass them into promoting me.'

'How do you mean?'

'You know Paddy Collins?'

'In the Victoria Infirmary? The stab-victim.'

'Stab-victim? He's got more holes than Haggs Castle. They didn't know whether to bandage him or play a round on him. He's been a dead man for days. They were just waiting for him to admit it. Last night he admitted it.'

41

'You know who did it?'

'No. But I will. I was with him a few times, but he never recovered consciousness. You know who he was?'

'Paddy Collins.'

'Aye. And Hitler was a housepainter. His name's just Paddy Collins, but you know what his connection is? Cam Colvin's brother-in-law. You know what that means?'

'Paddy Collins might not be the only dead man.'

'This could really be something big.' Milligan's blatant enthusiasm disconcerted Harkness, like someone offering guided tours of the mortuary. 'Imagine it. I saw Cam's sister at the hospital. She's really into the grief-stricken widow routine. She's had days to rehearse it. She's getting good. Great, isn't it? Her man's always been a bigger shit than two tons of manure. Nasty to birds, nasty to blokes. Living off Cam Colvin's reputation. Anybody who knew him would've voted him the man most worthy to be a corpse. But put him on a hospital bed and shove a tube up his nose, and it's bring on the angel choirs. She's going to make it seem like the end of the world. And Cam's not going to like that. He's going to want to give her a shroud to dry her tears. With somebody inside it. He can't let it go.'

Harkness shook his head, absorbing the implications.

'It makes Jack's worry seem less than major,' he said.

'Who, Laidlaw? He still your neighbour? St. Francis of Simshill. What's he up to?'

'I phoned my father there. Jack had been on the phone for me. Eck Adamson died in the Royal last night.'

'That's a worry? It's about as sad as breaking a bottle of meths. He must've been pure alcohol by now. Of course, maybe to Laidlaw he was just another example of suffering humanity. Christ, we've all got our worries, right enough. Anyway, as a tout Eck was about as much good as a budgie. He could hardly repeat what you told him, never mind tell you anything else. But I've got a real tout. Remember Macey?'

Harkness nodded. When he worked with Milligan, he had met Benny Mason several times. Macey had been what

policemen call 'a good ned'—professional, unviolent,
prepared to play the percentages and take the odds the
way they fell without complaint. He seemed to regard his
transition to informer as a self-determined promotion.
He wore it well, his nerves seemingly unaffected by the
hazards of inhabiting that criminal limbo. Harkness had
heard recently that on a break-in when an ill-informed
policeman chased Macey and caught him, Macey had calmly
explained, 'Ye're no' supposed tae catch me. Ah telt ye
about this job. Ah'm the one that jist manages tae get
away.' He did.

'You're still using him?'

'Never to stop,' Milligan said. 'I've got his balls in a vice.
He's mine. He's in with Hook Hawkins. I've told him he's
got to come up with something about Paddy Collins. I'm
sure he can. He better.'

'Just watch he doesn't make it up.'

Milligan laughed.

'Be like ordering his headstone. Nah. Macey's not that
simple. He'll do me a wee turn. I'm seeing him tonight.
Guess where?'

Harkness shrugged.

'The Albany.'

'The Albany? You're kidding. That's a helluva place to
meet a tout.'

'Isn't it?'

'Like asking him to advertise.'

'Isn't it? He was going to renege. Couldn't believe it.
Shouting down the phone. But I made him agree. I'll bet he
had to wade through his actual excrement to get out the
phone-box.'

'Why?'

'I want him feeling vulnerable. As if he's left his cover in
the house.' Milligan winked. 'You in a hurry?'

'Aye,' Harkness said. 'Jack wants me to meet up with him
early.'

'You going to get these dishes? I'll get ready. I want to be
busy-busy today. Listen. I'll be in "The Admiral" late this

43

afternoon, if you've the time. We could have a jar. If your guts have recovered.'

When they went down into the street, Harkness looked up at a sky like a dustbin-lid. It fitted his hangover. He was wishing he could share Milligan's joviality, when a long-haired young man in jeans, looking back, bumped into Milligan. The young man looked at Milligan without apologising.

'Fuck off before I step on you,' Milligan said and started laughing.

Harkness remembered something Laidlaw had said about Milligan's laughter—'It's the sound of bones breaking.'

He settled for his hangover.

8

In the bar of "The Gay Laddie", John Rhodes' favourite pub in the Calton, the beginning—and some said the end—of the East End of Glasgow, there was what felt like a crowd. There was Macey and Dave McMaster and Hook Hawkins. The rest of them were John Rhodes.

In spite of his experience, Macey never failed to be awed by John. It was nothing specific. It wasn't his size, which was considerable. It wasn't just the crazy lightness of his eyes, blue as a brochure sea. There was no external you could finally attach the feeling to. Perhaps it had something to do with the sense of accumulated past violence John carried, bad places been to and come back from. The effect his presence had on Macey was of conveying danger, as if his life was a matter of juggling with liquid oxygen. And always the feeling found itself relegated to recurring mirage by his easy naturalness.

Looking at John now, pouring four mugs of tea from the pot that Dave had brewed in the back, Macey was freshly aware of the combustible contradictions that were John Rhodes. Their presence here was part of them. They were meeting in the pub because John would allow no intrusion from the violent ways he made his money to disturb the home where his wife and two daughters might as well have had a bank-manager as the breadwinner.

The thought of that strangeness was echoed by the strangeness of the place. It was about half-past nine in the morning and, slanting down from the high windows that were slits of glass reinforced with mesh, the shafts of light were constellated with motes and gave the still, quiet pub an incongruous solemnity, like a chapel with a gantry. The ritual of the tea completed, the high priest spoke.

'Hook,' he said. 'Tell me the truth. You know whit Cam Colvin's on about?'

Hook Hawkins appealed to the bar. His upturned head moved as if deliberately displaying the scar that ran down his left cheek and under his chin. Some said his nickname came from that, because it had been given to him by a man with a hook for a hand. Others said the name belonged to his brief career as a boxer.

Remembering his meeting tonight with Ernie Milligan, Macey had more reason than his natural curiosity for paying careful attention. He knew that Hook and Paddy Collins had once had a fall-out but he had never heard why. He wondered if it had been about something which wasn't really over. But he found Hook's performance convincing.

'Honest to God. Ah don't know whit it's all about, John. Ah don't know.'

'Paddy Collins is dead,' John said. 'You don't know anythin' about that?'

'We were mates.'

'Ye weren't always mates.'

'That trouble was all finished, John.'

'Maybe Cam doesny think so. This Sammy's a friend of yours, Macey?'

'Aye. Well, an acquaintance, John. A harmless boay.'

John looked at Dave McMaster. Macey regretted his last remark. He had only meant to make it clear to John that he wouldn't have been responsible for introducing a trouble-maker to any of the pubs John looked after. But he realised that he had made Dave's position worse by implying he was letting innocent people get molested. He hoped Dave wouldn't hold it against him.

'But he's fine,' Macey offered as emendation. 'No damage done. Except that the jacket looks like a tie-dye job now.'

But in certain moods John was as easily amused as an old Glasgow Empire audience on a wet Tuesday. He was still looking at Dave. Being looked at in that way, Macey thought, would be like standing too near a furnace. You would want to back off.

'What's Mickey Ballater doin' up here? Who needs to re-import sewage? An' Panda Paterson? Ah've done shites that could beat him.'

'He wis no problem, John,' Dave said. 'But Ah didny want tae get involved wi' Cam without your say-so. That's serious business. That wis all.'

John was staring at him.

'Ah hope so,' he said. 'Minding a place means lookin' after everybody. Let wan wanker toss off in yer face an' they'll be organisin' bus-trips. Bein' cheeky in "The Crib" could get tae be a fashion.'

He sipped his tea. He wasn't really deciding anything. He was letting it be decided for him. Deliberation wasn't his forte. Anger was. Sitting there, he was coaxing it out of its kennel, presenting it with fragments of what had happened like giving it the scent of a quarry.

'Open-plan pub?' he said. 'Oh, ah doubt that won't do. We'll have tae see which way he wants it. If that's how he's goin' to be, we might have tae make his rib-cage open-plan. Ah'll punch holes in 'im big enough for birds tae nest in.'

He looked at Macey.

'Fix it up.'

'When, John?'

'Right now.'

'For here?'

'Naw. Let him choose. It doesny matter where. But be right back. Ah want tae see him right away.'

Macey left the tea that he had hardly touched and went for the door.

'Macey. Maybe ye'd better make it near a hospital.'

John Rhodes smiled, an event as cheerful as the winter solstice.

9

'Glasgow has them like every city, the urban bedouin. With the disorientation of the alcoholic and the down-and-out, they shift locations but their vagrancy has trade-routes. Places are in for a season and then get abandoned, like spas where the springs have dried.

Laidlaw knew Eck well enough to have a very rough chart of his preferences. There were brief spells—in the past few years infrequent—when he vanished into what some said was respectability, a proper house. Certainly, he usually re-emerged wearing a coat that looked less like a dump with buttons, but not for long.

Outside those times, he was roughly predictable. Even disintegration can be routine. Winters had been Talbot House or the Great Eastern Hotel, a name that sat on the Duke Street doss-house like a top-hat on a turd. In easier weather, he had favoured the East End around Glasgow Green and the decaying, still unredeveloped area south west of Gorbals Street.

Harkness had been worried about Laidlaw since they set out on foot from the office. He knew Laidlaw's belief in what he sometimes called 'absorbing the streets', as if you could solve crime by osmosis. Apart from being of dubious effectiveness, it was sore on the feet. Sometimes the preoccupied conversation that went with it wasn't a very soothing accompaniment, like watching a hamster desperately going nowhere in a revolving cage.

'Paddy Collins mentioned on Eck's bit of paper. Paddy Collins dead. What connection could Eck have with Paddy Collins' death? Did Milligan tell you anything else?'

'No. Just that.'

'Did he say anybody had been at the Vicky when he was there?'

'Paddy's wife. And I suppose Cam.'

They were passing a phone-box.

'It's weird. Wait and I'll try that number again.'

They went into the box and Laidlaw dialled it from memory. Harkness could understand why. It was the fourth time Laidlaw had tried it since they had started walking. This time it answered at the twelfth ring. Laidlaw's eyes were like a small boy's at Christmas. He nodded Harkness in to share the ear-piece as he inserted the money.

'Hullo,' Laidlaw said.

'Hullo?' It was a woman's voice.

'Hullo. Who's speaking, please?'

'Hullo, hullo?' She sounded elderly.

'Who's speaking, please?'

'Hullo. This is Mrs Wotherspoon. Who are you, son?'

'Excuse me,' Laidlaw said, winking at Harkness. 'I just want to check I've got the right number. What address is that you're speaking from?'

'Address? This is a public phone-box, son. I was just passin' there an' I heard it ringin'. I'm on ma way to the chiropodist's. Ma feet are givin' me laldy. It takes me about ten minutes tae pass a phone-box the way Ah walk. That's probably why Ah heard ye.'

Harkness was wheezing silently, his face red with suppressed laughter, and winking elaborately back at Laidlaw. Laidlaw looked as if he'd been given a stockingful of ashes for his Christmas.

'Where is the phone-box, love?' he asked.

'It's one of the two boxes at the corner of Queen Margaret Drive and Wilton Street. What is it, son? Ye tryin' to make contact with somebody? Can Ah help ye?'

'Look, love,' Laidlaw said. 'I'm sorry I bothered you. It's a wrong number. Thanks for your help.'

'Not at all.'

'I hope you get the feet sorted out.'

49

'So do Ah, son. So do Ah. Ah've got feet here like two Mother's Pride loafs. Ta, ta, son.'

'Cheerio.'

As they walked on, Laidlaw accepted Harkness's mickey-taking. But it didn't prevent him from quickly resuming his preoccupation.

'Well, it's something,' he said. 'That's that dealt with. Paddy Collins is incommunicado. "The Crib" is too general to mean anything to us just now. That leaves the Pollokshields address and the mysterious Lynsey Farren. We'll see what they yield after we check this out.'

Laidlaw and Harkness stayed north of the river at first. They checked part of the Green roughly, coming out past the strange, ornate façade of Templeton's Carpet Factory.

'Some smashing buildings in the city,' Harkness said. 'But you never notice them.'

Laidlaw agreed.

'This job gives you tunnel vision,' he said.

They wandered weirdly. Harkness began to worry even more about Laidlaw. There was a compulsion in the way Laidlaw kept walking. It was ruthless. He stopped strange people, described Eck to them and asked them if they had seen him lately. Harkness was beginning to get embarrassed.

This wasn't what they taught you in police college. This was as cute as walking naked down the street. And yet, in some odd way, it was working. Nobody got alarmed. Harkness reflected that in Glasgow openness is the only safe-conduct pass. Try to steal a march and they'll ambush you from every close. They hate to be had. Come on honestly and their tolerance can be great.

One man typified it. He was small, with a gammy leg. He was carrying what looked like a poke of rolls. When Laidlaw stopped him, he nodded with instant wisdom into his questions.

'Christ, aye. Big Tammy Adamson's boay. No problem. Ah can tell ye exactly. When Big Tammy sellt the shoap in Govanhill, Alec went tae sea. The Merchant Navy. As far as

Ah know, he's still there yet. A nice big boay. Aboot six-feet two.'

'Naw,' Laidlaw said. 'Not the same fella.'

'Well. He sounds awfu' like 'im. Good luck, anyway. It's the only Eck Adamson Ah know.'

'Thanks,' Laidlaw said.

'For what? Ah've enjoyed the chance tae rest ma leg. Cheers, boays.'

In their travels, they found a few isolated groups of derelicts and talked to them. One group round a fire directed them to the south side of the river. The information was probably as helpful as a wooden compass. But they had nothing else.

They crossed the river by the Suspension Bridge. Nothing happened for a time. But after a lot more walking, they saw five people behind the Caledonia Road Church. It was a striking moment. They were four men and a woman in a difficult conspiracy. One man had a bottle and a deep argument was going on. Plato never had it harder.

Against the backdrop of the church, they looked small and yet they put it in perspective. Burned in the sixties, the shell of the building remains a monument to nineteenth century confidence, an eroding certainty about what God's like. They bickered stridently in its shadow like a rival sect.

'Hullo there,' Laidlaw said, and for Harkness the remark tuned the day into another wavelength. Laidlaw's attempt at conversation with them was like trying to communicate with a ship sinking in mid-Atlantic when you're on the shore.

'Furraff,' one of them said, a small man whose face dereliction had made a gargoyle. 'Furraff, is oors.'

The woman giggled, an eerily coquettish sound that belonged behind a fan. She looked at the small man with roguish appreciation, as if he had just produced one of his better epigrams. The other three were still ignoring Laidlaw and Harkness.

'Furraff,' the small man repeated.

He moved towards Laidlaw in a way that was both

51

threatening and touching, a vaguely remembered style still carried around like an unloaded gun.

'I just want to ask you something,' Laidlaw said. 'Did anybody here know Eck Adamson? I know you.' Laidlaw pointed at the man with the bottle. 'I've seen you with him.'

They all paused. The man with the bottle stood swaying, drawing his dignity round him like an opera cloak. His irises had a furry look.

'Ah know all there is to know aboot boats,' somebody said. 'Can make a boat speak.'

'I beg your pardon, captain,' the man with the bottle said. 'You were addressing me?'

The formal politeness was a bizarre anomaly in his state of savage ruin.

'Yes,' Laidlaw said. 'You knew Eck Adamson.'

The man seemed to be leafing through a mental engagement-book of fair dimensions.

'I have that pleasure.'

'Had. He's dead.'

'Greedy wee man,' somebody said.

'Bereft,' the man with the bottle said. 'Bereft.'

He took a drink and passed it to the woman. While the others drank, Laidlaw explained what had happened and asked the man if he knew where Eck might have been hanging out lately. Only fragments seemed to register.

'One of our favourite spots,' the man said and started to walk. Laidlaw and Harkness went with him while the others straggled behind.

They didn't have far to go. He stopped on a waste lot where the ashes of a dead fire suggested an abandoned camp-site. The man was nodding. The others joined them.

'Did anyone get in touch with him that you saw?' Laidlaw asked. 'A stranger.'

'A young man perhaps. A benefactor perhaps.'

Harkness understood Laidlaw's expression. The questions were probably no more than the spurs to creative fantasy in the man. He had the drunk's disconcerting technique of hibernating between remarks.

'Yes. There was a young man. John? David? Alec? Patrick?'

'Thanks,' Laidlaw said. 'Do you remember his second names as well?'

'We don't use second names here.'

'He wouldny share,' the small man said.

'How do you mean?'

'Had a bottle. Wouldny share. Basta.'

Laidlaw gave the dignified man a fifty-pence piece.

'Many thanks. At the moment I'm slightly devoid of funds.'

They dispersed as vaguely as fog.

'Useful information,' Harkness said.

They were standing aimlessly on the waste lot.

'Let's look,' Laidlaw said.

'What for? A visiting card?'

'Anything. Just bloody look!'

They did. After a dusty half-hour, Harkness turned up a bottle in a niche of the wall and hidden with loose bricks. It was a Lanliq wine-bottle with a screw top. It contained something dark.

Lifting it gingerly by the neck, Laidlaw unscrewed the cork and smelt. It meant nothing he recognised. He looked at Harkness.

'We've got to go in and get a car anyway. Let's take it with us.'

'Sure,' Harkness said. 'We might get something back on the bottle.'

'But I'm not humphing this. We'll get a taxi.'

It seemed a simple enough idea but it led to one of those impromptu moments of Glaswegian cabaret in which the city abounds. Having flagged a cab down, Laidlaw, with a sense of camouflage that was instinctive to him, gave a destination near Pitt Street. And things began immediately with a green car pulling out without warning in front of their driver.

'Away, you!' their driver bellowed. 'Ah hope yer wheels fa' aff.'

53

He was a man who looked in his late thirties with thinning, curly hair and he was obviously an extreme sufferer from that contemporary ailment, urban choler.

'Bastards,' he said, jerking his head as if he was riding the world's' punches.

He was one of those taxi-drivers who do up their cab like a wee house on wheels. There was fancy carpeting and instead of advertisements on the base of the fold-up seats he had pasted on pictures of a couple of Highland scenes, the Three Sisters of Glencoe and the Ballachulish Ferry before the bridge was built. He had woollen baubles hanging from the inside mirror and plastic footballers, Rangers and Celtic, over the dashboard-switches. It was like taking a ride inside someone's psyche.

'Ye fancy some music, boays?'

His eyes in the mirror suggested refusal might be a capital offence. They murmured non-committally and he switched on a tape.

'Magic him, intae? James Last, eh? Ye need somethin' soothin' in this job.'

There was an almost full bottle of Irn Bru wedged upside down between the meter and the luggage-door. As he talked, it began to seem that its purpose might be more than a thirst quencher.

'Tell you two places Ah'll no' go.' He said it as if they had turned up especially to enquire about his taboos. 'Not any more. Blackhill and Garthamlock. No chance. Know why? Garthamlock. Take a bastard out there. In the back wi' the biggest alsation Ah've ever saw. Rin-Tin-Tin wi' elephantia-sis. Get there, no money. Gonny set his dog on me. Ah steps oot the cab. Before ye could say Jack Robinson, he's hit me the awfiest kick in the knackers. Oot the gemme completely. Ma balls were like wattermelons. Ah wis walkin' aboot like a cowboy for a week, wasn't Ah? But he wisny clever. Knew roughly where he stayed, didn't ah? Couple o' the mates an' me pay a wee visit, wait for him. We played at keepie-uppie wi' his heid. Don't worry about it. Big guy. He wis squealin' like a pig. Left his face like a

54

jigsaw-puzzle. Wan o' his lugs had nostrils by the time we stopped. Correct. This is a nice wan, boays.'

He turned up the music and hummed along with it briefly.

'Aye, ye meet some fuckin' lunatics in this job.'

In the mirror Harkness watched the driver's eyes contemplate the incidence of insanity with a kind of cosmic dyspepsia. There was a certain relief in realising they were almost at their destination. He couldn't hold in his laughter.

'Aye. Ye learn to trust nobody. Some o' them wid massage yer head wi' a screwtop as fast as look at ye. The world's a shambles.'

'Your tip's on the meter,' Laidlaw said as he paid.

Harkness realised that Laidlaw was justified. Behind his distracting talk, the driver had followed an unnecessarily circuitous route. But the man looked at Laidlaw as if deciding whether to fight a duel with him.

He flicked on his 'For Hire' sign and took off. Harkness imagined him cruising round Glasgow like a mobile manic broadcaster, Radio Armageddon, meter ticking like a time-bomb.

'We'll get this to the lab,' Laidlaw said and suddenly was laughing.

He pointed helplessly after the departing taxi, shaking his head. Harkness nodded, buckled beside him.

'How about that?' Harkness managed to say.

'Like going over Niagara in a taxi.'

'I wonder what happened in Blackhill?' Harkness said.

10

The "Top Spot", in the same building as the Theatre Royal, had changed since the theatre had been taken over by the Scottish Opera. But its continued nearness to the new Scottish Television building meant that it still got a lot of its clientele from there. Bob Lilley by-passed the public bar and went downstairs, where the arched alcoves and beer-barrel bottoms stuck on the wall to advertise Lowenbrau were like a rough set for *The Student Prince*.

The lounge was pleasantly busy. He saw Laidlaw sitting with Brian Harkness at one of the metal-topped tables. Harkness was saying something that Laidlaw didn't seem to agree with. When Bob joined them, Laidlaw waited a few minutes and then said, 'What do you have to do to get a drink here? Wear make-up?'

Harkness and Laidlaw had been talking again about the post-mortem Laidlaw had attended that morning. Harkness was glad Bob had come in.

While Laidlaw was at the bar, Harkness shook his head at Bob. Bob sat down and looked along at Laidlaw. He saw a tall, good-looking man who didn't look like a policeman, didn't look forty, staring at the gantry as if it was the writing on the wall. That preoccupied intensity was such a familiar aspect of Laidlaw to Bob that he wondered what was bothering Harkness.

'It's not a bee in his bunnet Jack's got,' Harkness said. 'It's a bloody hive.'

Sharing an office with Laidlaw, Bob was as close to him as anybody, with the exception of Harkness, although sometimes Harkness wondered. He had known Laidlaw for about a year and still found his presence a lucky dip from which any chance remark could draw a surprising response. He was about as easy to explore as the Louisiana Purchase. Among the other men on the Squad, Bob had appointed himself Laidlaw's defence counsel, a function which must have sometimes felt like a full-time job in itself.

'What's up?' Bob said.

'A few fruitless days for us. That's what I think's up. Jack thinks he's going to find out whoever did in wee Eck Adamson.'

'Eck was murdered?'

'Jack seems to think so.'

'How?'

'Ask *him*. So it would be all right if he just keeps his eyes open and hopes for something to turn up. But not him. I feel an obsession coming on. And it's hopeless, isn't it? You might as well point to a snowstorm and say, "See that snowflake at the end of the road. Go and get it." No chance. And you know what Jack's like when he's got a cause. Even a lost one. About as easy to ignore as a Salvation Army drum. He's going to start putting everybody's humph up. The Crime Squad'll look like the Loch Ness monster.'

'They should be used to him by now.'

'Who gets used to Jack? You know what I mean. I like the man. I just wish somebody would give him a lorry-load of Valium for his Christmas.'

Laidlaw brought Harkness's lager and a whisky for Bob and sipped his lime-juice and soda. Bob decided to help Harkness.

'Eck was murdered?' Bob asked.

Laidlaw nodded.

'Pulmonary fibrosis. Suspected paraquat poisoning.'

'Paraquat? Come on,' Bob said. 'If it's paraquat, what makes you think it was murder? Eck had a thirst that wouldn't have stopped at horse's piss. As discriminating as a public lavvy. He would find it and drink it. That's all. How can you say it was murder?'

'It was something he said.'

'Jack! You knew Eck. He made Pat the Liar sound like George Washington. You're not serious. You can't put any weight on that.'

'I think I can. He said something about "the wine he gave me wisny wine". I think somebody gave him a bad present.'

'How do they know?' Bob asked. 'Did they find paraquat in him?'

'No. It would've worked itself out by then, I suppose. I think he'd had it for a wee while. But it causes what they call proliferative changes.'

'What *is* that?' Harkness said.

'I'm not sure. I think it means that even after the stuff's gone, the damage caused goes on multiplying itself. I suppose it's the exact nature of the damage that suggests paraquat. Not a nice way to go.'

'You saw him?'

Laidlaw nodded.

'All right, Jack,' Bob said. 'So he had a bad time. You're sorry, but sorriness is no kind of substitute for common-sense. Get a grip, will you? Learn to settle for doing the things you *can* do.'

'Right Bob,' Laidlaw said. 'I think I've had enough of the Police College notes from Brian already. You think I don't know? If you want to commit the perfect crime, just a crime for the sake of a crime. What do you do? Wipe out a wino. Right? For two reasons: who cares? Indifference coming at you like a river. And you trying to swim up it. Second: to solve a crime, you check with neighbours, family, friends. Who's a wino's friend? Another wino. Like cross-examining an answering service. Neighbours? Pigeons. Family? If they're not in the Eastern Necropolis, they're keeping quiet enough to be there. You can depend on it. What was the sequence of events? Who the hell knows? As predictable as a pin-ball. And there's always the feeling that it might just have been a fun crime. A fly-swatting job. It's as if you're jay-walking in Hope Street. In the middle of the road you find a fly with its wings torn off.

58

You're going to track down the culprit? I know, Bob. I know.'

'Then why the hell don't you accept it?'

'Why the hell do you? I don't know what you feel about this job. But it fits me as comfortably as a hair-shirt. All right, I do it. Because sometimes I get to feel it matters very much. But not if I'm just a glorified street-sweeper. Filling up Barlinnie like a dustbin. There have to be some times when you don't just collect the social taxes. You arrange a rebate. If all I'm doing is holding the establishment's lid on for it, then stuff it. I resign. But I think there can be more to it. One of the things I'm in this job to do is learn. Not just how to catch criminals but who they really are, and maybe why. I'm not some guard-dog. Trained to answer whistles. Chase whoever I'm sent after. I'm not just suspicious of the people I'm chasing. I'm suspicious of the people I'm chasing them *for*. I mean to stay that way.'

'So?'

'So Wee Eck. If the law works for them, it should work for him. If he'd died in a penthouse, let's hear you say the same. You know the life he had. Its patron saint was Torquemada. So the least he deserves is that we should care about his death enough to understand it. Like laying a wee plastic wreath on his grave. Grave? He won't even have one. His body goes to the Anatomy Department at Glasgow University. I remember Eck telling me years ago he'd tried to sell his body to them for a fiver. Didn't know that when you're dead, your body belongs to your next of kin. So they get it free. He even lost out on that one.'

'When did you join the vigilantes, Jack?'

'Never. I'm not witch-hunting whoever did it. I just think some understanding is owed. The only healthy climate is the truth.'

Harkness said, 'So how do we get there, great white hunter?'

Laidlaw laughed.

'Don't ask awkward questions.'

59

Bob said, 'You could advertise: confessions wanted. I'd say it's your only chance.'

'I'd like to do something more practical,' Laidlaw said.

The attractive young waitress came up and took Laidlaw's empty glass. She had long, straight black hair and the kind of eyes that always seem to see something just past your face, maybe the dandruff on your jacket. They were dark eyes that assumed your interest, letting you get on with staring at her if you must. She hovered—waiting to take an order or be discovered?

'No thanks, love,' Laidlaw said.

The other two agreed. The waitress went away. There was a television personality being a television personality at a nearby table. The accompanying group were demonstrating the spontaneity of a studio audience.

'Another lime-juice and soda,' Laidlaw said, 'and I'll want to audition upstairs. There's only so much of those the human head can stand. Anyway, we've got another call to make.'

'I'm glad,' Harkness said. 'I was beginning to think your idea was to *talk* a solution to Eck's death.'

'We'll grab something to eat and go out to Pollokshields.'

'Jack,' Bob said. 'Take it easy.'

'Ignore him,' Laidlaw said. 'He hangs about here a lot. I'll tell the manager.'

Bob came out with them. The waitress said cheerio almost to them. Outside, Glagow had had a change of mood. It still wasn't warm but the sky had cleared. Harkness, his hangover gone, had that feeling that weather is subjective. Bob said he was going to the office, 'Back to sanity.'

Before they went over to Stewart Street for a car, Laidlaw hovered about the entrance to the Theatre Royal, looking at the billings.

'Life should be more like the opera,' Laidlaw said.

'Why?'

'You never die without a detailed explanation. If Wee Eck could've sung an aria in the Royal, we'd have no problem.'

They were walking up to cross Cowcaddens Road. Harkness, momentarily dazzled by the brightness of the day, thought about it.

'I was gee-ven the par-aaa-quat,' he sang, 'by Hec-tor McGob-leee-gin.'

'Still,' Laidlaw said. 'Maybe it's just as well he couldn't.'

11

They had settled for the function suite of the Coronach Hotel. Just beyond the south-eastern edge of Glasgow, at one of the points where the city suffers natural erosion from the countryside, the hotel seemed well enough named. A coronach is a dirge.

It belonged properly to the time before the Clayson Report relaxed the drinking laws, when only hotels had a seven-day licence and Sunday drinking was for what the law called bona fide travellers. Like a village pump in a place where the plumbing has been modernised, it stood as a slightly tatty monument to the old Scottish Sabbath, that interesting anomaly whereby the Kirk's insistence on the observance of the Lord's day of rest resulted in a country busy with Scotsmen transporting a thirst as heavy as luggage from one place to another.

The Coronach was still a drinking hotel, but quieter, especially on Sundays. To ask for a room there was as naive as expecting to meet Calpurnia in "Caesar's Palace". The only acknowledgment that hospitality could go beyond the dispensing of drink was the function suite.

It was called the Rob Roy Room, which meant that the carpet was MacGregor tartan and there were a couple of targes on the walls, framed in crossed claymores. Today its occupants were outlaws unromanticised by time.

When Macey ushered in John Rhodes, Hook Hawkins and Dave McMaster, Cam Colvin was already installed. Two of the small tables had been placed together with chairs around. Cam sat at the head of one of the tables, sedate as a committee-man.

John Rhodes and he were a conjunction of contrasting styles, like a meeting between shop-floor and management.

Cam was conservative in a dark-striped suit and black shoes as shiny as dancing-pumps. The shirt was demurely striped and the tie was navy. John looked as if his tailor might be Oxfam. The light-brown suit was rumpled, the shirt was open-necked. He was wearing a purple cardigan.

Cam registered nothing when John Rhodes came in. But the fuse was already lit in John's blue eyes. Cam and he nodded at each other. Cam indicated the man who was sitting on his right.

'This is Dan Tomlinson,' he said. 'He's the manager.'

Dan Tomlinson was a thin man in his fifties. He looked worried, as if he couldn't remember whether his hotel insurance was up to date. Mickey Ballater was standing nearby and nodded. The only other man in the room, who had been trying to stare down the one-armed bandit beside the small bar, ambled across to join them.

'Oh,' John Rhodes said. 'And Panda Paterson.'

'Correct, John. Your memory's good,' Panda said.

He extended his hand to shake and John Rhodes punched him in the mouth. It was a short punch, very quick and very measured, costing John nothing, the punch of a man in training, emerging from reflexes so honed they seemed to contain a homing device. It was only after it had landed you realised it had been thrown. It imparted awe to some of the others, as if thought was fait accompli.

The effect was reminiscent of the moment in a Hollywood musical when the mundane breaks into a Busby Berkeley routine. Suddenly, Panda Paterson was dancing. He moved dramatically onto the small slippereened square of dance floor and did an intricate backstep. Then, extending his improvisation into what could have been called 'The Novice Skater', he went down with his arms waving and slid sitting until the carpet jarred him backwards and his head hit a radiator like a duff note on a xylophone.

'That's the price of a pint in "The Crib",' John Rhodes said.

There was blood coming out of Panda's mouth. He eased himself off as if to get up and then settled back, touching his mouth gently.

'Ye've made a wise decision,' John Rhodes said, watching him refuse to get up. 'You're right. Ah've got a good memory. Ah don't know where you've been lately. Watchin' cowboy pictures? Well, it's different here. Whoever's been kiddin' you on ye were hard, Ah'm here tae tell ye Ah've known you a long time. Ye were rubbish then an' ye're rubbish now. Frightenin' wee boys! Try that again an' Ah'll shove the pint-dish up yer arse. One wi' a handle.'

If you could have bottled the atmosphere, it would have made Molotov cocktails. Practised in survival, Macey was analysing the ingredients.

John Rhodes stood very still, having made his declaration. What was most frightening about him was the realisation that what had happened was an act of measured containment for him, had merely put him in the notion for the real thing. He wasn't just a user of violence, he truly loved it. It was where he happened most fully, a thrilling edge. Like a poet who has had a go at the epic, he no longer indulged himself in the doggerel of casual fights but when, as now, the situation seemed big enough, his resistance was very low.

The others, like Panda Paterson, were imitating furniture. This wasn't really about them. Even Panda had been incidental, no more than the paper on which John had neatly imprinted his message. The message was addressed to Cam Colvin.

Macey understood how even at the moment of its impact John's anger had maintained a certain subtlety. Neither he nor Cam needed confrontation. People could die of that. John had repaid an oblique insult. The move was Cam's.

He took his time. His eyes sustained that preoccupied focus they usually had, as if the rest of the world was an irrelevant noise just over his shoulder. He seemed so impervious to outside pressure, Macey felt he could have rolled a fag on a switchback railway. He looked up directly at John Rhodes.

'You'll need to work on your fishtail, Panda,' he said. 'It's rubbish.'

It was style triumphant. Everybody laughed except Panda

Paterson, who stood up sheepishly. John Rhodes, like a bull lassoed with silk, sat down at the table. The others joined him. Dan Tomlinson brought drinks, port for John and beer for the others. Cam was drinking orange juice. Dan Tomlinson went out. The meeting was convened.

'It was really Hook I wanted to see, John,' Cam said.

'So Ah heard. But Ah thought Ah would jist come along. Ah had a wee message to deliver.'

He looked at Panda, who happened to be looking down.

'What did ye want tae see Hook about? Ye seem to have been impatient.'

'I still am.'

Cam sipped his orange juice carefully, his calmness seeming to belie his own words.

'Paddy Collins is dead.'

He said it with a kind of innocent expectation of immediate response from the others, the way a king might await the alarm of his courtiers if he sneezed. But this was divided territory. John Rhodes was tasting his drink as if he had suddenly become a bon viveur from the Calton. Cam's concern and John's indifference created an impasse of neutrality in the rest. Looking at the table, Cam chose his line of thought as carefully as threading a needle.

'Not that Paddy Collins matters much,' he said. 'I've seen better men in Burton's window. But he was our Pauline's man. He was connected. She's in a state. Don't ask me why. She's like most women. Seems to keep her brains in her knickers. But that's the way of it. And I don't like it. Nobody shites on my doorstep. Or I wipe their arse with razor blades.'

The words were a ritual exercise, like the noises an exponent of the martial arts might make preparatory to combat. He seemed separate from them at the moment, rehearsing the basic gestures of his nature, locating his will. He was distant, almost formal. But you knew he would soon be coming on.

'Who do they think they are? Where do *they* live? Whoever

killed Paddy Collins I'm going to find. There won't be enough of him left to make up a tin of Kennomeat.'

It was spoken quietly. Since he felt no doubts, the statement needed no force to assert itself. It occurred as evenly as breathing.

'He was never able to tell me what happened. But somebody knows. Do you know anything, Hook?'

'Wait a minute,' John Rhodes said. 'How wid he know anything?'

'I'm asking him, John. I don't want one of these fucking conversations by post.' The pitch of his voice hadn't changed. Only the swear-word was like an abstract signal of a quickening mood. 'His mouth's here. Let it answer.'

'Aye, maybe,' John said. 'It depends whit the question means.'

'John. What you do to Panda's your affair. He's not one of mine. He just happens to be with me. But don't try to piss me about where I live. Somebody killed my brother-in-law. I didn't choose him but that's what he was. They're going to have to join him. I'm asking a straight question. All it means is what it says. Does Hook get to answer?'

Macey felt the axis of the room tilt delicately in favour of Cam. He watched John Rhodes judge whether he was letting too much happen, smile easily and nod to Hook.

'But how wid Ah know anything, Cam?'

Cam was watching Hook. 'Tell him,' he said to Panda.

'Well, Ah'm livin' quiet these days. But Ah do all right.' He couldn't resist tentatively trying to reinstate himself in their eyes a little, let them know he didn't get his mouth punched every day. 'We've got a few things goin' for us.'

'You're not on "This is Your Life",' Cam said. 'Tell him about Paddy.'

'Well, Ah've kept in touch with Paddy back and forward. Paddy was a friend of mine.'

He seemed to be offering loyalty as a compensatory quality.

'Ye shouldny talk ill o' the dead,' John Rhodes said.

Panda was like a banana republic threatened by two contending major powers who don't want direct conflict. He

66

felt the pressure, began to speak in a deliberately neutral voice.

'Last time Ah spoke to him, he was very chirpy. Reckoned he had money comin'. Somebody owed him. It was somebody he met in "The Crib".'

The others waited but that was all Panda had to say. He sat like someone who can't remember the punch-line.

'That's it?' John Rhodes said.

'Not quite,' Cam said. 'Mickey.'

Macey was interested in Mickey Ballater's presence. Panda was a scavenger off other people's reputations. It was easy to see why he was here. But Mickey Ballater was different. Macey was wondering about him.

'Ah'm up here to see Paddy,' Mickey said. 'By the time Ah get up, he's in the Vicky. There was somebody he talked about up here. Wis going to introduce me. Seemed a right oddity. Fella called Tony Veitch.'

Cam was still watching Hook.

'That's the only two things Ah've got to go on,' Cam said. '"The Crib" and somebody called Tony Veitch. Hook?'

'Ah'm sorry, Cam. Ah'd help ye if Ah could.'

'A minder should mind. It's your job to know everybody.'

'How can ye do that, Cam? Come on. A place like "The Crib" has a name, gets tourists. What counts is they should know me. Know Ah'm around.'

'I want this Tony Veitch. It seems to me it might be the same one he met in "The Crib". Hook, you were still friendly enough with Paddy, were you? There was that bit of bother.'

'Years ago, Cam. A daft fall-out over a wumman. We laughed about it after. He musta told ye.'

'I probably wasn't listening. Women. The bastard. Anyway . . .'

A stranger had walked into the function suite. He was a fairly big man around whom middle-age had set like a podium. Not much had happened to detract from his sense of his own importance, or if it had he had managed to forget it. His mouth was open in one of those smiles that suggest the joke is private.

'Oh-ho,' he said as he came towards them. 'Thought Ah heard voices. Ah wis at the lavvy there. A wee fly party, boays. Well, how's about a ticket? Any chance of a drink?'

He had had enough already to suggest he should be taken into protective custody. It was Cam Colvin he had interrupted. John Rhodes was watching him without amusement. The others waited.

'Cat got yer tongues? Any chance of a drink?'

'Aye.' Cam looked up at him. 'How about a pint of blood? Siphoned off your face.'

The man started to sketch a laugh and erased it instantly. Losing its self-assurance, his face was clumsily rehearsing expressions as he looked round the table, slowly assimilating the drift of the plot from the appearance of the cast. It wasn't a comedy. 'Huh,' he tried, to convince them he could take a role here. It was a bad audition.

'Wait a minute. There's no need—'

'Fuck off,' Cam said precisely, as if he was giving elocution lessons.

The man went out, his mouth bumbling a rearguard of aimless noise to cover the retreat of his self-esteem.

'I must tell Dan Tomlinson,' Cam said. 'He's not supposed to decorate the place with balloons till Christmas. Anyway. I think Hook should help me, John.'

'How?'

'He knows the people that go about "The Crib". He can ask around. Just for starters, I'm going to find this Tony Veitch. Just for starters. If it's him, he's dead. And anybody that gets in my road'll get hurt sore. I wouldn't like to think Hook was being less than helpful.'

John Rhodes smiled. They were watching each other.

'If anything happens to Hook or any of mine through you, Cam, ye better book a family plot. Paddy Collins'll have a lot o' company.'

The others were utterly still. Professional criminals are essentially conservative, perhaps because they have to take

68

the law so seriously, can only operate effectively where rules are rules. They were all aware of how threatening to the tight order of things this confrontation was, like a nuclear stand-off in the terms of their narrow lives.

Macey understood the tension. If you were choosing a winner out of such a conflict, it would have to be Cam. His interests were bigger and more varied and he was far more highly organised than John. But among several people who were in any organisational sense more powerful, John Rhodes still commanded a lot of respect.

There were sound reasons for it. Like a traditional family firm overtaken by pushy corporations, John Rhodes retained one quality which had so far guaranteed his survival: he dispensed a pure and undiluted product—100% proof violence. When he had to go, it would be to the death, preferably other people's. Everybody knew that if you went against John Rhodes it was serious business. You weren't going to conclude it by breaking a couple of knee-caps here and there.

Cam seemed to be contemplating that old-fashioned set of values that would let John make a bonfire of everything he had just to warm his sense of honour at it. Cam could deal with it if he had to, but he would rather not. You could never be sure what would be left.

When he spoke, his face had an expression almost of pleading but it was a complicated plea, including a desire not to have his own violence activated, since he couldn't himself see the end of it.

'John. You want trouble, your wish is granted. But does it have to be now? All I'm asking is for Hook to show willing. Show whose side he's on. He can help. Is he going to?'

John Rhodes finished his port. 'Doin' what, like?'

'Mickey here's going to be asking around a bit. It's handy. He's handy. He's not known about here the way he was. But he could use a guide. He thinks Hook could help him. Okay?'

Mickey looked at Hook, who put the question back to John Rhodes. John nodded.

'Okay. He'll help. But don't come back to any o' ma pubs, Cam. And you, Action Man.' He pointed at Panda Paterson. 'If it even rains on any o' ma pubs, Ah'm gonny blame you. See it disny. Macey here'll pass on anything else we get. Okay?'

'Okay. The fella's name is Tony Veitch. I'll be looking for you soon, Macey.'

Macey nodded briskly to cover his worry. In a marriage as uneasy as this one the best man could finish up being the purvey.

12

This should have been a Saturday but it didn't feel like one to Harkness. This had to be the eighth day of some deformed week, a kind of thirty-first of June. It didn't fit. Maybe the moon had blown a fuse.

They weren't in the office. They weren't preparing for a court case. They weren't on surveillance. They weren't on the streets soliciting information. They were in Pollokshields.

It was a part of Glasgow Harkness didn't know too well, a place on the South Side to drive through sometimes on his way to work, trying not to let the houses bother him. All fur coats and no knickers, he had often told himself as an antidote to the envy that hit him here like lack of oxygen.

But it wasn't true. The wealth was more real than apparent. Some of the huge yellow sandstone houses had been converted into flats, it was true. A few had become self-contained Pakistani villages. But the infiltration of some of the merely well off or even the poor was hardly enough to change the basic impression this part of Pollokshields gave.

The house they were visiting confirmed it. It was a turreted sandstone castle separated from the street by a low wall and a high hedge, like a soft-sell moat. The conservatory at the side was an interesting piece of architecture in itself, a domed colony of humid vegetation. Inside the house, Harkness had half-expected to be handed a catalogue. The wide hall had two abstract paintings and a small terracotta frieze set into the wall—some ancient punters naked among the leaves. The staircase looked a suitable place for losing a glass slipper. A stained-glass window guled the fawn carpet faintly.

The room they had been shown into was furnished richly

in leather and wood, nothing more parvenu being permitted. There was so much space around that the armchairs they sat in felt to Harkness like stations on a steppe. Watching their host nursing a nugget of Chivas Regal in his hand, Harkness wondered why Laidlaw hadn't taken one, obliging him to abstain as well. It wasn't as if Laidlaw had never indulged on duty before.

Milton Anthony Veitch, as he had declared himself, was wearing his late forties as if anything else was merely apprenticeship. The hair was beautifully grey, fairly long and precisely cut, looking not just washed but professionally laundered. The slightly worn face was carried proudly, like a trophy. The lines were earned. As far as women went, Harkness imagined, he was still a runner. If any lady didn't fancy him, that was her problem.

He was a big man but had stayed nearly trim. The weight was only now beginning to hang like slightly inferior tailoring. The way he was sitting in his real leather chair, the stomach bulged delicately. But that was a tasteful cairn, memorial to good times. Maybe he couldn't make it happen everywhere any more, Harkness thought, but then he wouldn't have to. Money would allow him to move through invented habitats and there he must still be special, an aging lion at Longleat. Harkness thought he wouldn't like to be looking at his host down the wrong end of a business decision.

Milton Veitch had listened to Laidlaw explaining about Eck, Eck's piece of paper, and his address on it. He sighed.

'You have the piece of paper with you, do you?'

Laidlaw took it out, went over and gave it to Mr Veitch, came back and sat down. The time it took in this room, Harkness thought, a bus-service would have helped. Mr Veitch watched his drink, looked up.

'Tony,' he said.

'Tony?'

'My son. He wrote that.'

'You're sure, Mr Veitch?'

He smiled.

72

'I think I would know his writing. Besides, I was privileged to receive a communication recently from him myself. A letter, in a manner of speaking. That script is very fresh in my mind.'

He rose and crossed to the door and called, 'Alma.' The woman who appeared, like most women, interested Harkness. He felt that this time Laidlaw, who said that studying good-looking women was one of the non-taxable perks of the job for Harkness, must be agreeing. She was tall, maybe late thirties. She clarified for Harkness why it was that older women interested him so much. It was very simple: she had been where he hadn't been but where he wanted to go. As soon as he saw her, he saw a doorway he wanted to go through.

'This is Miss Brown,' Milton Veitch said to them, which was like pointing to Rheims Cathedral and saying, 'This is a church.'

She smiled and Harkness's head turned a somersault. It was a beautiful smile, slow and undeliberate and unselfconsciously strange. Harkness decided it was an Amazon of a smile and he knew what he wanted to be: an explorer.

'She keeps house for me.'

Everybody in the room knew what he meant and Harkness was deeply disappointed. She could be so much more than that, he knew. He started to have misgivings about her.

'Alma. Do we still have that letter Tony wrote me?'

'Which letter?'

His look told her not to play games.

'Which letter would it be?'

'You threw it out. Remember?'

'Anyway, it doesn't matter. It was just to convince the police force that I know my own son's writing. Maybe you'd better stay.'

He did the introductions and they all sat down again.

'What was the letter about?' Laidlaw asked.

'A good question. A tantrum against fatherhood is about as near as I could get.'

73

'Your son doesn't live here?'

'Not for a while, no. In fact, we don't know where he lives at all.'

'That's only been for a week or more,' Alma said. 'Give him time.'

'I've got no more time to give him,' Mr Veitch said. 'Not another day.'

They were looking at each other, the absent Tony forming a frost between them.

'Does the letter have something to do with that?' Laidlaw asked.

Mr Veitch noticed him again. He sighed.

'It's a long and largely unsavoury story. My son is a student at Glasgow University. Was. He was sitting his final exams recently and disappeared before he had taken all the papers. The letter was written to explain—I use the term loosely—his behaviour to me. Not so much a letter, really. More like a novel by post.'

'But before that he hadn't lived here anyway?'

'In a flat in the city. The wild freedom of youth, I suppose. But since he left there we haven't a clue where he is.'

'You haven't tried to trace him?'

'Well, he's patently all right. His letter was nothing if not full of the vigour of condemnation. I think he has at last found a way of expressing his rejection of everything I stand for. He's been trying to get the message through to me for long enough. I deliberately didn't contact the police. If he wants to disown me, that's his right. He *is* over twenty-one. Just. Perhaps you could let Alma see your piece of paper? A corroborative witness, do you call it?'

Alma didn't linger over reading it. Milton Veitch was watching her closely but she didn't look at him.

'It's Tony's writing, all right,' she said.

'The man who had it on him was a vagrant. Eck Adamson. He's dead. Paraquat poisoning.'

'Suspected,' Harkness said.

Laidlaw ignored the footnote.

'Did either of you know him?'

'I run a rather large business. I don't meet a lot of vagrants.'
Alma Brown shook her head.

'He was a nice vagrant,' Laidlaw said. 'The other names.
Paddy Collins. A small villain. Bit-parts only. No? I don't
suppose a pub called "The Crib" means anything?'

Both looked as if they had forgotten he was there.

'No, you won't have any branches in the Saracen, Mr
Veitch. Lynsey Farren?'

That was the name that changed the thermostat. You
could feel the room freeze slightly. Alma Brown looked
involuntarily at Milton Veitch. It was like calling the name
of someone who was in hiding. It blew his cover. He looked
annoyed.

'We both know Lynsey Farren,' he said. 'She's Lord
Farren of Farren's daughter. Lady Lynsey Farren. I think
she may know even fewer vagrants than I do.'

He said it as if that was the matter closed. Harkness
doubted that.

'But Tony knew her, I take it?' Laidlaw asked.

'Yes, he did. Our two families have known each other for
years. Since Lynsey and Tony were children. But I really
don't think I want her bothered with whatever mess my son
has got himself into. What *has* happened, by the way?'

I thought you'd never ask, Harkness thought.

'It may not all come down quite to what you want, Mr
Veitch. Paddy Collins was stabbed to death. That's two
corpses connected with this piece of paper your son wrote
on. We don't know what happened. But I think you'll agree
there's a certain urgency in finding out. Eck and Paddy
Collins are keeping quiet. What's "The Crib" going to tell
us? It would be like interviewing a football crowd. That
leaves yourselves and Lynsey Farren. We're talking to you
and we'll be talking to her. By the way, the telephone
number on the paper is a public box in Queen Margaret
Drive. Does that mean anything to you?'

His head was shaking first but hers caught up quickly.

'Could I have Miss Farren's address, please?'

'I'm not entirely sure I like your manner.'

Laidlaw was looking down as if waiting for the irrelevances to pass. But Mr Veitch wasn't going anywhere except towards a confrontation.

'I said I'm not sure I like your manner.'

Laidlaw looked at him. 'That's all right,' he said quietly. 'I'm not sure my manner likes you. But it hardly seems relevant.'

'Milton!' Alma Brown was appealing to him. 'Please. If something's wrong with Tony, we must help. We must. Lynsey would want to help. She won't mind being involved, will she?'

He conferred with his drink before giving them an address in East Kilbride, which didn't seem to Harkness the likeliest place for the titled to live.

'Does she work?' Laidlaw asked.

'There I do draw the line. She has her own business and I don't think the presence of the police would help it.'

Laidlaw let it pass and Mr Veitch's sense of himself seemed assuaged.

'There are reasons for my reluctance to involve Lynsey,' he said in the manner of a cabinet minister responding to a naive interviewer. 'Lord Farren is an old man. He lives essentially in the past. The sordidness of much of what passes for life today passes him by. It would be nice if it could stay that way. If Lynsey were dragged into anything unsavoury, it would kill him. And Lynsey herself has had enough recently, I should think.'

Laidlaw was interested.

'Why is that?'

'An incident where the police were involved. A visitor to her flat who got nasty. Violent, I think.'

'Do you know who or what happened, Mr Veitch? What was it about?'

'I've no details, I'm afraid. I didn't press the poor girl. Was there anything else?'

'A couple of things. Do you know Tony's friends or where he might be staying? Anyone he might get in touch with? Places he might go? Anything like that?'

'I'm sorry,' Alma Brown said.

'No to everything,' Mr Veitch said. 'He's been a stranger to me for years. I hope he keeps it that way.'

'How will he be living?' Laidlaw asked.

The question seemed to puzzle Mr Veitch.

'What do you mean?'

'Money. Hiding out somewhere. How can he get the money to live?'

Mr Veitch smiled.

'He has his own money. My wife died some ten years ago. She left all of her money to her son. When he was twenty-one. Which perhaps explains the timing of his great rebellion. Like quite a few rebels, he presumably wants to do it in comfort.'

'Do you have any photographs of him?' Laidlaw asked.

'Well, if we do, I don't keep them next to my heart.'

'I'll find something,' Alma Brown said and went out.

Milton Veitch added to his drink and sat back down.

'You think Tony has done something terrible?' he asked. 'Been responsible in some way for what's happened?'

Laidlaw shrugged.

'Not necessarily. Not necessarily at all. But two people have been murdered.' He glanced at Harkness, letting him know he didn't need the intervention of purists at this point. 'This is the only pointer we have. That's all.'

'You know,' Mr Veitch was staring ahead. 'I'm afraid it wouldn't surprise me. It wouldn't surprise me at all.'

His voice faded out of earshot as Miss Brown came in. She gave Laidlaw two photographs.

'You can keep those,' she said. 'I have copies.'

Mr Veitch stood up. There was nothing to do but the same. Standing beside Mr Veitch in his light grey suit that looked expensive enough to be tailored from hand-stitched tenners, Harkness felt the way his shoes always looked when he was trying on new trousers—suddenly shabby.

'Oh, a last thing,' Laidlaw said. 'I don't know if you paid much attention to what Tony wrote on that bit of paper.

But it seems to me worryingly interested in wrongdoing. Was that like Tony?'

'Don't ask me,' Mr Veitch said. 'I hardly knew him.'

'Perhaps you shouldn't take that too seriously,' Miss Brown said. 'Tony wrote an awful lot of things. He had masses of papers. We never paid them much attention. Perhaps we should have.'

'But that letter was the only communication since he left?'

'Once was enough. Believe me,' Mr Veitch said.

As they all moved awkwardly out towards the door, Harkness felt the strangeness of these two people living together in this house, having conversations full of shadows. He thought it would take a house as big as this to accommodate the ghosts he had sensed in their relationship. He wondered if property did that to people, if big houses in some of the ghost stories he had read were really being haunted by the guilt of unjustly having while others were deprived. Certainly he couldn't remember reading about too many haunted single-ends.

Sitting in the car, Laidlaw took out the photographs and looked at them, passed them to Harkness. They showed a fair-haired young man, unsmiling, with intense, startled eyes. One was in colour, taken with a flash, and he was looking up from something he was reading. The other was taken outside, black and white. Tony Veitch was in an overcoat, standing outside a house. He looked like a refugee who had just arrived wherever he was.

'What do you see, Boy Robin?' Laidlaw said.

'A murderer?' Harkness asked.

'A mystery. That'll do for just now.'

Laidlaw took the refugee, left Harkness with the reader.

'Milton Veitch seems less vague about him,' Harkness said.

'Aye, he was in a hurry, wasn't he? I wonder why. But I'll tell you something. You know who casts the first stone? The guiltiest bastard in the crowd. You've got a son in the kind of bother he thinks Tony Veitch might be in, what do you do?'

'How would I know?'

'And how would I? But I would bet. I'd find him for myself. I'd need to know what happened. If wee Jackie grew up and got involved in this way, I'd have to know what I had done as well. Jesus, I could make a better father than him out of raffia.'

Harkness looked at him worriedly. Laidlaw was too vehement. Harkness had been working with him for over a year now. In that time he had seen an intensification take place in Laidlaw. Whatever forces were working themselves out in him, they were accelerating. Laidlaw was forty now but that anger against so many things that ticked in him like a geiger-counter was in no way mollified by middle-age.

Harkness thought he knew some of the pressures that relentlessly maintained the tension of his nature. He had been at Laidlaw's house a few times and had seen that in the wreck of his marriage he was using himself as a lifebelt for his three children. Laidlaw's insistence on staying during some important cases at the Burleigh Hotel in Sauchiehall Street could hardly be due to the comfort and cuisine to be found there. It was more due, Harkness was sure, to Jan the receptionist. When you added Laidlaw's natural tendency to look for any storm in a port you had a recipe that might have blown the lid off a pressure-cooker.

'Okay, Jack,' Harkness said. 'Where to? East Kilbride?'

'She won't be in. Back into the city, Brian. Anyway, even if she was in, we couldn't outdrive a phone-call.'

'What?'

'Mr Veitch is phoning her right now. You can bet on it. Galahad is alive and well. And playing with himself.'

Driving, Harkness remembered something.

'Here. Why no whisky again? This could get monotonous.'

'I take water with my whisky,' Laidlaw said. 'Not condescension.'

13

'. . . in this crowd deaf to its own cry of hunger and misery, revolt and hatred, in this crowd so strangely garrulous and dumb.'

Gus Hawkins was reading the end of the sentence again when the knock came at the door. He was eating a folded slice of bread and jelly, a Saturday lunchtime return to the comfort food of childhood, and drinking the last of his tea. His mother was clearing the table. His father sat in his armchair, a telly cataleptic. Gus made to get up.

'Ah'll get it, son,' his mother said. 'It's likely Maggie from downstairs.'

But her startled 'Oh' as she opened the door made Gus look up to see his brother standing there, wearing his scar like an embarrassing admission in front of his mother of the kind of work he did. He gave her an operatic embrace and winked over her shoulder at Gus. His jollity was a smoke-screen.

'How's the best wee ma in Britain? Aye, Da. Ah've got a mate with me, Ma. We're here to talk to Mastermind there.'

'Jimmy! Ah thought ye'd forgotten the address.'

What should have been anger became laughter in her mouth by the alchemy that enables mothers to transmute their children into what they believe them to be.

'No chance. This is a mate up from Birmingham. Mickey Ballater.'

Gus looked at the big man who stepped in behind his brother. Whatever he did in Birmingham, he wasn't a bank-clerk. Gus's mother shut the door.

'Come in, son. Come in. Mickey, is it? Ah'll make a cuppa tea. We're just finished. Gus comes every Saturday fur his

80

dinner. Then Ah know he's gettin' at least wan good meal in the week. Ah don't know why he canny stay here a' the-gither. But that's the young yins nowadays.'

'Ah know whit ye mean,' Mickey Ballater said.

'Ma. Don't bother wi' tea. We're on our way somewhere. We were passin' an' we jist came in to settle an argument. Ah told 'im ma brother's a genius. He would know.'

Gus realised that his brother was improvising desperately, didn't know what to say next. Hook Hawkins noticed that the doorway to the balcony was open and continued talking.

'Look, we'll no' disturb ma Da's telly. We'll nip out on the balcony. Okay, Gus?'

He went out onto the balcony, followed by Mickey Ballater.

'Fair view, innit?' he said.

'No' bad at all.'

Gus put down his book slowly. He looked at his mother and couldn't be sure whether her expression was what she really felt or a determined cover-up. It seemed to suggest her older son was an awful wag. Gus crossed and stepped out onto the balcony.

Three was a crowd out there. It was thirteen storeys up and Mickey Ballater seemed impressed.

'Never seen the Gorbals from this high up. Seen it from doon there, right enough. Surprised how wee it is. When Ah wis in among it, Ah thought it went on forever. Ah suppose this is progress, eh?'

Gus said nothing. Half of his head was still dealing with Aimé Césaire's *Return to my Native Land*. He hadn't worked out how he came to be standing on the balcony of his parents' house with his brother and another heavy. He was waiting to catch up with events.

'Gus,' Hook said. 'Mickey wants to ask you about Tony.'

'Tony who?'

'Come on, Gus. Tony Veitch.'

'Tony Veitch? What's this about?'

'Tony Veitch,' Mickey said.

'What's he to you?'

'Money,' Mickey said. 'That's what he is. Just money.'

'What do you mean?'

'He owes me money.'

'Tony owes you money?'

'Ah've come a long way,' Mickey said. 'It's gettin' to feel longer. Ah didn't do it for nothin'. He owes me money.'

Gus saw his father still watching television, his mother clearing up. The programme was an old film on BBC2, a grey actor talking nonsense to a grey actress listening nonsensically. It was the kind of film about which the clever Sunday papers would find something clever to say, like 'a delicate sense of period' or 'survives in spite of itself'. It was just crap, a lot of people making what money they could in the way they knew best.

Gus felt angry. Why was his father watching it? He had had a life more harrowing than any of their melodramas. And he hadn't once seen what had happened to him shown on that screen. Gus saw his parents in cameo, peripheral to this moment, peripheral to their own sons, frozen into decoration. He resented it. His anger spilled over.

'What's this about?' he said to his brother.

'Mickey's just askin' a question,' Hook said. 'Where's Tony Veitch?'

'Naw.' Gus was staring at his brother. 'What's this about?'

'Where's Tony Veitch?' Mickey said.

Gus didn't look at him.

'I'm talking to my brother,' he said. 'What's this about?'

'Gus,' Hook Hawkins said. 'People are lookin' for Tony.'

Gus looked at his parents a moment.

'Why don't you organise gang-fights in the kitchen?' he said. 'You bring a hoodlum to ma mammy's house?'

'Listen,' Mickey said.

'Naw. You listen.' Gus Hawkins looked like a bomb that

might soon explode. He was staring at Ballater. 'This is where good people live. We don't need you.'

A signal went off in Mickey Ballater's head. He remembered a chip-shop in the Calton. He had been young and hard and drunk, and he had casually insulted a small, middle-aged man. He had said for the titillation of by-standers, 'Somebody in here's fartit. It wis you!' pointing at the small man. The small man had said nothing, paid for his chips and gone out.

Mickey Ballater had forgotten he said it by the time he came out the door, when he forgot everything for several minutes. He worked out later that the small man must have hit him from the side as he came out, presumably with a gib-crane he had handy. Since then, Ballater had understood that the fiercest man is the one who has had his incomprehensibly private values encroached upon. Attack a mouse in its hole and it will try to nibble you to death.

This was no mouse. He saw one of an endlessly repeated species, the young who haven't found their limits yet and wonder if you could help them. Gus Hawkins was puffed out like a cockerel with his own aggression. He had started before Mickey had even thought of it.

Mickey knew that steel to steel the boy had no chance. Six days a week, Mickey would kill him. But this was one of those seventh days—wrong time, wrong place. It wasn't why he had come. So he had recourse to a feeble gesture.

'Wait a minute!' he said.

Gus Hawkins waited. Mickey found it useful that Hook Hawkins intervened.

'Listen, you,' Hook said.

'Jim!' Gus said at once. 'Don't give me your routine. I'm your brother. In my book you're just a liberty-taker. We're where you come from. Don't try to frighten us. I'll put up with you. But I really don't need his nonsense. He doesn't behave, I'll show him a quick road down.'

He nodded to the pavement thirteen storeys below. Mickey Ballater couldn't believe how silly the boy was but he was trying to. This was unbelievable but it was happening. What struck him was how seriously Hook was taking it.

'For Christ's sake,' Hook was saying. 'You get a grip. The man's just askin' a question. Tony owes him money.'

'I don't believe that.'

'But it's true,' Mickey said.

'Tony Veitch's got money. His mother left him it. He doesny need to owe anybody.'

'Ah don't mean he borrowed it,' Mickey said. 'Ah just said he owes it.'

'What for?'

'That's ma business.'

'Fine. Take it with you when you go out. Like as fast as your legs'll carry you.'

Hook held up his hand to forestall Mickey. He looked down at two boys playing with a ball.

'Gus. Ye're no' in a book now, son. This is serious business. Ah didny want to come here. Ah tried for ye at the flat. Then Ah knew ye wid be here for yer dinner. There's people in a hurry tae find where Tony Veitch is. Mickey's just one o' them.'

'How do you mean?'

'Big John Rhodes is lookin'. And Cam Colvin.'

Gus looked from one to the other, unbelieving.

'Come on. Tony blew his finals.' He laughed. 'Is Cam a member of the University Senate?'

'Whatever that is, Ah think your Tony did a bit more than that,' Mickey said.

'They reckon he did Paddy Collins,' Hook explained.

Gus stood looking over the balcony as if he had never seen the view before. He started to laugh and stopped and looked at the sky. When he looked back at them, his certainty was already clouding.

'Tony?'

'Tony,' Hook said.

'But why would he do that?'

'He owed Paddy as well,' Mickey said. 'I came up and

84

we were gonny collect together. By the time I get here, Paddy's dead. Veitch's shot the crow. Looks a bit that way, doesn't it?'

'You reckon?' Gus was looking at Hook.

Hook nodded.

'So what's it got to do with me?'

'You shared a flat, Gus,' Hook said.

'And what's it got to do with you?'

Gus was completing his thought, running through Hook's statement. Hook was shifty.

'Cam isny too sure about me. Paddy an' me fell out a wee while back.'

Gus's stare left Hook wanting a shield against it.

'Anyway, Ah know you liked him, Gus. Better if Mickey finds him. If he does, he'll have a chance to check if the boay did it, before Cam gets there.'

'I don't know where he is,' Gus said.

'You must have some kind of information,' Mickey said. 'Ah'm holdin' Cam Colvin off. He doesny know about you.'

'Then tell him.'

'It's no' you that's gonny get the napalm. It's yer brither. That wouldny do yer mother a lot o' good.'

Gus looked into the living-room. His father was sitting like somebody found at Pompeii. His mother was reading the paper. Seen from outside, the room looked small, some chairs and ornaments, the pathetic sum of two hard lives. And here on the balcony was what those lives had produced, a hooligan whose existence mocked their decency and a student who still hadn't begun to repay them for what they had given.

He felt an anger that was never far away from him. He looked down at what had been the Gorbals. This was improvement? His parents lived thirteen storeys up in a building where the lift broke down if you looked at it askance. His father's life had made him an offshoot of the bookie and the pub. His mother still offered the world an irreducible decency the world didn't deserve. Something had to be done. In the meantime, he couldn't bear to add one more worry to their lot.

'Gus,' Hook was saying.

Gus looked at Hook, then at Mickey Ballater.

'Don't you two come back,' he said.

But he knew himself the aggression of the remark was no more than stylish surrender. Why should he protect Tony Veitch? Let Tony look to himself. Gus's parents were more important. Yet he resented how his brother was teaching him to hate himself. Family shouldn't matter that much, but here it did. He thought how his father admired Hook more because he lived by his body, whereas Gus was just a reader of books. For his father it was better to batter one aggressor into the ground than try to help all the non-aggressors like himself. It was a strange philosophy, but not uncommon where Gus lived. What did this place want?

'Okay,' Gus said. 'I'll tell you the only thing about Tony that might help you. There's a girl called Lynsey Farren. Lady Lynsey Farren. Lord Farren's daughter. She was with Tony. Then Paddy Collins. Then Dave McMaster.'

Ballater knew he was getting close.

'Where do Ah find 'er?' he asked.

'She's got a shop in East Kilbride. Called "Overdrive".'

'Thanks, Gus,' Hook said.

'For being a shite? Don't mention it.'

Distantly, Gus watched them go into the living-room. He saw how animated his father became because Jim was inviting him down to the pub. When they had gone, he saw how contented his mother looked, as if all was well with the world. He saw how Hook was probably nearer to them than he was, though he loved them in a way he sometimes thought might destroy him. He came slowly back into the room. He lifted his book.

'Oor Jimmy's lookin' well,' his mother said.

Gus didn't look up. He was thinking that he would soon be with Marie and he was glad.

'Is everything all right, son?'

'Fine, maw. Everything's fine.'

He tried to concentrate on his reading. But it was strange how he felt on the opposite side of the book from that with which he had identified before Jim and his friend came in. He felt he was one of the people Aimé Césaire was talking about rather than to.

'In this disarming town, this strange crowd which does not gather, does not mingle: this crowd that can so easily disengage itself, make off, slip away . . .'

14

'A distinct tendency to sculpture whimsy,' the tall man said. His eyes contemplated nothing thoughtfully.

'Not unlike Joyce's poetry.' The small man was fat with black hair like a bush. He spoke with an assurance that suggested it was burning. He wore the kind of intense spectacles that draw the pupils like a poultice. 'But at least he had his prose. Isn't it strange with Joyce how the originality of the prose never seems to transfer to the poetry? As a poet, he remained slightly sub-Georgian. "Lean out of the window, Goldenhair." My God.'

'Or like Emily Dickinson. Reducing all experience to lace doilies.'

'At least it makes a change from the spurious passion of Lawrence. You can't read his poetry without feeling drenched in saliva.'

'Jesus,' Harkness said quietly.

'If we're dropping names, that's a good one,' Laidlaw said.

'How *about* this?'

They were sitting in the Glasgow University Club bar where Mr Jamieson had left them. He was a senior lecturer in English who had known Tony Veitch but he had gone to look for a younger man who had been Veitch's tutor in his final year. Laidlaw was staring at his lime-juice and soda. Harkness was taking his lager like anaesthetic. Around them the heavy buildings and empty quadrangles seemed to shut out the city, giving them the feeling of being at the entrance to a shaft sunk into the past. Certainly, the only other two people in the room were having less a conversation than a seance, though they only seemed to summon the dead in order to rekill them.

'Have there not been any good writers, like?' Harkness asked.

The talk of the two university men reminded Laidlaw of why he had left university at the end of his first year, having passed his exams. He found that the forty-year-old man agreed with the nineteen-year-old boy. He suspected that a lot of academics lived inside their own heads so much they began to think it was Mount Sinai. He disliked the way they seemed to him to use literature as an insulation against life rather than an intensification of it.

He liked books but they were to him a kind of psychic food that should convert to energy for living. With academics the nature of their discipline seemed to preclude that. To take it that seriously would have annihilated the limits of aesthetics.

Listening to their exchange of attitudes in what amounted to a private code, he didn't regret the youthful impulse which had pushed him out into the streets and now brought him back here, by a circuitous and painful route, as an alien visitor. He didn't want to be included in that clique of mutually supportive opinions that so often passes for culture.

He remembered what had finally crystallised his rejection of university. It had been having to read and listen to the vague nonsense of academics commenting on the vague nonsense of much of what D. H. Lawrence wrote. Coming himself from a background not dissimilar to Lawrence's, he thought he saw fairly clearly how Lawrence had put out his eyes with visions rather than grapple with reality that was staring him in the face. You needn't blame him for hiding but you needn't spend volumes trying to justify it either; unless, of course, it helped to make your own hiding easier to take.

'A lot of what passes for intellectuality's just polysyllabic prejudice,' Laidlaw thought aloud.

Harkness remembered Laidlaw telling him that he'd left university at the end of his first year.

'Were you glad to get out of here?'

Before Laidlaw had answered, they saw Mr Jamieson come back in alone. Laidlaw rose to get him a drink. Mr Jamieson took a whisky and joined them.

'I'm sorry,' he said. 'Tony's tutor isn't in today. It's a pity. He knows Tony well. But the academic year is really over, of course.'

He was a frail man with thinning grey hair and pale eyes. His voice was gentle.

'But you know Tony Veitch quite well,' Laidlaw said.

'As a student, yes. He had what I would call a serious intelligence. By that I mean he thought ideas were for living, not just thinking. Hm?'

He nodded infinitesimally towards the other two, who were still talking. He bit his lip briefly as if dismayed at the garishness of his own indiscretion.

'Academicism, of course, can be mental formaldehyde. A way for people to put their brains on display without actually doing anything with them. Tony wanted more. For him any idea he accepted carried a responsibility to living along with it. He was an interesting thinker. Is, no doubt. It's some time since I've seen him.'

Laidlaw was set to ask something, Harkness could see, but Mr Jamieson was preoccupied in following his own thought, like someone out to net a butterfly.

'That's rare, of course. Though less rare here than in some other places. I was glad to come back to Glasgow for that reason. The borders are crossed more easily here, of course.'

Laidlaw noted the intellectual trick of that 'of course', a way of stating something you might only just have realised as if only fools could be unaware of it. It disarmed close examination.

'How do you mean?' he asked.

'You get a lot of first-generation academics here. And some of them are not inclined to endorse the rules of academe too quickly. There's a strong autodidact tradition in Scotland, you see. I happen to believe it's especially strong in the West. Such people don't submit too happily to academic categories. They can have a refreshing swingeing freedom of mind. Mind you, too often career seduces them and they conform to get success. Every year some Visigoths arrive. And every year I feel renewed hope. Perhaps among them there's an Attila of the mind—if you'll excuse a racially mixed metaphor. Someone who will re-animate our rituals by attacking them. Tony had possibilities in that direction.'

Laidlaw was beginning to be more and more interested in Tony Veitch.

'As far as his crossing of borders went? I mean, did he associate with people who didn't seem to fit with university life?'

'Hm? Well, I was his tutor, not a social worker.'

When he stopped talking, the voices of the other two men seemed never to have let up. They weren't reading or drinking or even looking at each other. They just sat casually communing with their own profundity.

'A despair as actual as leprosy.'

'Imagine a Somme,' Mr Jamieson said, 'where everyone is immortal. Nothing can happen, of course. But, oh my God, the noise!'

'Mr Jamieson,' Laidlaw said. 'About Tony Veitch.'

'Yes. Tony hated that.'

'Is that why he ducked out of his finals?'

'I should imagine so. He seems to have been doing well in the papers he sat. He was rejecting us, I suppose. Perhaps not without reason.' For the first time his eyes achieved a clearly specific focus, emerged from the abstract. 'Do you think you'll find him?'

'We were hoping you might help,' Laidlaw said, not without some recrimination in his voice.

'Yes. I'm getting an address for you. We tried ourselves, you see. At first. We hoped it might be possible to make some arrangement for him to take the other papers. But he obviously didn't intend that anyone should find him.'

'Did he seem to you a violent person at any time?'

The pale eyes smiled.

'Isn't everyone?' The remark was unexpected in his mild mouth. 'He was certainly intellectually violent. Iconoclastic. But then many young people are.'

A woman with glasses came in, wearing a smile that was like opening a window in a stuffy room. She gave Mr Jamieson a piece of paper and went out.

'Thank you, Sybil,' he said and passed the paper to Laidlaw.

'Who's Guthrie Hawkins?' Laidlaw asked.

'He shared a flat with Tony Veitch. The other addresses are Tony and Guthrie's home addresses. The flat may be vacated by now, of course.'

Laidlaw drained his lime-juice and soda. A bit of ice, eroded to a lozenge, slid down the glass as he replaced it.

'Thank you, Mr Jamieson,' he said. 'I appreciate the time and all the help you've given us.'

'I hope that he's all right. I think I understand him a little. I think I understand his decision. One of the terrors of academicism is that our criticism becomes absorbed as merely one of its own techniques. Hm? It's an endless maze. Every exit from one dilemma is merely an entrance to another. Hm?'

It should have been eerie as a man carving his own epitaph. He sat looking old, gentle, charming and hopeless. He gave off a sense of defeat. Yet he spoke without feeling, seemed merely to be commenting. It was as if he had reduced himself to the status of a gloss on his own life.

'There is something. Guthrie Hawkins is perhaps an example of the crossing of borders I was talking about. Tony Veitch once mentioned in tutorial that Guthrie had a brother in the criminal world.'

'Do you know his first name?'

'I'm afraid not.'

'Observatory Road,' Laidlaw said as they came out into University Avenue. 'That's just round the corner. Off Byres Road. We may as well try it. The other address is in Hutchesontown.'

92

They got into the car. Laidlaw lit a cigarette. As usual, Harkness was driving.

'You think Eck knew about Paddy's death and had to be shut up?' Harkness asked.

'Could be, I suppose.'

'Nice old man.'

'Brave enough, too. When you think how near his heart the hemlock is.'

15

The peg-board in the window showed a couple of bright blouses and a sweatshirt with a lurex butterfly. The name painted across the glass in cursive red letters was 'Overdrive'. Beneath it the black printing said: 'If you like top gear, why not come into Overdrive?' He went in.

He felt like a visitor from a spaceship, but an interested one. The piped music made him feel alien, as rock always did. His musical taste had stopped at Country & Western. The smell of what could have been incense annoyed him into wondering again what the hell teenagers were up to. The clothes didn't help, racks of the kind of colours that suggested a dressing-room at a circus.

Besides the long racks and circular racks he noticed bright Indian-looking scarves tied from a beam. There was a display of thonged sandals, a section for beads he would have refused as a prize at a fairground. He heard a voice.

'Try it on. I think you'll see what I mean.'

He walked along a rack of dresses and a girl emerged at the other end. She was wearing a shocking-pink blouse with one shoulder and sleeve missing and leopard-skin trousers that would have fitted a gnat. She was doing everything but carry a megaphone. She smiled a smile that was twenty years ahead of its time and condescendingly acknowledged the awkwardness of his hulking invasion of her trendy world.

'Yes, sir. Can I get you something?'

'No thanks,' he said. 'Ah'm no' holdin' Hallowe'en this year.'

He looked casually past her at the slatted saloon doors that were the entrance to the two small fitting-rooms.

Beneath one set of doors he could see a good pair of legs that were trying on a denim skirt.

'But don't mind me. Ah can wait.'

He looked back at her and enjoyed the way her face had lost its composure and was fumbling for the right reaction. She looked properly young again and her accent had got lost in the post.

'Lusten, mister. Whit is it ye want?'

'Well. Nane o' these is quite ma colour. Could Ah see the manageress? Is Lynsey Farren in?'

'Whit for?'

'Hen, suddenly Ah'm in a hurry. Tell 'er.'

'Whit for?'

He looked round and located a beaded curtain blocking a doorway. He walked towards it. Coming behind him, the girl called, 'Miss Farren!' The curtain was pulled aside and the face that looked past it renewed his interest of last night. It looked as if it had ordered the future, which would be coming along on a silver tray. The face took him in like passing traffic and referred itself to the girl.

'Janice?'

Janice absorbed the accent like a refresher-course.

'It's this gentleman, Miss Farren. He says he wants to see you.'

'Very good, Janice.'

Janice went back to her customer. Miss Farren came through the curtain. He appreciated the revelation.

'Yes?'

'Yes.'

'You wanted to see me.'

'Yes. Ah enjoyed that. But Ah'd like to talk as well.'

'What is this?'

And then she recognised him.

'This is Mickey Ballater. A friend of Paddy Collins. Ah'd like a word with ye. In private.'

She handled it well, converting a flicker of panic in the eyes to instant boredom. She studied the wall beside him as if there were printed instructions there.

'You've come at an awkward time. I'm afraid I'm rather busy.'

'Times'll likely get a helluva sight more awkward if you don't speak to me right now.'

'I can't imagine what it could be about.'

'Don't waste yer time. Ah'll tell ye. Paddy Collins. Tony Veitch. Dave McMaster. Cam Colvin.'

'Are all of these names supposed to mean something to me?'

'Naw. Ah got them out the telephone directory. Let's go inside.'

A woman had come out of the fitting-room and was talking to Janice. Lynsey Farren hesitated, perhaps gauging how much more complicated it was going to be playing to two audiences. She turned and went through the curtain. He followed her.

It wasn't an exceptional back-shop, a table with an electric kettle on it, a couple of chairs, a small calor-gas heater, two cartons stacked one on the other, the top one spilling an opened cellophane pack of multi-coloured blouses—but she contrived to inhabit it as if it were fully furnished with antiques. She was quizzically amused, demonstrating what a clash of styles they were.

As she took a menthol cigarette from a packet, he lifted the slim metallic grey lighter from the table and lit her cigarette. He kept the lighter in his hand as he sat down, flicking it into flame two or three times. She sat easily against the table, crossing her legs. He fidgeted a moment with the big, empty metal waste-bin on the floor and looked up. She was still wondering what it was all about.

'Paddy Collins is dead. You knew that?'

'Is this a joke?'

'Fourteen stab wounds? If it is, Paddy didny see it.'

She said nothing.

'Where's Tony Veitch?'

'Who's Tony Veitch?'

'Money for me.'

'I'm afraid I can't help.'

'Oh well. Ah doubt Ah'm wastin' ma time.'

'It looks that way.'

'Aye.'

He stood up, seemed nonplussed. He picked up one of the blouses from the cellophane and studied it. The label inside the neck said 'Baumwolle Cotton'.

'Nice that,' he said.

'It wouldn't suit you.'

In one action he flicked the lighter, lit the blouse and dropped it into the waste-bin. In the tightness of the room it flared like an explosion, a quick geyser of flame the heat of which she felt. It brought her off her table, mouthing outrage that died as quickly as the fire.

'What the hell? Do you . . . I'll get the police.'

Both understood what the quickness of her silence meant. He was looking at the lighter in his hand. He shook his head.

'You don't want the police,' he said. 'But this place could burn down very easy. Not the day. Maybe later.' He looked at her. 'Ye want to tell the wee lassie to go out? Ye could talk freer.'

She paused only briefly, putting down her cigarette. She lifted a blouse from the pile and went out into the shop. When she came back in, he was sitting down again. Sitting against the table, she took up the cigarette but it was no longer a prop. She dragged on it anxiously.

'Janice is still in the shop,' she said pointedly. 'She's changing the window.'

He nodded.

'Lady Lynsey Farren. Don't think Ah've spoken to an actual lady before. We weren't trippin' over them in Crown Street. It's nice. But then ye're not really any different, are ye, love? Paddy told me about you, ye see. The pair o' ye seem tae have got up tae some very unladylike capers. That was before Dave McMaster came on the scene, wasn't it? Ye know Cam Colvin apart from last night?'

She shook her head. He decided there was no way to know if she was telling the truth. She probably smiled by committee decision.

'Fair enough,' he said. 'We'll do it that way. You in your small corner and me in mine. All ye have to do is listen. Tony Veitch is due me money. Paddy Collins was going to help to collect. Tony Veitch has disappeared. Paddy Collins is extra dead. That's where we are. Ah'll tell ye where we're goin'. Cam Colvin is Paddy's brother-in-law. If ye don't know him, Ah'll tell ye who he is. The Black Death in a pinstripe suit. Ah take money, he takes lives. He's angry about Paddy and lookin' for anybody connected with him recently. Ah know a lot of things Cam doesny know. You were there when Paddy met Tony Veitch. You had a wee thing with Paddy. Then you moved on to Dave McMaster.'

'What's Tony supposed to have done?'

'Ye miss the point. Ah mean, we both know what he's done. But ye miss the point. Ah'm not here to answer questions. Ah'm here to ask one. Just one. Where's Tony Veitch?'

'I don't know. I honestly don't know. How am I supposed to know?'

'Ye're either lyin' or ye're not. Ah haveny the time to worry about it. But Ah know one thing. Ye can find out. You an' him was close. An' that's what ye're goin' to do. Ye got a pen?'

He tore a strip of paper off the bottom of the calendar behind him. Automatically, she picked up a pen from the table and handed it to him. He wrote something down, handed pen and paper back to her. He had written a telephone number, the pen-point having gone through the paper a couple of times.

'What am I supposed to do with this?'

'You've got the rest of the day. You phone me there. And tell me where Tony Veitch is. If Ah'm not in, you keep phoning till Ah am in.'

'You can't be serious.'

'Ah thought Ah was.'

'There's no way I can find out. He's disappeared.'

'Ye've got two choices. Ye find him or Ah pass on what Ah know to Cam Colvin. You tell Dave McMaster that. Ah

98

don't think Dave wid like that to happen. The bother could be very bad. You're a tourist here, hen. Ye don't know what it's really like. Ah can arrange tae show ye. Ye like mixin' wi' tearaways, do ye? Ah can mix ye in that much, ye'll never get loose again.' He pointed at her. 'You're in serious trouble, milady. Ah'm offerin' you an easy road out. Take it. Tell me what Ah don't know, an' Ah tell nobody what Ah do know.'

He stood up.

'Ah'm goin' now. Phone Dave.'

He went out. As she looked at the number he had given her, she heard Janice speaking to a customer about jeans. She wished that was all she had to worry about. She lifted the phone.

16

'Yesterday all my mogres seemed so far away.
Now Ah'm paintin' every bloody day.
Ah've chinged ma mind. Gi'es yesterday.'
The singing led them to the house. It was near the top of
the road, past Hillhead Parish Church. The big double
doors were lying open with a piece of cardboard against the
jamb with 'Wet Paint' painted on it. Two men in stained
white boilersuits were painting the groundfloor windows
on either side of the door. The one on the left, a florid man in
his fifties, was working at ground level. The other, about
thirty and in need of a shave, was up a ladder because his
window was above the basement flat. He was the singer.
His improvised lyric had tailed off into Glaswegian mouth-
music: 'Ta-ta-reetin-deetin-beetin-bu-Pa-reeting-du-da-
reeting-du.'
It was a big, handsome house, three-storeyed with a
long, low modern dormer window. Its Victorian porten-
tousness, basking in the sunshine, was undermined some-
what by the nine push-buttons inset in its front. The names
listed beside the buttons testified to the contemporary identity crisis being undergone by a building constructed out of
a formidable self-assurance. No doubt it felt a certain affinity
with James R. P. S. MacKenzie and Miss L. S. Booth-
Williams. But the basement claimed to be occupied by
'Maggie, Jeanne, Sarah and Mad Liz.' Flat 9 said 'The
Friends of Che.'
'Lookin' for Mad Liz, boays?' the singer asked. He pointed
downwards. 'She dwelleth in the nether regions. A right big
cracker. An' daft as a brush. The perfect combie.'
Laidlaw laughed and Harkness waved and they went in
past the payphone in the hall. As they climbed the stairs,

100

they heard the preoccupied conversation of the painters through the open door.

'She's no' that mad that she fancies you anyway,' the older man said.

'Harry! They all fancy me. Ah carry a pocketful o' stones tae throw at them. Ah've got tae protect maself. Why d'ye think Ah go hame a different road every night? Tae avoid all these birds in ambush.'

'Ye couldny get yer end away at an orgy.'

'Anyway, Ah don't think yon was Mad Liz.'

'The big blondie?'

'Nah. Ah didny fancy her anyway. Like a prop-forward wi' tits. Pa-ra-dee-pa-ra-rutin-dutin-beedle-be . . .'

Flat 9 was up a final small stair to what had been part of the attic. Laidlaw knocked on the Yale-locked door.

'Aye. Who's that?'

Laidlaw made a face that meant he didn't talk to doors and knocked again. There was something said that sounded like 'Oh to hell,' a pause, and the door opened.

'Guthrie Hawkins?'

He grimaced. 'Gus Hawkins.'

He wore only a pair of jeans. He was early twenties, with blue direct eyes that looked as if they wouldn't have been intimidated by a regiment. His hair was black, cut rough and ruffled. He was fairly short but his bare torso was so blatant with power height would have been overstatement. When his eyes came up from Laidlaw's identity-card they had grown a skin of distance.

'What's this about?'

'It's about Tony Veitch.'

'Again?' he said and smiled. 'You going to wait there a minute, please?' He closed the door on them.

When it opened again, he was carrying a v-necked sweater. He pulled it over his head as they came in.

The door opened directly on to the one-roomed flat. To the left of it hung a curtain of blue and white plastic strips, separating the cooker, sink and some cupboards from the rest of the room. There were three beds, two of them with

101

cushions decorating their neatness. The third bed had signs of having been hastily made up, suggestive wrinkles showing beneath its coverlet.

But the essence of the place wasn't in the sparseness of its furnishings. It was in what had grown in their interstices. The walls were a collage defying interpretation. Che Guevara was surrounded by Thurber cartoons, his handsome romanticism as decontextualised as a tragedian on a tube-train. There were various photographs and drawings obviously cut out of books: Marx, Camus, T. S. Eliot, Socrates, John Maclean pointing an admonitory finger at the world, Marlon Brando refusing to give Eva Marie Saint back her glove in 'On the Waterfront', Hemingway studiedly being Hemingway. There were prints of 'Old Woman Cooking an Egg', Pisarro's 'Peasant Digging' and Breughel's 'Icarus' with a typewritten sheet beside it containing Auden's 'Musée des Beaux Arts'. There was a post-card from Pollok House showing 'Adam Naming the Beasts' and 'Eve Naming the Birds'. Most conspicuously, there were books, the real furniture. They covered the place like a fungoid growth, having proliferated from the single three-tiered bookshelf into piles on the floor.

The images all around were like holes drilled in the drab walls, offering strange vistas. Together with the books, they were a denial not just of the room but of the city beyond it, a refusal to have vision circumscribed by circumstances.

Laidlaw felt immediately two things: that just by standing here he was closer to Tony Veitch, could take the pulse of his comprehensible strangeness, knew a little better where he came from; that he was looking at a lost part of himself. He stood among the complex and incompatible idealisms of youth and remembered having been there. Remembering that, he had the grace to be aware that he was alien. Middle-age was foreign country here. This was a shrine to youth, where compromise was like a profanation.

The girl emphasised the feeling in him. She had pulled on jeans and T-shirt. She had mules on her bare feet. Her recent vulnerability was her embarrassment now. Her breasts seemed too conspicuous, as if she knew the three men in the room were too aware of them. The intense privacy of what she had been involved in had been made public before she was ready. Her shyness was an indictment. Laidlaw felt guilty.

'Look,' he said. 'I'm sorry we disturbed you. I'm Jack Laidlaw. This is Brian Harkness. We won't be long.'

'That's all right,' Gus Hawkins said. 'This is Marie.'

Laidlaw liked him at once. Considering the varieties of embarrassment and aggression and deceit the arrival of the police gave rise to, Laidlaw liked the cool directness of the boy's response. Gus leaned back on his elbow on the bed they had been making love on, and wore his preposterous health like an aureole. He knew whatever happened he could handle it.

Marie put out two chairs for them and sat on the third remaining chair. Gus gestured them to sit down. Laidlaw admired his style and, admiring it, couldn't resist trying to disconcert it.

'You said "again",' he said.

'Sorry?'

'When I mentioned Tony Veitch. You said, "Again?" Who's been asking about him?'

'People.'

'I'd worked that out. What people, though? You see, it could be important. You could be withholding vital information.'

Gus Hawkins held out both hands, palms up, wrists together. Laidlaw and Harkness managed not to smile.

'Naw,' Gus Hawkins said. 'Don't take me away. Just friends at the uni. There seems a lot of fuss about Tony. So what's he done?'

'As far as I'm concerned, he's disappeared. We'd like to find him.'

'I don't know where he is.'

'No ideas at all about where he might go?'

'I've checked them all. D'you think I wouldn't?'

'Well, maybe you could tell us something that might help us to find him.'

Gus sat up on the bed and clasped his hands, elbows resting on his knees. He stared at the floor for a time and looked up, seeming to have made a decision.

'You want a cup of coffee?'

'That would be great,' Harkness said.

'I'll get it,' Marie said.

'Would you, love? Thanks. Okay, I'll tell you what I can.'

Laidlaw wondered why.

'Did you know he was going to take off? I mean, did he give any indication of it?'

'Not really. Not any more than at any other time. He could've shot the crow at any time during the last year or so, Tony. He had become allergic to the uni.'

'So how did it happen?'

'Well, I'd given him the place to himself for the week of the finals. I've just finished Junior Honours, right? I look in a couple of times during the week. To see if I could help. Like Anglo-Saxon vocabulary or something. Or check references for him maybe. Last time I saw him was on the Thursday night. He seemed all right. Bit of a zombie, the way everybody is at the finals. Your head standing in for a filing-cabinet. But he was all right. Reckoned he had done pretty well so far. Then Saturday.'

He shook his head. His eyes rediscovered the puzzlement he must have felt then.

'I come in on Saturday morning. The door's not even shut. It's lying open. I push it. And it's like coming aboard the *Mary Celeste*. I *knew* there was something wrong. I mean, there was no reason why he should be here. It wasn't that. It was just—the room hadn't been left, it had been abandoned. There was a full cup of coffee sitting on the floor. A couple of drawers hanging out where he had emptied them. About half-a-dozen books scattered round the floor, all open. I looked in the cupboard and his travelling-bag was gone. And that was it. Never seen him since.'

'What did you do?'

'I checked with the uni. He hadn't turned up. I went round some of the places I thought he might be. Pubs and that. No joy. I don't know why he went, but he really meant it. Even took his music centre.'

'Was he in any kind of trouble that you know of? We spoke to Mr Jamieson at the University—'

Gus Hawkins allowed the distribution of coffee-mugs to defer the question. Laidlaw had Snoopy. Harkness was drinking out of a 19th-century remedy for rheumatism. Marie gave out milk and sugar. Harkness thought she was an attractive girl.

'Not that I know of.'

'Did Tony know a man called Paddy Collins?'

Gus tested the hotness of the coffee.

'That sounds familiar. I think he's mentioned him.'

'He knew him well?'

'Tony didn't know anybody well.'

'What do you mean? He was a loner?'

'Not by choice. He tried to mix. But he was oil and everybody else was water. He just sat on the surface. He *thought* he knew people. He probably thought every casual chat was soul-talk. He was naive.'

'In what way?'

'Look. You could show Tony's development geographically. Without going outside Byres Road. And that's pathetic. You know what he did? When he came here? He was here before me. We've talked about it often. He spent a year in The Salon in Vinicombe Street. Just down the road there. Seeing some pictures three times. Whatever they were showing, that's what he saw. If it was Tom and Jerry, he was there. He was hiding from the shock of real life. Then in his second year he did his Captain Scott. He started to go into "The Rubaiyat". Then "The Curlers". Then "Tennents". Do you know what I mean?'

Laidlaw thought he knew. The three pubs are all in Byres Road. He supposed Gus Hawkins meant that Tony's progress had been towards some idea of a working-class pub.

'Then he went beyond Partick Cross. He was Vasco da Gama. "The Kelvin". "The Old Masonic Arms". Next stop, outer space.'

'That's where he seems to be now. There must have been some indication of him being under pressure.'

'Everybody doing finals is under pressure. You don't need the doctor's bag to work that out.'

'You think that's all it was?'

Gus seemed to be savouring his coffee.

'As far as I know.'

'So you think he'll turn up again?'

'Haven't a clue.'

'Did you ever meet Tony's father?'

'No. He mentioned him a couple of times.'

'Not more than that?'

'Well, he seemed to put him in roughly the same bracket as leukaemia. I don't suppose that's something you'd want to bum about a lot.'

'Lynsey Farren?'

'I've seen her.'

'And?'

'Pleasant enough to talk to if you've got the dark bins on. She dresses like Blackpool Illuminations.'

'What more do you know about her?'

'She's some kind of hand-knitted Scottish aristocracy, is she not? I just thought somebody should've taken the after-birth out of her eyes. I thought she was dangerously naive. But then I think most people are.'

'Including Tony?'

'Aye. Especially to himself.'

'Does the name Eck Adamson mean anything to you?'

'The old wino?'

'That's right.'

'He's been here a coupla times. Bumming off Tony.'

'Not off you?'

'I don't invest in lost causes.'

'You know when they're lost, do you?'

'I've got a fair idea.'

'Lucky you. You reckon Tony's one? A lost cause.'

'I don't know. I just think his naivete's dangerous. Like psychic TNT, that stuff. And he had every pocket stuffed with it. It was like he'd lived so long in a sterile unit. I suppose money's like that. Every half-boiled idea that touched him, he came down with it. He had no resistance. Because reality wasn't where he lived. It was where he was trying to go. I mean, he's very bright. But his brightness has no antibodies.'

'I don't get you,' Harkness said.

Gus's eyes took in the girl, looked at Harkness.

'He gave you his face like a blank cheque. You know?' He was enjoying holding court. 'Anything different from what he'd had was hooking him. He mainlined anecdotes about working-class life. I used to tell him daft things. Like eating porridge out a drawer. Things I've only heard of. And say they happened to me. I wasn't being nasty. Well, maybe just a wee bit.' He smiled reflectively. 'Mainly, I was taking the piss to teach him a lesson. Like cold turkey. But it never worked. But I liked him. Tony was all right at that time.'

'Your liking's past tense,' Laidlaw said. 'What happened?'

'Aw, listen. I still like him. When he's gone the rest of the road, I hope I catch up with him again.'

'But you wouldn't know where?'

'No. All I mean is when the revolution comes, I hope they don't shoot Tony. He's one rich guy worth saving.'

'Eck Adamson's dead. Did you know that?'

His face gave no response.

'No. I didn't. But I knew it was coming.'

'How?'

'He worked hard at it, didn't he?'

'Well, actually, he got a bit of help. He was poisoned.'

'How did they find one he hadn't tried already?'

'Paraquat.'

'Aye, I suppose that would work.'

'Oh, it did. Had you seen him lately?'

'Tony mentioned he had been here the last night I saw him.'

'Did he mention anything specific about the meeting?'

107

Gus shook his head.

'Anything else you can think of?'

Gus shook his head. Laidlaw looked at the girl. She had spent almost the whole time watching Gus Hawkins. She looked as if her eyes were voting Gus for God. Gus looked as if he would second that.

'What does your brother do?' Laidlaw asked.

Gus looked up at him very carefully.

'Sorry?'

'I hear you've got a brother. What does he do?'

Gus gave him a slow, dazzling smile like the beam of a searchlight: halt, you have been spotted.

'I wonder,' he said. 'I must ask him sometime.'

Laidlaw surrendered.

'Well, thanks for your help.'

'And for the coffee,' Harkness said to Marie.

Laidlaw paused, noticing two picture frames on the bookshelf. They didn't contain pictures. Inside each was a hand-written poem. Laidlaw recognised Tony Veitch's writing. He went over for a closer look.

> *I am the one*
> *Who scratches before he itches*
> *Brings the weather indoors*
> *Sees the pig in the rasher*
> *Eats an egg and tastes feathers*
> *Is everybody else's pupil.*

'Tony called them word-photos,' Gus said.

'Has he written to you since he disappeared?' Laidlaw asked.

'He did, actually. A long letter about Marxism. Trying to show me the error of my ways. I've lost it.'

> *We are big, abandoned, bleached by sun.*
> *We are the absence of everyone.*
> *Held by void, we hold it,*
> *Finite dimensions round the infinite.*
> *We are the bones of the many*
> *Housing the bones of the few.*

'But photos of what?' Laidlaw said.

'Well, they're riddles.' Gus was laughing. 'You're supposed to work them out for yourself.'

'Just like some people's conversation,' Laidlaw said as they went out.

'Not a silly boy,' Harkness said in the car.

'No. A bit more clued up than we are at the moment. You going to drop me off at the Burleigh? Must be this case but I'm going to need the migraine pills. You take time off and see the lady of your choice. Pick me up later for East Kilbride. How many women are you perming from these days?'

Harkness didn't think it was funny.

'Checked the shops along Queen Margaret Drive,' Laidlaw said. 'Nobody knew him. For all he shows himself he could be living in a cave.'

'Find the lady,' Harkness said, enjoying driving on the dual carriageway. 'Maybe Miss Farren can help.'

Lying close to Glasgow, the modernity of East Kilbride is demonstrated by the good roads that converge on it and the roundabouts that mark their confluence like whirlpools. The town occurs among them like an archipelago.

In one of the islands is the police station. There Laidlaw and Harkness found something interesting. The Uniform Log contained an entry for over a week previously, concerning a girl called Lynsey Farren. The police had been called to her place to deal with a disturbance involving a man.

Hearing the sounds of a violent quarrel, a neighbour, Mr Watters, had knocked at her door. The door was opened slightly. Before it was slammed shut again by a man who told him to go away, he heard Miss Farren's voice saying she was a prisoner and urging him to call the police. This he did. When the police arrived no man was present in the flat but Miss Farren showed signs of having been violently treated, notably severe bruising on her arms. Miss Farren, however, insisted that she had merely meant to threaten the man with the police and declined to identify him. 'Miss Farren refused to proceed with the matter.'

She lived in Old Vic Court, in a ninth floor flat. It was a well kept building. Coming out of the lift, Laidlaw checked the names on the landing and rang the bell to the flat that said 'Michael E. Watters'. Harkness looked at him.

'She seems a hider,' Laidlaw said. 'Like you might need radar to locate her. Let's see if they can help.'

The door was opened by a tall, thin man whose caution suggested that only muggers called on him. He looked worn.

'Yes?'

'Mr Watters?'

'Yes?'

'Detective Inspector Laidlaw. Scottish Crime Squad. This is Detective Constable Harkness. We wondered if we could talk to you.'

Laidlaw held out his wallet with the identification-card. Mr Watters stared at it as if it were a knife.

'Police?'

'It's all right. We're just following up something that might be connected with the incident in Miss Farren's flat. We thought you might be able to help us.'

'Excuse me. Could you wait a minute, please?'

He disappeared into the house.

'Probably away to stash the sub-machine guns,' Harkness said and took a mock kick at the door. 'Okay, baby, this is a raid.'

The man came back.

'Come in, please. I was just explaining to Molly. The wife. She can't take too much excitement.'

Harkness felt flattered, as if they were a ticker-tape parade. They came into a room that was oppressively cosy. Knick-knacks abounded. It was like a stud-farm for ornaments. Wee horses faced big horses, dogs cohabited with cats, a china donkey, china ducks. Wall space was at a premium. It looked as if they would soon be hanging stuff out of the window. 'The old curiosity room,' Harkness thought.

'Mrs Watters,' Laidlaw said. 'I'm Detective Inspector Laidlaw. This is Detective Constable Harkness. It's kind of you to see us.'

She nodded in agreement. Mr Watters gestured them to sit down.

'Oh dear,' she said. 'What we've had to put up with. You

111

live decently all your days. And when you've got the place you want, this is what you have to put up with.'

She had the high colouring and the faint wickerwork of veins in her cheeks of someone who might have heart trouble. With her very black hair unmarked by grey, she had a kind of hothouse bloom that contrasted with the washed-out appearance of her husband.

'I don't know. The way some people live. *We* keep ourselves to ourselves. We're never out.' She tapped her chest delicately. 'It's my heart, you see. But she's a trial to us.'

'You mean Miss Farren?' Laidlaw asked.

She nodded.

'In what way?'

'Ho!' She stared at the electric fire, leaned over and fractionally moved the dish of water in front of it as if she knew exactly where the atmosphere needed moistening.

'You mean there have been other incidents?'

'Don't you think one was enough?'

'I'm sorry. I don't understand. What then?'

She paused and looked at her husband.

'Men,' she said. 'Comings and goings.'

She looked at Laidlaw and nodded. Harkness enjoyed watching Laidlaw's face trying to deal with the invitation to share her shock. He chewed the side of his mouth and was nodding very slowly. Harkness wondered what he was agreeing with.

'Mr Watters. Maybe you could tell us exactly what happened three weeks ago.'

'The noise was terrible,' Mrs Watters said. 'We stood it as long as we could. Then Michael went to the door. It took them a while to open it.'

'Who opened it?'

'It was a man.'

Laidlaw took out his photograph of Tony Veitch and made to pass it to Mr Watters.

'Was it this man?'

Mrs Watters intercepted it. She looked at it and gave it to

112

her husband. He covered the left-hand side of the face with his hand.

'I only saw his eye round the edge of the door. It could've been *his* eye.'

Laidlaw looked at Harkness. 'That your right eye did commit a severe assault,' Harkness thought.

'Then he told me to go away and shut the door.'

'What exactly did he say?'

Mr Watters looked at his wife and paused. He cleared his throat.

'Fuck off,' he mumbled.

They all sat waiting for the word to disperse like a noxious smell. Harkness had an insight he didn't enjoy. It was of Mr Watters spending his days attached to his wife like a life-support unit, a human pacemaker. Since they had come in everything had been focused on Mrs Watters. The room was her sterile area. Illness has its uses, he thought. Life must approach her in a medical mask. He imagined the two of them in hiding here, interested in nothing more than the beat of her heart.

'But she shouted to you to phone the police.' Mrs Watters said. 'Then she wouldn't prosecute. She must have known she was in the wrong.'

'Did you see the man leave?'

'We keep ourselves to ourselves. What is it you're trying to find out exactly?' Mrs Watters was stern.

'We're not sure yet,' Laidlaw said. 'What does Miss Farren do?'

'She's not short of a shilling, the same girl. Some kind of new-fangled shop she has. What is it they call it?'

'It's a boutique in the town here,' Mr Watters said. ' "Overdrive".'

Laidlaw thanked them and they left. Mr Watters saw them to the door. Mrs Watters waved abstractedly like a queen in a passing coach.

'Which of them do you think's in more danger?' Harkness asked.

'Aye,' Laidlaw said. 'I know what you mean.'

113

Lynsey Farren seemed like a different species. She opened the door at once, saying 'Forgotten your key . . .?' She obviously hadn't bothered to check the spyhole that looked as if it had been recently inserted in the door by an amateur joiner. The excitement in her greenish eyes hardened into distrust. She stared at them. They didn't mind staring back.

She was a big blonde girl, say late twenties, subtle as a fanfare. The face was handsome, wide eyes, strong nose, slightly ferocious mouth, and the body was generous. She made Nell Gwynn look peaky. She was dressed to go out, if not to emigrate, in a long green dress with something that looked like an overgrown waistcoat over it, big earrings, a necklace and so many bangles they almost constituted luggage. She gave the immediate impression she was wearing her boutique.

'Good evening,' Laidlaw said, and seemed to Harkness to be showing amazing presence of mind.

'Who are you?' she asked. She had one of those slightly butch upper-class voices.

Laidlaw showed his card and said who they were.

'What do you want?'

'Miss Farren?'

'Yes.'

'It may be connected with that business about a week ago.'

'That's over with. I've nothing to add. I told them that.'

The door was closing.

'Something else has come up.'

The door opened again and she re-emerged from behind it like a quick-change artiste. It had been pleasure, then distrust. Now she was bored. Her eyelashes seemed to weigh a ton. Harkness decided she had been preparing for them. She had overdone it.

'Oh look. What is it?'

'Murder,' Laidlaw said.

'I'm just going out.'

'Two people already have. Permanently.'

114

'*Two* people? Oh, come in if you like. But I can't give you long.'

She walked away, leaving the door open. Harkness closed it as they came in. You almost had to climb over the smell of perfume to get in the room. It was a studied place, Harkness thought—kitsch tapestries, a big, round glass table, a half-acre of painting above the imitation fireplace showing horses posing on the foreshore. One of those studio mock-up LPs of recent hits recorded by Joe Soap & Company was playing, authentic as a wooden penny. It belonged. Harkness wondered if that was why she wore her hair long: her ears were made of tin.

She didn't ask them to sit down. She took a cigarette and lit it. Laidlaw and Harkness stood like members of the audience who have wandered on to the stage.

'Well?'

'What exactly happened three weeks ago, Miss Farren?'

'A misunderstanding. It's personal.'

'So's murder. Very.'

'*I* wasn't murdered.'

'Miss Farren. We're trying to find out if whoever was here three weeks ago might have been involved in a stabbing that's happened since then. It's important for us to establish who it was who was with you.'

She glanced at her watch. She sat down. Laidlaw and Harkness did the same.

'I hardly knew him,' she said.

'Do you know his name?'

She checked the brand name on her cigarette as if it tasted strange and looked across at Laidlaw suddenly, boldly.

'No. Look, I'm embarrassed about it. I'd had too much to drink. I met him and brought him back here and it all went sour. Very sour. Never again. It's embarrassing but I honestly don't know his name.'

'His first name?'

'Not even that.'

The silence was the sound of incredulity. Laidlaw took out Eck's piece of paper and passed it to her. As she read it, she stopped over-acting like a tic-tac man. Her face became still.

'You recognise the writing, Miss Farren?'

'It's Tony's writing.'

'He's written to you, has he?'

She nodded.

'When?'

'About a week ago.'

Harkness felt she was about to tell them the truth. He reckoned the phone-call from Milton Veitch foreseen by Laidlaw had happened. She had decided what she would tell and what she wouldn't. He was convinced this was something she had chosen to be honest about, perhaps because they knew her connection with him already or perhaps because she cared about him or perhaps just because good lies need a leavening of the truth to make them palatable.

'It was a letter. We had stopped seeing each other. Tony and I've known each other for years. At one time it felt like love. But it wasn't. Not for me. Not that kind, anyway.'

'It was you that packed it up?'

'That's right. It was a long letter.'

'Do you have it?'

'I destroyed it.'

Harkness reflected that Tony Veitch wasn't having a lot of luck with his writing. Maybe he should have enclosed a stamped-addressed envelope for return of manuscripts.

'He must have been affected by the break-up,' Laidlaw said. 'You think that might have something to do with his disappearance? You know he's disappeared?'

'I know. But I don't think so. It was a very calm letter. Just trying to analyse our relationship, I suppose.'

'That piece of paper you have. It was found on a vagrant. Eck Adamson. Does the name mean anything to you?'

It didn't.

'He's dead of paraquat poisoning. The other names?'

She looked at Laidlaw condescendingly, returning to the dismissive style she had adopted on first seeing them. Her moment of truth was evidently over.

116

'My own means something to me,' she said.

'Not Paddy Collins?'

She shook her head.

' "The Crib"?'

'It's a pub Tony and I sometimes went to.'

'A bit down-market, isn't it?'

'Tony liked that.'

'And you?'

'It makes a change. Look. I'm not quite finished getting ready.'

Harkness couldn't imagine what else she was going to do—apply varnish? But she had made up her mind. The rest was a lock-out and her impenetrability was double-bolted when the outside door of the flat suddenly opened and a young man came in, whistling like a bush of blackbirds and walking at the head of an invisible parade. He halted dramatically, observing the group. Laidlaw and Harkness recognised Dave McMaster.

But it didn't do them much good. He and Lynsey Farren might as well have dropped in for the weekend from Mars. What they didn't know about Glasgow was compendious. Dave had seen Tony Veitch in "The Crib" but that was all. Was Paddy Collins dead? Who was Eck Adamson? By the time Dave had taken up with Lynsey, Tony was out of the picture. Neither could understand how Lynsey Farren's name could come to be on Eck's piece of paper. It made you wonder what Tony Veitch was up to. They were just a happy young couple going out for a meal. And they didn't want to miss the table they had booked.

At the door, Laidlaw said, 'By the way, Miss Farren. When I mentioned that there were *two* people murdered, you repeated it. You sounded surprised. Did you know that there was one dead already?'

But she was firmly esconced again as the lady of the manor. She smiled.

'I suppose two just seemed so—extravagant.'

But as the door closed on the police, she came apart very quickly.

'Dave! He asked me about Paddy Collins.'

'You didn't tell him anything?'

'I said I didn't know him.'

'That's good. Everybody's after Tony, right enough.'

'Dave. Eck Adamson's dead.'

'Auld Eck? Is he? Still, maybe it's whit they call a blessed release.'

'He was murdered.'

Dave stared at her disbelievingly.

'Eck? Come on. Be like bombin' a grave. Who'd want to murder Eck?'

Before he had finished the question, their stares had locked, seeming to find the same possibility in each other's eyes. Dave looked away and shook his head too determinedly.

'Behave yerself, Lynsey. It couldny be Tony.'

'He's done it once.'

'We canny be sure o' that.'

'Can't we?'

'Anyway, there wis a motive then. Whit reason could there be for killin' Eck?'

'Maybe he knew something.'

'Eck didny know the time o' day.'

'Oh, Dave.' She was huddled against him. 'I don't think I can take this. Poor Tony. Have you phoned Mickey Ballater yet?'

'Aye. Just putting him off. He could be real bother. Ah'll have to phone him again the night.'

'What are we going to do?'

'We're going to go out and enjoy ourselves.' He bear-hugged her. 'See if they're away yet.'

She crossed to the window and held the curtain back. Their car hadn't moved. Inside, it was being agreed that Harkness would drop Laidlaw off at Pitt Street. Afterwards, Laidlaw was going to meet Eddie Devlin at the Press Club and Harkness might see him there. Harkness turned the ignition and put the car into gear.

'Dave McMaster,' Laidlaw was saying. 'She's really

118

crossing borders with him, isn't she? Maybe Mr Veitch should update his sense of Lady Lynsey Farren. She's definitely stopped playing with dolls, the lassie. What a con-artist! She looks as if she hires her expression by the day. From Haughty Faces Ltd.'

'Aye. No Oscars for Miss Blandish,' Harkness said. 'She lies like a car-dealer. Why?'

18

Milligan climbed the hill to where, overlooking what had been Anderston, now redeveloped into anonymity, the Albany Hotel stood. He had parked in Waterloo Street. The Albany is a huge glass-and-concrete fortress to the good life. The drawbridge is money. It's where a lot of the famous stay when they come to Glasgow. It's maybe as near as the city gets publicly to those embassies of privilege by which the rich reduce the world to one place, although in Glasgow few public places would have the nerve obtrusively to discourage certain clients. They merely give discreet financial hints.

Milligan had stipulated the main lounge, so he passed the basement bar, The Cabin. That was a kind of servants' quarters where the punters drank, surrounded by people such as Charles Aznavour and Georgie Best, photographs like the leftovers of big occasions.

The glass doors parted politely in front of him. The lounge was an extension of reception with the bar at the far end. Milligan infiltrated the polite crush at the bar and came out with a glass of bottled lager. There was nothing as vulgar as draught.

He sat in one of the two vacant black chairs. He was sharing a table with a couple of businessmen. 'But compared with last year's profits.' 'A new factory in Sheffield.' 'The overheads.' They were talking in dialect.

Milligan was glad they didn't wait long before going into The Carvery. They were part of an intermittent departure. Every so often a Glaswegian voice would come over the tannoy dressed in Pukka English like a Moss Bros suit that had been delivered to the wrong person. 'Mr Somebody to the Carvery, please,' it would say. A group would rise from its glass-topped table and go into the restaurant, still roped loosely together with conversation.

Milligan settled for the women. There were a couple he wouldn't have minded adding to his problems. One was a big blonde in a red satin dress. The other was more subdued, with less of a lighthouse's ubiquity of vision. But she was the one Milligan really fancied, brown-haired, sending him on by never having noticed him. He would have liked to upset her style. He shot the man she was with a couple of looks of curare, but he went on living.

'Thank God for Macey,' Milligan thought.

Macey was coming towards him, walking not quite tall in his platform shoes. He had on his grey striped suit with the four-lane lapels, red shirt and a tie that might have doubled as a table-cover. Macey believed in hiding his bushel under a light. The youthful face, well fed but with a nose you could have shaved with, was brightly interested in everything. Born and brought up in Govan, living in Drumchapel, he seemed to be saying to himself about everywhere else, 'Fancy me bein' here.'

What happened when he saw Milligan would have been a double-take in somebody else. In Macey caution reduced it to an infinitesimal pause. He nodded pleasantly and made to go past, still looking.

'Macey,' Milligan called softly. 'Over here.'

Macey hesitated like a cat testing an opening with its whiskers. He came across.

'Aye, Ernie.'

'Can I get you a drink?'

The time it took Macey to decide, he might have signed the pledge. His livelihood, if not his life, depended on caution and foreknowledge. He welcomed this place the way a cardiac case does chest pains.

He seemed to be checking for a murmur at the instincts, then nodded and sat down.

'Ah'll take a pint of heavy.'

'No draught here, Macey,' Milligan said.

'A glass of export then.'

121

While Milligan told a waitress, Macey looked round in the blinky way he had, innocent as a tourist's Kodak.

'Whit's these then?'

He was referring to the etchings and paintings of Norman Ackroyd that hung round the walls of the lounge like black holes in which whispers of light and shape were conspiring to survive.

'Macey,' Milligan said. 'These is art. I like them.'

'Uh-huh. Whit's his secret? All the people I know get put in the jile for stealin' money.'

Milligan laughed and Macey turned that naive face towards him as if he'd like to be included in the joke. Milligan wasn't taken in but he appreciated the tradition in which Macey was working. Macey was a practitioner in the ancient Glaswegian art of the double-con. He was a master of the upturned palms and the kind of innocence that could pick anybody's pockets of suspicions. A lot of the people he dealt with, Milligan thought, must have been home in bed before their self-congratulation went sour and they realized that Macey had been taking the mickey out the mickey they thought they were taking out of him. He was so simple he could have sold life-insurance in heaven.

'Your export, Macey,' Milligan said and paid.

Macey wet his lips with the beer. Unlike a lot of touts, he never used alcohol as a way of getting his mouth out of reach of his misgivings. If you bought him two drinks, one would have to be a carry-out.

'Whit d'ye reckon tae Danny Lipton, Ernie?'

'It's porridge, isn't it?' he said. 'Unless Danny can prove that somebody broke into *his* house and dumped the stuff there. We found enough loot to keep the Barras going for a fortnight?

'Dampt shame, intit?'

'He was careless, Macey. You should always fix your depot before you move. You don't bring it home like the Christmas shopping.'

'Ah know that. So does Danny. The polis are at his hoose that often, ye'd think it wis a sub-station. But the chance

122

comes up fur a wee job, ye're in there, aren't ye? Professional instinct, intit?'

'No, it's not. Professional instinct's when you go three stops past your first thought and then walk back. Danny didn't do that. He jumped off while the idea was still moving. Right into Barlinnie.'

'The Bar-L.' Macey shuddered. 'Gads.' He had only been in Glasgow's prison once. He had no plans for going back. 'Hellish, though. He's sich a nice big fella.'

Macey was right. The only thing Danny Lipton had ever shown violence to was a window.

'Ah wis speakin' tae his wife the day,' Macey said.

'Big Sarah?'

'She'll miss 'im that much. Great relationship, ye know. Any time he's no' brekkin' intae hooses, he's doin' up his own. 'S a fac'. Sarah aye says if Danny's no' in, she knows exactly where he is. No' like some people's men. She knows he's just out screwin'.'

Macey meant houses.

'Ye back wi' the wife yet?' Macey asked.

'No. But I soon will be.'

Milligan recognised the tout's pride in having an easy familiarity with the police. He supposed touting was a back door into the establishment, like the servant at the big house thinking he's got the edge on all those who never even get in. The money often seemed secondary. But this was long enough to have been playing at equals.

'Macey.'

Macey reluctantly confronted the changed tone. Milligan reached into his inside pocket and passed something across for Macey to look at.

'Whit's this?'

'Promotion,' Milligan said. 'You're looking at D.C.I. Milligan there.'

Baffled, Macey looked at a photograph of a young man the rawness of whose face was just about enough to make Macey look for the eggshell on his head. He was looking up from something he was reading and his expression suggested he had never seen a flashbulb before. Macey looked at Milligan from behind his own mask of innocence.

'That must've been taken a few years back. Ye're that young-lookin', Ernie.'

'Uh-huh. Tony Veitch, Macey. Tony Veitch.'

The name almost startled Macey out of his performance but, being less than a world war, not quite. Watching him, Milligan suspected there might have been a response in there somewhere.

'You know him?'

Macey shook his head.

'I'm looking for him. It's my feeling that if he did what I think he did, I could be one of a crowd. Macey.' Macey brought his eyes up from the photograph. Milligan indicated himself with his thumb. 'I'm first. I don't wait in queues. Follow?'

'What's it got to do wi' me, Ernie?'

'Macey. I had to take out a mortgage to buy you a drink in here. I don't like wasting money. I know you're in with the right people for this one. All you have to do is want to know. You better want. You drag your feet on this one, I'll see you get plenty of time to drag them. You thought Barlinnie was bad, Macey? Barlinnie's Butlin's. Full of jolly redcoats. You want to try Peterhead? They've got a bit of that nick they just call the married quarters. You're a nice-looking boy, Macey.'

'Ah'll do ma best, Ernie. What about money?'

'C.O.D., Macey. C.O.D.'

'There's been talk about 'im. Ah don't know the fella. But he's disappeared, it seems.'

'I know. All I'm asking is when they find him, I'm there first.'

Macey handed back the picture, a small transaction observed from further along the lounge, nearer the reception area. There Lynsey Farren was surprised to have her dignified entrance interrupted by Dave McMaster. He grabbed her elbow and turned her back the way they had come.

'We'll go up the side way,' he said. 'Get a drink at the table.'

'Why?' she asked, as he led her into the side passage that ran parallel to the lounge.

'Ah've just clocked something very interesting,' he said.

19

When you opened the street door to the Glasgow Press
Club in West George Street you were confronted with an
old, stone, curving staircase, an act of contrition steep
enough to take the wind out of most pomposity. Once you
negotiated the locked door at the top (in Harkness's case by
getting Eddie Devlin to sign him in), you came into a small
place articulate with that Glaswegian instinct for finding the
off-hand remark which freezes pretentiousness in its tracks.
It was a de-briefing room for the spy network the press runs
on celebrities.

Mainly, it was two places: the snooker room and the bar,
which had a small, compact gantry and a scatter of tables. In
either room, there was no problem finding someone to
deflate you. Eddie Devlin was merely one of many always
ready to oblige.

'Uh-huh,' he was saying. 'Then we could run a society
column for down-and-outs. Who's getting off their mark
with *whom* from the Salvation Army Mission. Have a series.
Who was out mind with the bevvy on Custom House Quay
last week. Which are the smart derelict buildings to be seen
in these days. Hey. I could become the William Hickey of
Caledonia Road. It's a good idea, Jack.'

Harkness was glad he had a pint of pain-killer. He knew
he had made a mistake coming in here and he sympathised
with Eddie. It was a moment he recognised from a case like
this, one of the lay-by times when there was nothing actively
they could do and Laidlaw was left going over the thing
obsessively in his head. He was still on the lime-juice and
soda, which couldn't be helping.

'Come on,' Laidlaw was saying, staring through Eddie's
ridicule. 'Just give him a mention.'

'Where? In the dead derelicts column? We discontinued it, Jack. Doesn't sell a lot of papers.'

'A paragraph. One small paragraph.'

'Why?'

'Because he deserves it. Your mob invent fame. Like playing stocks and shares with people's reputations. So invest a paragraph in Eck. This glamour crap gets me. Same in our job, Brian. Steal enough money from an institution and you'll get the entire Crime Squad after you. Steal a widow's last fifty quid and who cares? It's only people. Eck deserves to be acknowledged.'

'Why?'

'Because he was there. But even playing it by your rules he still deserves it. I think he was murdered. That's still news here, isn't it? What's happened to this city? It used to be the life of the streets was properly respected here. It got attention. What about Hirstling Kate? Or Rab Ha' the Glesca Glutton? They were Eck's kind of people.'

Hirstling Kate had been a cripple who pulled herself along on her knees by means of spiked boards held in her hands. Rab Ha', who was said to have eaten a calf at a sitting, had died as a vagrant in a hayloft in Thistle Street. Laidlaw had touched on one of Eddie's hobbies.

For the next few minutes Harkness was introduced to some other nineteenth-century landmarks of Glasgow, like Old Malabar, the Irish street juggler, and Dungannon, the barefooted porter of the Bazaar at Candleriggs. He heard a four-line rhyming sermon from the 'Reverend' John Aitken. He discovered that Penny-a-Yard's job had been making brass chains for wall clocks. His favourite was Lang Tam, an imbecile beggar who inspired people's charity by waving goodbye to the Paisley coach at Jamaica Bridge and waving hello to the same coach as it arrived in Paisley.

The memory of those people who had found preposterous niches in a hard life, like kittiwakes nesting on a sheer cliff face, worked on Eddie, while Laidlaw argued Eck's place in the tradition.

'And another thing, Eddie. Whoever did this thinks

127

they've caused about as much fuss as running over a stray cat. I want them to feel differently. It doesn't mean a lot but I'd like to get them worried if I can. Who knows, it might help. You might put in an appeal for information.'

'What's the point? If it's not an accident, it has to be rummy obliterating rummy. How many rummies do you think read the *Glasgow Herald*?'

'I don't know, it makes a good big blanket on a cold night. And you know what might help? If you could pass it on to the *Evening Times*.'

'Right, Jack. Stop there. I've got no influence with the London *Times*. Look, I'll see. All right? I'll see.'

'Thanks, Eddie. There's another thing.'

Eddie looked round his raised whisky the way the negro house-servant used to look round doors in old Hollywood films.

'I know,' he said. 'You want me to do a piece on stray dogs.'

'Not this week. Remember that stuff the paper ran a while back? On the vagrant thing. "Skid Row" idea.'

Eddie nodded.

'You think you could get me that to check through? Just in case. It's probably hopeless. But just in case.'

'You're mellowing. You're beginning to ask reasonable things.'

A man came over from the bar to their table. He was tall and very fat.

'Five minutes,' he said to Eddie. 'I hope you're fit.'

'I'm not likely to be less fit than you, Stan,' Eddie said. 'Look at him. If they cleaned him out, he'd make a good garage. Pollokshaws Fats, the one-man crowd. You've got to wait in the bar while he's making a shot.'

'Gallows humour,' Stan said. 'Can I buy you boys a drink? I believe it's customary at a wake.'

The voice was appropriate to the remark, slow, deep and mournful, every sentence a small cortége. Laidlaw had barely touched his lime-juice and soda. Eddie and Harkness didn't need anything at the moment.

128

'Five minutes,' Stan said.

Eddie checked his watch. It seemed a typical gesture to Harkness. That broad face with its kindly inquisitive eyes always seemed to be slightly abstracted, thinking ahead. It was as if the pressures of the job had invaded his private life so that even his pleasures needed the adrenalin of having time-limits. He was a junkie for deadlines.

'How about the lab tests?' Harkness asked Laidlaw.

'Oh yes. Guess what? Paraquat in the bevvy. That was Eck's bottle we found, all right.'

'Hey, maybe you're not so daft. Mixing that stuff with the wine means premeditation, doesn't it?'

'Not just that. Two sets of fingerprints on Eck's bottle. Only one of them Eck's.'

'And if it's true that he didn't share . . .'

'Find the fingerprints, you find your man.'

Eddie got up to take on Stan. He was smiling.

'I've got it, boys,' he said. 'Go round the off-licences fingerprinting people and you're home alone. I'll buy you a drink with my winnings.'

Harkness stared after him, turned back to Laidlaw.

'He's got a point. If you've got two lots of fingerprints on the bottle, that's got to be the other lot, hasn't it?'

Laidlaw refused to be dismayed.

'Don't take Eddie too seriously. That journalism makes you cynical. Not like police-work.'

'No. But he's right.'

Laidlaw took his lime-juice and soda as if it was a wisdom-potion, and winked.

'I would bet he isn't. Cynicism's just a failure of imagination. Those fingerprints are a solid investment. They'll work for us. Well, where did you bestow your charms tonight?'

Harkness had a drink.

'I didn't,' he said. 'I phoned Mary and we decided we wouldn't be seeing each other again. I'm going to get married.'

'You make it sound like a death-sentence.'

'No. You know what it was? Mary sounded really happy about it. I thought she fancied me. I worry my arse off about telling her. And she takes it like a prezzy. Like Christmas was early.'

Laidlaw was laughing.

'You know what's worrying me now?' Harkness said. 'I ask Morag to marry me and she hunts me. If she does that, I couldn't take it. The equipment'll shrivel up and fall off. After Mary went off the phone singing, I went and got bevvied. I'm going to have to leave in time for the last bus. Just leave the car.'

'I'll drive you to Fenwick,' Laidlaw said.

'You not staying at the Burleigh tonight? You going home?'

'Well.' Laidlaw had a clowning expression on his face, like Pagliacci. 'More or less home. That's where I'm going, if that's what it is.'

Harkness had a feeling about Laidlaw he had had before, an almost irresistible compassion for him. Laidlaw came on hard, could be a bastard, sometimes gave the impression that if God turned up he'd want Him to take a lie-detector test. But he so obviously cared about people, was so unmistakeably hurt by what happened to them, sometimes through his doing, that he would have put a stone under pressure to feel things. Out of concern for him Harkness moved the conversation away from where they were headed.

'I don't want to sound cynical,' he said. 'But how is it those fingerprints are going to be use to us?'

'Brian. Imagine it. You're putting paraquat into a wine-bottle. Some down the sides. Right? You wipe the whole bottle. Because you don't want the bottle to look suspicious. Isn't it true? Then you're giving it to a wino. Who cares if your hand's been on it? Where is it going to finish, anyway? In the Clyde? You're going to be careless. You're going to give it to him with panache. Oh yes, you are. If it's Tony's fingers on it, Brian, it's Tony. If it's somebody else's, it's somebody else. We've found the combination to this safe.

I'm telling you. Hey. I like being bright. Don't you? It's good fun, isn't it?'

He was laughing. Harkness was pleased to see him arrogant again. Harkness believed that Laidlaw had certain small rights in that area.

20

There was a girl wearing white trousers, tight enough at the buttocks to let you count the pores. She gave the impression she was practising how to atomise. Every part of her body seemed to be making strenuous efforts to separate from every other part. Her eyes were closed. She had a partner somewhere. The music had given up following her.

She wasn't particularly noticeable, except to one of the only two older men standing at the bar. They were probably no more than late thirties but the context and their mood made them feel like two face-lifts that fell. Poppies Disco wasn't a haunt of theirs.

'See that yin wi' the white breeks on, Pat?' one of them said.

'Ah've got somethin' in ma eye,' Pat said.

'Probably her left tit. She's throwin' them about all over the place.'

Pat was conducting a delicate operation on his left eye. He teased his upper eyelashes carefully towards his eyebrow and rolled the lower rim of his eye up and down. He blinked a few times and seemed satisfied.

'Ah feel like Methuselah's daddy, Tam,' he said. 'This wis your idea, ya bam.'

'Gets us the late drink, doesn't it?'

'Right enough. But they're all that young.'

'If they're old enough to bleed, they're old enough to butcher.'

'Be your age. Where'd ye read that? The *Gestapo Gazette*? Ah'd be embarrassed tryin' with wan o' these. In case Ah couldny undo her nappy. When's the go-go dancer on again?'

'Ah thought ye wereny interested,' Tam said.

'That's different, intit? The lassie's just doin' a job. Ye can kid yerself on an' go hame. Her an' you can both get a good night's sleep. No problem.'

Tam looked round the place. He liked the decor. The seats round the edges were designed as dice, the wall-lights as poker hands. The small stage the go-go dancer would come back to was a roulette-wheel. It appealed to his love of risk.

'Fella that used to own this,' he said. 'He cut his throat.'

'He musta felt like me. Know somethin', Tam? There's nothin' can age ye more than seein' all the cuff ye'll never get near. Ah'm greetin'. Ah'm greetin'.'

'Naw. He wis a poof,' Tam said, as if that explained the inevitability of suicide. 'Ye gonny dance?'

'Ah thought ye wid never ask me.'

'Naw. Ye gonny?'

'The first Canadian Barn Dance they play, Ah'm up like a shot.'

'You know whit it is wi' you?' Tam said. 'You feel out your depth. Ye see, Ah don't. Ah can see people here Ah recognize. Can you?'

'Tam. Ah'm no' sure Ah recognize me.'

'Look over there.'

Tam swivelled Pat's shoulders towards a corner of the room. Pat focussed on a couple. To him they were a woman with a man vaguely attached. Neither was speaking. She was a big, blonde woman that he wouldn't have had the cheek to claim seriously. He felt he wouldn't know what to say in the morning. She was somewhere he wouldn't have minded taking his holidays but he knew that she wasn't a place for him to live. Then he noticed the man. He looked as if they might have made him in Dixon's Blazes, a piece of heavy engineering, Pat thought. He looked as if he could arm-wrestle a crane.

'Uh-huh,' Pat said. 'Ye gonny show me somethin' else?'

'That's Dave McMaster,' Tam said. 'Ye've heard of Dave McMaster?'

133

'Aye,' Pat said. 'Ah just wish that big burd wisny wi' him. Look at her!'

She was staring ahead. Lynsey Farren wasn't liking having her enjoyment of this place compromised by Dave. It expressed so much of what she felt about him that she resented his willingness to let in outside air. He was bringing in cold draughts from the streets outside.

'We have to sort this out,' he was saying. 'One way or the other. We have to.'

She looked around. The energy took her breath away. She saw these young people dancing, bodies throwing themselves about, so careless, like casual conversation. They were a message that fascinated her because she could never quite understand it or imitate its tones, that unselfconscious declaration of self before departing into the dark. She imagined what boring jobs they must go back to, if they had jobs, that girl with a face tallow in the strobe lights, that boy who looked like a seedy angel and sneered at himself.

They explained her flat to her. She had rejected her own taste and just bought kitsch because she felt that where she lived no longer mattered much, should be as anonymous as a railway station. Tony had taught her that. He had said, 'Houses are ways of hiding from a more complicated reality, I think. They should have porous walls. The less they're you, the nearer they are to communal places. Like the best working-class houses.' These dancers reminded her of that, were all open doors.

She looked at Dave. He was drumming on the table, absorbed in his worries. She understood why she had finished up with him. Tony was the idea, Paddy Collins was the imitation of the idea, Dave was the fact. He couldn't walk into a room without his eyes asking what was the game here and his body saying he could play it. His vigour was a train you thought you'd better catch if you wanted to go somewhere. She had caught it. Though she didn't know exactly where it was going, she believed it was better than where she had been.

'So what do we do?' she asked.

134

'We try to help Tony. But Ah've got tae phone this Mickey Ballater the night. Ah give him a nonsense, right? Ah mean, Ah'll tell him where tae find auld Danny McLeod. That keeps 'im busy a wee while. But he's gonny phone back. An' he'll not be a pleased man. So then we have tae move intae the real game. Ah have to start doin' real tricks. Ah need your help. You've got to find out where Tony Veitch is. It's as simple as that.'

'I'm sure Alma knows.'

'Then you go and see Alma. The morra mornin'. Fair enough?'

'I suppose I could. Milton will be at the golf. He always plays golf on Sunday morning. Sometimes has lunch at the club and plays again in the afternoon. I'm sure I can get her alone. Are you going to give Mickey Ballater my number?'

'Ah'll have to. Ah'm goin' to let him phone me back. Ah give him that, he'll give me back some trust. It'll steal a few hours. We're gonny need them. See. You want to help Tony, what we've got to do here is play for time. Ah can get the right people to find him. An' still kid Ballater on. Ye understand?'

She wasn't sure that she did but she didn't know anything else to do but let Dave handle it.

'You going to phone?' she asked.

'Ah'll phone right now. Ah said before the day's out. The day's not out.'

He got up and walked across a red carpet that nobody else could see. But she believed it was there. And certainly nobody encroached on his progress.

Reaching the phone, he dialled the number he had dialled earlier today. The same woman's voice answered, saying the same thing, 'Gina?' Did she not know who she was? He didn't bother confirming. He asked for Mickey Ballater. The voice that was as gravelly as a cement-mixer came on at once. 'Aye?' He must be in bed with her, Dave thought. She must be kinky for no-users. He gave his message and waited.

'Who's he?'

'He wis a friend of Eck Adamson's. He must know

somethin' about Tony. Ah told ye about Eck, right? Ah'm tryin' all Ah know. You have a word wi' him. No joy, you phone this number.' He gave him Lynsey's number. 'That all right?'

'It better be. Ah'll tell ye how all right it is the morra.'

Ballater put the phone down. Dave gave the dead tone the fingers. Go and frighten Birmingham, he thought. He walked back into the dance-area, hoping somebody would try to intercept him. But he had a clear path to Lynsey. She looked up. He nodded and sat down.

'There's a man at the bar,' she said, 'trying to have a fight.'

He looked across. He saw a man who wasn't as drunk as he was trying to be. He was gesticulating in that ambiguous way that was both a threat and a plea. 'I'm warning you but don't take me too seriously.' Dave didn't. He sipped at his vodka and orange.

Tam stopped gesturing at one of the men behind the bar and subsided into his whisky. Surrounded by imagined enemies, he was muttering to himself. 'Ah could sort this whole place out.' He looked over his shoulder and saw Pat sitting suave at a table. The girl he was with was almost all eyes. He wondered what they could be talking about that was so interesting.

'After that,' Pat was saying, 'I played at inside left.'

21

'Blankets? Pull this over the head, ye've got a fallout shelter. Hand-knitted from Polar berrs. Ah'm tellin' ye. Wake up in the mornin', ye see the frost on the windae in the shape o' two hands up. It's surrendered. At a fiver a whack, Ah've got to sell them quick. Polis see me, Ah'll get arrested for insanity.'

Mickey Ballater moved on. He wasn't in the market for blankets. Paddy's Market in Shipbank Lane was a nostalgic experience for him, a walk into the past that momentarily blurred his present purpose. There must be streets like this in any city, he supposed, but this one was different for him. It was where he came from, a re-enactment of the way he used to live. He felt as if they were flogging his own past.

What struck him wasn't the blanket-seller's spiel. That was untypical of this street, more like an echo of the Barras, the city's official market where the brashness of commercial success came out at you like a lasso. This was a quieter place, mute with resignation. It was a street of dead eyes and indifferent glances.

Down one side there was a series of holes in the wall, lock-ups where a conglomerate of scruffy goods were howked out of the dimness to be sold. The catch-as-catch-can quality of the articles was indicated by the fact that few sellers specialised in anything but most sold whatever they could get their hands on. Down the other side were those whose premises were no more than a patch of ground on which they laid what looked like the remnants of their private possessions. The market still lived up to a name that implied a place where mendicant Irish immigrants could buy.

Mickey became angry at the thought of those who, sitting

in plush places, said there were no longer any real poor. If this stuff was being sold, who else would buy it but the poor?

He remembered the house in Crown Street and an old bitterness came back. These were people he had once been part of. He thought of his father using the booze as blinkers, of his mother not able to live one day in which a penny wasn't important. He thought of his sister, broken-hearted because the joiner she was going with packed her up, his mother keening in the background that Prince Charming had ridden away.

He was different. His wife lived in a private house. Where a second-hand bike at thirty bob had been something he waited two years for, his three daughters took a personal stereo for granted. He was going to keep it that way.

'Excuse me, aul' yin,' he said.

She looked up as if a glance was a boulder she was tired of lifting. Her face was a derelict cul-de-sac. The junk behind her was like a load she was yoked to, ensuring that she would never move anywhere else.

'Ah'm lookin' for Danny McLeod.'

She nodded along the street.

'Auld Danny's up there. The wan at the very end. Silly auld bugger.'

As he got nearer he saw what she meant. Danny McLeod had a piece of felt spread on the cobbles. On it lay a few boxes of matches inside metal holders, two second-hand paperbacks, a pair of spectacles in an open case and a tin ashtray. The man himself had a face blotched with drink, a map of bad places he had been.

Mickey bent down and lifted one of the metal holders. The holder was cheap metal, three-sided. The idea was you fitted the matchbox into the metal with the striking-surface facing out. One side of the metal box had what looked like a snake on it. Mickey put it back and picked up another. The design was a sun.

'These is fae Peru,' Danny McLeod said. 'Lima in Peru. That's the capital, but. Ye get these in Lima.'

138

'Peru?'

'Correct. They're a right rarity. 50p.'

'How d'ye get these fae Peru? Ye got a branch there?'

'World Cup, right? Scotland playin' in the World Cup. Right? Ah know some people goin' over to support the boys in Argentina. So they're goin' overland. Down through Peru. They got me these in Lima. Cost them a bomb. But they know Ah like precious metal. Ah'm losin' like. But Ah'm selling off the stock. Very few left. Ye get the matches free wi' the holder.'

Mickey put down the sun, picked up a lion.

'That's a beauty. That's ma favourite, like. That wan there. Looks real enough tae bite ye. Chow holes in yer pocket, that yin.'

'50p?'

'Special offer, big yin.'

Mickey put his hand in his pocket, pulled out a pound.

'Know what? Gave away the last o' ma change there.'

Mickey smiled at the expectancy in the old man's eyes and replaced the pound in his pocket. He started to count the change in his hand and stopped. He replaced the coins and, for a reason he didn't understand, gave him the pound.

'Aye. If ye're ever headed for Argentina, that's yer best road. Straight through Peru.'

As Mickey was handing him the pound, he was saying, 'How's Eck doin' these days then?'

Danny McLeod paused with the money in his hand, seemed transfixed by it. He carefully folded it and put it away.

'Eck Adamson. How's he doin'?'

The old man was finished rehearsing. His head came up and his eyes were an old, old baby's.

'Ye've got me, big yin. Am Ah supposed tae know whit ye're on about?'

Mickey had seen enough.

'Anyway,' he said. 'Thanks for the bargain. Ah'll pass it on in ma will.'

He walked a little way on, just past the market. Leaning

against the wall, he turned his purchase over in his hand before putting it in his pocket. Then he just looked, letting the old man fry in his stare. He knew it wouldn't take long.

Danny McLeod seemed to have found the equator passing through Glasgow. He wiped his brow with his hand a couple of times, flapped his grubby shirt out from his chest. When a spit of rain happened, he wrapped up his goods immediately in the piece of felt and started in the opposite direction from Mickey. Mickey followed casually.

As he saw the old man about to turn left, he called out, 'Hey, auld man.' Danny McLeod glanced back briefly and was round the corner. Fancying his chances in any geriatric marathon, and not wanting to make anybody else notice him, Mickey didn't change his pace. The rain was really starting to come down.

He came round the corner and began to walk more briskly. As he got a clear view up ahead, he was briefly nonplussed to see no sign of Danny McLeod. He walked a little way on and stopped. He was beginning to get annoyed when he realised he was standing outside the old Fish Market. Its entrance loomed to his left. There was nowhere else he could have gone. Mickey smiled to himself.

He walked in under the high glass roof and looked around. He saw a caravan, some parked cars and a van that told him the place was now a storehouse for the Parks Department.

'Hello there,' he called.

Nobody answered. The silence was what he had wanted to hear. To his right planks of wood were piled over head-height. The ground was cobblestone. The building was an oval of wooden frontages, discontinued by the entrance. Above the ground-floor was a projecting balcony along which the names of fishmongers were withering in the wood. Two rickety stairways led up to the balcony.

He listened. Upstairs there was the sound of rain dripping on wood. He walked quietly round the ground-floor, checking. There was nobody. As he started to go up one of the creaking staircases he heard a furtive scuttering above him, like an overweight rat. He climbed steadily. At the top, he looked round the empty balcony.

He pushed open a door and was in a dusty corridor where puddles of water indicated the warping of the floor. He started to walk carefully along it. It was strange how far away the city felt from here.

He was pushing doors open as he went, looking briefly into mouldering rooms. At the turn of the corridor he heard the smallest whimper, a shaving of fear that had fallen almost inaudibly into the silence. He cocked his head carefully, letting it pivot towards the source of the sound. The peeling door was ajar. He kicked it open.

'A-a-a-h!'

The bundle tumbled from Danny McLeod's hands, the felt unrolling as if he was open for business. He was crouched in a corner, his head half-turned away, looking over his shoulder. Mickey smiled at him.

'Hullo, Danny McLeod. Is this yer office? I'd like to make an appointment.'

He came in and painstakingly rolled up the bundle again, handed it to the old man and, holding him under the armpits, lifted him upright. He dusted him down solicitously and looked at him, as if admiring his handiwork.

'Who *are* you?' Danny asked.

'A local boy made good. Just up on a visit. Ma mammy's budgie died. Ah'm up for the funeral. Lookin' up some old friends. Like Eck Adamson.'

'Ah don't know who ye're talkin' about.'

'Ye got off yer mark quick enough.'

'Ah thought ye wis the polis.'

'You got a reason for joukin' the polis?'

'Everybody's got a reason for joukin' the polis.'

'Eck Adamson.'

'Ah don't know who ye're talkin' about.'

Mickey stared at the old man and realised why he had given him the pound. He reminded him of his father. A reflex saved him from his own compassion.

He hit the old man once on the nose with the heel of his

hand and he bled. The blood ran over his mouth and into the several days' growth on his chin. It was enough. He had started to cry. Mickey was looking at the windows opaque with grime.

'Two choices, aul' yin,' he said reasonably. 'Ye tell me whit ye know or pick a windae. Ye're goin' out it.'

Danny had started to cough, a whirlpool of phlegm that seemed threatening to pull his bobbing head down into it. Besides bleeding, his nose was running. He fumbled something out of his pocket and it was a rag, encrusted and filthy, that looked like instant tetanus. He rubbed his lower face clumsily, leaving a streak of snot across his cheek.

'Eck's deid,' he said tearfully.

'Eck Adamson's dead? When did this happen?'

'A day or two back. Ah don't want anythin' to do wi' this, mister. Ah'm not involved.'

'So just tell me.'

'Well, he's deid. Drank somethin', like. Ye know?'

'No, Ah don't.'

'Well. Somethin'. Word is it wis paraquat.'

'Ye mean he tried it?'

'Aw naw. He wis fond o' a drink right enough, Wee Eck. But Ah don't think he tried it.'

'Whit wis his connection wi' Tony Veitch?'

Danny hesitated, looked up at him. Mickey wagged a forefinger.

'Eck seemed to do messages for 'im. That boy's got money, ye know. But there wis somethin' wrang. Eck told me the boy wis hidin' out some place.'

'Where?'

'Honest, mister. Ah swear to God. Ah'd tell ye if Ah knew. Eck wouldny tell anybody. For fear of Paddy Collins gettin' tae hear. Tony never liked Paddy Collins since he stole his girl. An' then gave her a doin'.'

'What girl?'

'Some lassie. A kinna toff. Ah think she's a Lady Somebody-or-ither.'

'What else d'ye know about her?'

'She's got a shop o' some kind. No' in the city.'

'Lynsey Farren. Lady Lynsey Farren?'

'Ah don't know, mister.'

But Mickey was talking to himself. It took him a moment to remember Danny was there.

'Where did Eck Adamson live?'

'Around and about. Just around and about. Mainly inside a bottle.'

'Where did Tony Veitch live?'

'Honest, mister.' The question made him cringe because he couldn't answer. 'Ah never knew. An' latterly Eck wis the only wan that knew. Nobody else knows.'

'Ah doubt it,' Mickey said. 'Ye're sure that's all ye know?'

'As God is ma judge, mister.'

Mickey turned suddenly and went out. Danny suspected he was coming back, listened carefully. The footsteps were receding. There was a faint splash and the sound of the big man cursing at a puddle. When he heard the footsteps going down the wooden stairs, Danny emerged very cautiously to look down through the dirty glass of the balcony. As he watched him cross the cobbles, Danny held his handkerchief under a water-drip and wiped his face more effectively. He saw the man pause in the doorway to check the rain.

Danny felt a sudden anger in safety. He couldn't re-member much of his past but he could remember it had been there. Pride in who he had been made him want revenge.

'Big guy!' Danny whispered against the glass. 'Ah'm glad there's only fifteen matches in yer box.'

22

Dave McMaster was staring at the object again when he heard Lynsey coming back into the flat. In his head he referred to it as a 'beady'. That was what Lynsey had called it. He watched it while the bubble-bath moved around the hardness of his body as if he was getting a fitting for velvet. Maybe it was because you could get it to throw up beads of water. At first he had thought it might be a toilet for dwarfs. He smiled at himself, remembering the old joke about the girl who was told to use toilet water and got a lump on the back of her head when the lavatory seat fell.

Lynsey came in. Looking up at her, he did a mental double-take in disbelief that she was with him. She was wearing cords and boots and a striped shirt and her hair looked as if it had been mussed by Vidal Sassoon. He remembered that he was in a place he didn't want to leave. The proof he was going to give her of his concern for Tony should help to keep him there. He tried to tell from her face if she had found out what they had to know. But in certain moods her face told you as much as a clock with no hands.

She sat on the toilet with the lid down and looked at him. He liked the way the water would be outlining his torso like grease. He smiled but she didn't respond. He tested.

'Ye gonny get me a drink, Lynsey?'

'At this time, Dave?'

'Well, Ah've seen them doin' it in the pictures. Drinkin' in the bathrobe an' that. Ah always fancied it.'

He knew she liked the idea of the hard man who was really a waif at heart. It worked again.

'Well, something civilised. Gin and tonic?'

144

'Aye. Wi' lemon and ice. Ye've got tae learn not tae pick yer nose an' chew it sometime.'

She went out. Having half-dried himself, he had a quick go at the beady. No wonder there were a lot of upper-class poofs. Drying himself and putting on the Paisley-pattern dressing-gown she had bought him, he thought about it. That was how things had been arranged. Everything was a kind of beady, to make you feel bad and realise you didn't belong because you didn't know how it worked. Well, he knew now, and he wasn't impressed.

When he came out, the drink was waiting for him. He sat at ease and sipped it. He wished he was as sure about how *she* worked. She was flicking the pages of a magazine in that way she had, as if the goings on of others were strange and she could never quite get interested in them. He realised that no matter what they got round to doing in bed, there was always a piece of herself stayed cordoned off, like the part of the stately home the punters just get filing past and the notice says 'Private'.

'Ye saw that wumman?' he said.

She nodded.

'Well?'

'I know where Tony is.' She looked up from her magazine. 'I was tempted to go and see him.'

'But ye didn't?'

'No, I didn't.'

She told him where it was. He was surprised how close it was to where Tony had been.

'Ye know what we're gonny do?' he said.

'I'm just hoping you do.'

He was going to tell her when the phone rang. He shook his hand at her, crossed, still holding his drink, and lifted the phone. His guess had been right. Mickey Ballater sounded as if he was trying to arrive through the earpiece.

'Listen, you! Ma legs are tired goin' the long road. All Ah'm findin' out is that you two know more than ye're sayin'. It's talkin' time.'

As Ballater raved on, Dave held the phone out so that

145

Lynsey could appreciate the reality of what they were up against. The voice raged faintly like a trapped wasp looking for something to sting.

'We've been workin' on it,' Dave said, watching Lynsey. 'We think we can find out the day. Ye'll get a phone-call at that number o' yours. Ye'll be there?'

The silence at the other end was Ballater's anger communing with itself.

'How long?'

'A few hours at the most.'

'Ah'll be there. If Ah don't know where Veitch is by the night, ye can emigrate."

Dave had other plans. He put the phone down and sipped his drink.

'Ah could get tae like that,' he said. 'It's like drinkin' shaddas in the summer.'

He crossed and ruffled her hair.

'Lynsey,' he said. 'Two choices for aul' Tony. The polis or the Clyde. Ah think he's better wi' the polis. Fair enough?'

She looked up at him.

'He could get away.'

'Tony? Tony couldny negotiate an adventure playground. You know 'im, Lynsey. What chance has he got? Cam Colvin'll kill him. Very easily and very painfully. That's what'll happen if we don't help.'

'So what do we do?'

'Two things. Help Tony and keep ourselves in the clear.'

'How?'

'Macey. First, we find Macey. He's in far more trouble than we're in. Or Ah can put 'im there. If ye're lookin' for a favour, always find somebody that needs wan.'

'Dave. Will this work?'

'By tonight Tony'll be in the nick.' He winked at her. 'Protective custody, they call it.'

23

'I have called this extraordinary meeting of the Society of the Friends of Eck Adamson . . .' Eddie Devlin said.

'The venue's extraordinary enough, anyway,' Laidlaw said, and adjusted his collar.

The strange method of calling the meeting was perhaps appropriate to the strangeness of its setting. Danny McLeod had phoned Eddie Devlin, having kept Eddie's card as carefully as if it had been American Express since the time Eddie had been involved in the series about down-and-outs. Eddie had phoned Laidlaw to see if he was interested. Laidlaw was. Laidlaw had phoned Harkness to make sure he was available. Harkness was. Eddie had phoned back Laidlaw to tell him where they would meet. Laidlaw had told Harkness.

They had all come together on a bench of the Kibble Palace in the Botanic Gardens. The choice was Danny's, who was perhaps training for the Foreign Office. They sat in a row among exotic vegetation. Laidlaw felt like an extra in a script Danny was reconstructing from some jungle film he had seen.

'When does the native bearer stagger out?' Laidlaw asked. 'Gaspin', "Drums say no go on, B'wana".'

Eddie said, 'One thing, Jack. Whatever Danny tells you, it's got to be hot.'

Laidlaw winced.

'Know what we should do?' Harkness said. 'We should all hide behind plants. And communicate in bird-song. That way the security's really tight.'

He cupped his hands over his mouth and demonstrated quietly.

'Well,' Laidlaw said. 'Is that the warm-up act over? Any chance we get to hear the star?'

147

'Jack. I remember once you almost relaxed.' Eddie winked along at Harkness. 'Anyway. Danny phoned me. He's got something to tell you. The right. The honourable. The Danny McLeod.'

'Ah've asked youse boys here,' Danny said, ' 'cause this is quiet. Ah'm runnin' risks here. There's people could be after me. Bad people. So what? Ah'll take ma chances. Like, Ah wis in the merchant navy. Ah've been around. That's one of the reasons Ah like tae come here. Reminds me. The world's a big place. It's not just Glesca. Not at all. That's why Ah'm not worried about hard-men. Ah've rounded the Horn often enough tae get tae keep it. When ye've faced the wrath of God, whit's a hard man? Ye know whit Ah mean?'

Harkness was loving it. He was at one end of the bench with Eddie at the other. They were exchanging reactions. Between them, Danny and Laidlaw were an interesting free show. Danny was determined to play his fragment of information as if it was the theory of relativity. Laidlaw was studying plant life like the first man on the planet. It occurred to Harkness that for such a fearless man Danny had found it necessary to sup a fair amount of the liquid vine.

'Well, Daniel,' Laidlaw said. 'You're good at the Bernard Shaw prefaces. But I hope you can write a better play.'

'Sorry?'

'Danny. Going to tell us? As you say, we're quiet. You're safe here. Unless they've bugged the greenfly. What is it you have to tell us, Danny?'

'Well. That's really why Ah asked ye here. Ah had a wee visit the day. Ye see, Ah've got a wee business in Paddy's Market. Not a great turnover. But it keeps me workin'. So the day. Here's what happened. Ye see, Ah've a special line. From Peru. Lima in Peru. That's the capital. It's like. Well, it's not pure gold, certainly. But it's like matchbox-holders. All different designs. Some of the boys brought them back from the World Cup an' Ah sell them. 50p a time. It's a bargain.'

'It's a fair comment on what Scotland got out of that World Cup,' Eddie said. 'Matchbox-holders at 50p a whip.'

'Aye,' Harkness said. 'Some caper that. A B-picture remake of the Darien Scheme.'

'Danny,' Laidlaw said. 'No offence. But are you going to tell us, before I melt in this place, what happened to-fucking-day?'

'Oh aye, certainly. Certainly. Anyway. This big yin comes up to buy. He buys one o' these, right? Gives me a quid for it, actually. Fair enough. He's not the loser. But then. Aha. Then. He asks me about Eck Adamson.'

'What did he say?' Laidlaw asked.

'He asks me how Eck's gettin' on.'

'Not well,' Eddie said.

'And what else?' Laidlaw said.

'Well. Ah twig this could be bother. So Ah've just arrived, haven't Ah? Ah've still got the hives. Ah don't know what he's talkin' about, do Ah? But he follows me. Duffs me up a bit.'

'So what did you tell him?'

'As little as possible. About that lassie wi' the shop. An' Eck bein' deid. But it's whit Ah didny tell 'im. An' Ah'm gonny tell you.'

'Before you do, Danny,' Laidlaw said. 'Who was this man? Your visitor.'

'Ah don't know 'im. He's Glasgow right enough. But not livin' here any more. Up on a visit, he says.'

'But what was he like?'

'Big fella.'

'That could be a coupla people, Danny. Nothing else?'

'A bastard.'

'Christ, you've widened the net. There must be three of them in Glasgow at least. Think, Danny. Think. Going baldy? Purple hair? Anything!'

'He had a wee toatty birth-mark on his left cheek.'

Laidlaw put his memory on it like a scanner. There was a troublesome bleep somewhere but he couldn't locate it.

'He was at the Vicky on Friday night,' Eddie said.

149

'So who is he?' Laidlaw asked.

'I don't know, Jack. A big man. Looks like Burt Lancaster with the flu. I didn't know him. One of Cam's barnacles. Panda Paterson was another one.'

'Panda's not one of Cam's,' Laidlaw said. 'Sounds like a scrubbers' reunion to see Paddy off. Mind you, who else would want to see Paddy off? If decency was food, Paddy would've died of malnutrition years ago.'

A boy of about two had stumbled stiff-legged towards them, like John Wayne running downhill. He was dressed in a way that only somebody who had no say in it would be dressed. He had those aggressive eyes of childhood, as if the world had just been waiting for him to look at it and, all right, he was doing it the favour. He stopped in front of Laidlaw and said something that sounded like Sanskrit passing through a scrambler. He seemed waiting for an answer. Laidlaw pointed his finger in the boy's face.

'Make your move any time,' Laidlaw said. 'I'm a killer. I'll wipe you out in a oner.'

The boy started to slap Laidlaw's legs ferociously, making high-pitched noises that seemed to imply pleasure.

'Hell,' Laidlaw muttered. 'That's supposed to work.'

Having made sure her son had had plenty of time to get out of hand, his mother timed her arrival. She wasn't pretty but she didn't have to be. She wasn't touting anybody's responses. She was deliciously full of her own life. She shook her head at her son for their benefit.

'He's an awfy handful,' she said.

'See that?' Laidlaw said to her, smiling. 'One word from me and they do as they like.'

Everybody except Danny watched her shepherd the boy away, wondering what it must be like, for a moment, to be the boy's father.

'Mammies is great,' Laidlaw said. 'She'll have ten stories to tell about him by the time she gets him home. Danny. You were going to tell us something else.'

'Ah saw Eck no' long before he died,' Danny said.

With one sentence Danny had effectively shifted the mood

150

of their meeting. He no longer seemed such a comic figure. His air of self-importance was something they were taking seriously.

'How soon before he died?' Harkness asked.

'Well, we don't know, do we? But Ah'd say it musta been one o' the last times he wis out an' about. He wis doon at the Market. See, Ah'd given 'im a message before that. Fae Paddy Collins.'

'You knew Paddy Collins?' Laidlaw said.

'Well, Ah knew who he wis, all right. An' a lot o' people knew Eck an' me wis friends. An' Paddy Collins asked me tae tell Eck somethin'.'

Danny paused. Attention is a drug. The only point of it is to savour the high, for the withdrawal symptoms are on their way.

'What was that?' Laidlaw asked.

'Well. Ah'll tell ye. Ah'm at the Paddy's, right? Okey dokey. Paddy Collins comes up. He knows that Ah know Eck. So he wants me to pass on a message. He wants tae meet Eck an' talk about somethin'.'

'Did he say what?' Even Eddie was involved.

'Did he say what?' Danny said it as if he didn't know the answer himself. He was enjoying the suspense so much he was identifying with it. 'Well. No. He never said. But he wis one keen fella. As anxious as a cloakin' hen. Ah don't know whit he wis hatchin' out. But he wis sittin' on eggs. Ah know that. Ah know people. See that Sigmund Fraud? Ah coulda learned him about people. Anyway. So Ah give Eck the message. An' the next thing . . .'

'Danny,' Laidlaw said. 'Where did Paddy Collins ask to meet Eck?'

'Well. He asked me tae help him there. Well, Ah know Eck, don't Ah? Whit wid be a good place to meet Eck. That's what he's askin' me. Well, it's obvious, isn't it? Eck wis a South Side man. For years. He'd come over the river at times. Of course, he would. Like, his sister's north o' the river. And . . .'

'His sister?' Laidlaw looked like a small boy who has

151

discovered yet another wondrous fact about the world, like the existence of giraffe-necked ladies. 'Eck's got a sister alive? He never mentioned her to me.'

'He wouldn't, would he? Eck wis a decent man, ye know. He knew he wis an affront to his sister. So he never talked about her. Out of respect. But we wis close. So he's mentioned her tae me. Eck loved his sister.'

'D'you know where she lives?'

'It's Anderston. The new buildin's. That's all Ah know.'

'What's her name?'

'Jinty.'

'But her second name.'

'Well. She never married. Must be Adamson.'

Laidlaw looked at Harkness, shook his head and smiled.

'That's great. We'll find her. Danny. You're like an albatross on land. Beauty in the mask of the commonplace. Oh, pray continue.'

'Aye. Fair enough. Well, anyway. Ye know?' Danny was fumbling slightly for a road out of his embarrassment. 'Well. He arranges to meet Eck in the park. The Queen's Park. So Ah tells Eck. But in the evenin'. He's gonny meet 'im.'

'The Vicky,' Eddie said. 'That's the obvious place to be taken to from there.'

'That's right,' Harkness said. 'Paddy Collins was found outside the park. Don't tell me Eck did him in.'

'But that was the second last meeting you had with Eck?' Laidlaw expressed it as a question but he didn't wait for an answer. 'You saw him after that. Wait a minute. What did Eck say about that meeting? Before he went, I mean. When you told him about Paddy's offer. Can you remember?'

'Eck wis worried. Who wouldn't be? Paddy Collins? Who wants a date wi' a disease? An' Eck says to me. He's gonny take out insurance. That's what he says. Ah remember it. He's gonny take out insurance. That's all he says.'

'But with what company?' Laidlaw said. 'That's all we need to know. Who Eck's company was that night. What about the last time you saw Eck, Danny?'

'Happy as Larry. As if he'd come into a fortune. Money on 'im an' more to come, he said. He gave me two quid. The boat wis in.'

'That's all?'

'Well, Ah think Ah know whit it wis.'

The others couldn't have been more attentive if an angel had descended through the domed glass roof. Danny gave them time to appreciate the splendour of his presence.

'He saw who did in Paddy Collins. Wis a witness. An' ye know who Ah think that wis? That boy Veitch.'

Laidlaw was considering it solemnly, staring ahead. Harkness was nodding. Eddie was watching the two of them.

'He's got the money,' Harkness said. 'We know that. Who could better afford to buy people off?'

'This Tony Veitch is well off?' Eddie asked.

'He got a lot of loot in his mother's will,' Laidlaw said. 'But come on, Brian. Who couldn't afford to buy off a witness to a murder you've committed? You'd print the money if you had to. That doesn't prove too much.'

'But he had a reason.'

Surprises were getting to be routine with Danny. They all looked at him.

'He hated Paddy Collins since the time Collins battered his old girl-friend.'

Harkness and Laidlaw looked at each other. Harkness winked and gestured to Laidlaw to stay quiet.

'Lynsey Farren?' Harkness asked.

'That's what that big eejit called her,' Danny said. 'The wan that duffed me up. Paddy Collins gave her a doin'.'

'And how do you know Tony Veitch was angry about that?'

'Eck told me, didn't he? Said Tony Veitch wis bealin'. An' he wis a funny boy, that Tony Veitch. From what Ah've heard.'

Harkness looked at Laidlaw. The prosecution rests.

'Danny,' Laidlaw said. 'I don't know what you've said

153

means. But it sure as hell means something. Thank you, sir.'

'Maybe this'll let me off the hook,' Eddie said. 'I mean, from writing a London *Times* obituary on old Eck. I don't suppose I even need to get you that information.'

'Naw. Forget it, Eddie,' Laidlaw said.

He reached into his pocket and found a fiver. His hand rested on his knee, holding the note.

'Tell me something,' he said to Danny. 'I'm always curious. What possessed you to come and tell us all this now?'

'The big yin,' Danny said. 'The man who hit me. Ah'm no' takin' that from anybody. This is me hittin' 'im back. The only way Ah can these days. Ah'm no' deid yet. If he finds out, Ah might be. But no' yet.'

Laidlaw slipped him the fiver and the three of them stood up, leaving Danny occupying his seat proudly, like a throne. They all said cheerio.

'Hey!' Danny called and they turned back. He was looking at Laidlaw. 'Ah didny do it for the money!'

Laidlaw came back a little way.

'Hey!' he said. 'I know you didn't.'

They went out along the Kibble Palace towards the exit. Danny sat smiling to himself. Circumstances had kissed the frog. He sat like a prince, remembering how much he had once mattered to certain people.

24

For Macey the familiarity of the day had fragmented when Lynsey Farren walked into the lounge of the Lorne Hotel like a mannequin parade and the two mates at his table watched her approach as if they were buyers for a surplus store who had wandered into a salon. Since then each next thing had been another shake of a kaleidoscope his hand wasn't holding.

Walking beside her, he felt as conspicuous as a lapel-badge and about as self-determining. The Central Hotel was another strangeness. Its big, weathered exterior, constructed in a time when the power issuing from the steam train had obscured the possibility of alternatives to itself, had been a familiar landmark to him since boyhood but had never seemed more relevant to his life than the Necropolis.

He was entering it for the first time and a couple of porters looked at him as if they knew that. Put a monkey in a toy uniform, Macey thought, and it will try to pull rank. Lynsey Farren went up the wide carpeted staircase in a way that suggested she owned it. Macey watched her buttocks move in her fawn cords as if they were chewing a very sweet caramel. He followed her through the first double doors on his right and along the corridor past the empty lounge-bar to where the weirdest moment of a weird day was waiting for him.

In the coffee-lounge looking up from an armchair like Lord Saracen receiving guests in his mansion was Dave McMaster. On the table in front of him was a silver coffee service, three cups and a plate of dainty biscuits. One of those Sunday papers that look like a paperback library was open on his knees. What was he doing with it, Macey wondered. Looking at the pictures?

Dave McMaster gestured them to sit down. Macey was relieved. He had thought maybe he was supposed to stand at attention.

'Coffee?' Dave said and poured two cups. 'Ah've had mine.'

Macey took his white and, watching Lynsey Farren not bother with milk, the unfamiliarity of where he was came to him again, heightening his senses. He had never understood people taking coffee black. You might as well lay into a cup of cascara. He put three lots of sugar into his own and checked the room.

You could have more fun in a coffin, he thought. There was a man sitting across from them with used coffee-things in front of him. He was reading typewritten sheets of paper and making notes. Probably early thirties, he looked so set already. Macey thought he had probably been born in a pin-stripe suit. The only other people were a middle-aged couple. The man was having a staring contest with the carpet.

'Lynsey wid tell ye,' Dave said.

Macey found himself too busy chewing a biscuit to answer at once.

'Ah know about yer connection wi' Big Ernie Milligan.'

Macey had his line ready, might as well try it.

'He wis tryin' tae nail me for somethin'. But Ah managed tae wriggle out.'

Dave looked at Lynsey Farren and smiled. When he turned the smile on Macey, the eyes had gone dead above it.

'Good for you. Ah'm that pleased. Very decent of the polis. Tae charge ye in the Albany. Lucky he didny throw you into a pent-house cell.'

'It wisny a charge, Dave. More a kind of—'

'More a kind of load of fucking shite,' Dave said quietly. 'You want to explain it tae Big John? Wriggle out? Be like tryin' tae wriggle out fae under a steam-roller.'

Dave offered him another biscuit but he wasn't hungry.

'You're a tout, Macey.'

Macey sat sickly still, a man who might just have heard

his own epitaph, while Dave held up the reality of his situation against the light, an X-ray plate that only he could interpret.

'You've pissed on Cam Colvin. And John Rhodes. You shoulda done something cleverer, Macey. Say, playin' at tig wi' King Kong. Macey, Macey. You're very fragile now. You could die of a phone-call.'

'Ah've never given away anythin' that matters, Dave. Never. Just a lotta stuff that everybody knows anyway. Honest. It's just tae keep Big Ernie off ma back.'

Dave was smiling, solicitous as an undertaker.

'Maybe ye're tellin' the truth, Macey.'

'Ah am, Dave. Ah am.'

Dave was considering.

'Tell ye what. You do somethin' for me an' Ah went blind on Saturday night. Okay?'

In Macey's experience nothing was more suspicious than inexplicable generosity.

'Whit—'

'Macey. Whit ye tryin' to do? Drive a bargain or somethin'? The firin' squad's lined up. You tryin' to get a price for the blindfold?'

Macey had to admit to himself he *was* against the wall.

'Ah'll do it,' he said.

'Correct. Here's the score. Ah'm more than a wee bit fond o' Lynsey here. An' Tony Veitch is a family friend. He's got to get it from somebody. We want it tae be the polis. Anybody else, it's gonny be awfy sore for him. So Ah'm gonny tell ye where tae find Tony Veitch.'

He did. Macey's day was in such small pieces he could no longer see any shape to it all. Why was he being told this?

'Because Ah want you tae use that information in a special way. Mickey Ballater's on the hunt for Tony. You're gonny tell 'im where Tony is. There's the number tae phone.'

Macey was wishing he had his name sewn on the inside of his jacket. He would have liked to check.

'But Ah thought ye want the polis tae find him.'

'Don't think. Just listen. *Before* you phone Ballater, you

phone Ernie Milligan. Once ye're sure the polis'll get there
first, then you phone Ballater. It won't be your fault the
polis knew before him. And everybody's happy. You. Me.
Lynsey. Ballater. Everybody. An' Tony's safely in the nick.
A happy ending. Just call me Walt Disney.'

He smiled at Lynsey and she touched his arm affection-
ately. She had been willing throughout the meeting to let
Dave handle everything. Macey wasn't sure that he shared
her willingness—not that he felt like saying.

'Agreed, Macey?'

'It's agreed, Dave. Ah'll do it the way you tell me.'

Dave stood up and Lynsey joined him.

'Tomorrow Ah've never been in this place in ma life,
Macey. Have you?'

'Never.'

They went out, leaving Macey concussed. Dave doubled
back in immediately on his own.

'Oh, Macey,' he said. 'Try the wee ginger nuts. They're
smashin'. By the way. If ye mix up the order of who ye tell
first, Ah won't be worried. As long as ye don't mention it
tae Lynsey. Okay?'

Macey was still sitting there trying to work out what was
happening when the waitress came up and handed him a
piece of paper. It was a bill for coffee and biscuits for three.
He sat staring at it, wondering how much was going to be
added to it if he wasn't careful.

25

Sometimes the pragmatic leads to wonder, like Columbus setting out on a business enterprise and discovering a new world. They went to Eck Adamson's sister's for information and Laidlaw found a lost part of himself. She was where he came from and had lost touch with.

Anderston wasn't a place where he would have expected to find it. It's an area of the city that memorialises a part of Glasgow's confused quarrel with itself, a warm and vivid slum expensively transformed into a cold and featureless one. Jinty Adamson lived high up in a grey block of flats, as accessible as a bald Rapunzel.

She would be about seventy going on seventeen, with eyes still alive with interest. Once she had established that their credentials made them trustworthy they weren't so much let in as they were ambushed.

'Ah haveny spoken to anybody since last Thursday. When Ah went out for ma messages. Ah'm surprised ye made it up here wi' the lift broken. An' no even wearin' grimpons.'

The mountaineering references surprised Laidlaw. The accuracy of the pronunciation suggested an aural source. There couldn't be too many sherpas in Anderston. But she explained it.

'See that,' she said, pointing at the television. 'Ma best friend. Ah watch everythin'. Ah can tell ye about silver-backed gorillas, life in Bogota or what Annie Walker had for 'er tea. Ah feel like an eagle up here. These wid be great hooses for folk wi' wings.'

It seemed a pity to spoil the pleasure with which she was taking to words like a disembarked sailor to drink. But Laidlaw felt that, if she was going to treat their visit like an unexpected present, they'd better open it for her quickly.

'It's about Eck,' he said.

'Oor Alec?' She sat down. She went inside herself briefly till she found the admission that she had been expecting something like this for a long time. The expression she gave Harkness and Laidlaw seemed to say they couldn't surprise her. 'Siddoon, boays. Whit's happened?'

'You haven't heard anything?' Harkness asked.

'Son. Is the war over? Up here ye widny know. Whit's happened?'

Harkness waited for Laidlaw to tell it.

'Alec was brought into the Royal Infirmary on Friday night. He had asked for me. I saw him just before. Before he died. He died peacefully.'

'Of course. You're Jack Laidlaw. He's talked about ye. Whit wis it? The drink?'

'Well. In a way.'

'It wid be. Oh Alec. It wid be.'

'But it was more than that. We think he died drinking wine that had been mixed with something. Paraquat.'

The word infiltrated her preparedness, undermined it. It became obvious to them that the calmness with which she had talked past hearing the fact of his death was just delayed action, like a body still trying to run before it realises it's gone over the edge of a cliff. She knew now. She cuddled herself as if against the cold and closed her eyes. Rocking very gently, she started to cry. Her quiet grief was a fact so sheer, consolation couldn't have found a handhold on it.

Laidlaw and Harkness could only let it happen for the moment. Laidlaw became aware more clearly of the room she sat in. It was comfortably furnished, with several old photographs positioned around, fading sepias in which the figures seemed threatening to recede into darkness. One that he thought must be her family showed mother and father, daughter and son in those stiff clothes they used to affect for photographs, like cardboard cut-outs that would stay when the people walked away. Jinty Adamson had eyes that looked as if they were trying to see beyond the horizon.

160

Had Eck ever been so young? The parents were statues of self-assurance. Ah, Laidlaw thought, no amount of self-assurance worked. Jinty had laboured and polished and made a small, bright fortress of this place but she was found just the same. And there was nothing you could do for her.

He got up and crossed towards her. He put an arm round her shoulders, leaning down.

'I'm going to make us a cup of tea,' he said quietly.

'Oh, Ah'll get it, son,' she said through the tears. A sense of the proper way to treat others was a reflex with her that would die when she did.

'Naw. Ah'll get it. Hey.' He put his head down till his face rested sideways on her head. 'He wisny a bad man. Most of the damage he ever did was to himself. You remember that.'

'Oh dear,' she said. 'Oh dear, Alec.'

He straightened up and smoothed her hair slightly and went through to the kitchen. For the first time, Harkness understood what Laidlaw had felt about Eck's death. He had been right. No death is irrelevant. It's part of the pain of all of us, even if we don't notice. Watching them, Harkness knew how relevant Jinty Adamson's tears were to him. It was one world or no world, no other way. She wasn't just paying tribute to Eck, she was dignifying living, no matter what form it took.

Harkness felt vaguely ashamed of something he had done recently. At first, he managed not to remember what it was. Then it came to him. He had given the photograph of Tony Veitch to Ernie Milligan. That didn't matter in itself. It was fair enough to help Ernie if he could. But he hadn't told Laidlaw. That was what he was ashamed of. He should have told him. Why hadn't he? He would do it now.

But when Laidlaw came through with three cups of tea on a tray with a poke of sugar and a bottle of milk, it seemed to Harkness an indulgence to insist on his small confession here, like announcing during a funeral service that you've cut your finger. He would do it later. This was Jinty's time. Over her tea she talked the nearest thing to an elegy Eck

161

would have. It was just fragments, less a monument than a home-made wreath of already withering flowers.

'He wisny a bad man. You've said it, son. He wisny bad' and 'The last time Ah saw him, he wis greetin' for the wastry of his life. Like a wee boy' and 'He wis that soft-hearted. Ah mind when he wis three or fower. Ma mither found him greetin' ower a picture o' Jesus with a' the thoarns in his heid. An' he said, "Look whit they did tae him, mammy." An' she couldny console 'im' and 'He wis a grand drawer, Oor Alec. Could draw a bird on a bit o' paper ye wid think could fly away. Always could draw. Coulda made something o' himself. But a luckless man. All his days a luckless man. The kinna man woulda got two complimentary tickets for the *Titanic*.'

The unintentional humour of the remark was like her natural appetite for life reasserting itself. Harkness couldn't stop smiling. It was as if Glasgow couldn't shut the wryness of its mouth even at the edge of the grave. Laidlaw seemed to be feeling something similar because he decided it was all right to speak.

'It's a bad time to be bothering you with questions,' he said. 'Forgive me. But there's things I want to ask.'

'No, no, son,' she said. 'You carry on. You've yer work to do.'

'If Alec was poisoned. And I think he was. Can you think of anybody who might have wanted to do that to him?'

She shook her head.

'Ah canny believe it, son. Oor Alec? Ah mean, Ah'm no' talkin' as some daft, dotin' sister. But you think about it. He wis that busy bein' bad to himself, he hadn't the time to make a lot of enemies. Ah canny see it.'

'He didn't say anything to you that might have suggested he was in trouble?'

'Son. Ye know the kind of life he led. God bless 'im. He wis only here when he couldny stand it any more. He wis always welcome. He knew that. But he couldn't forgive himself for whit he'd become. So every second blue moon Ah saw him. Ah always tidied him up and gave him whit

Ah could. Ma mither would've wanted that. She wis a kind wumman, ma mither. Woulda bought extra cheese if she'd knew there wis a moose in the hoose.'

'But Eck must've raved a bit. Coming to you like that. I mean, he must've been coming when he was out his mind with the drink. Otherwise, he couldn't have faced it. Because of his own guilt, I mean. I know what I'm like on that stuff. I'll talk for a week. So what did he say the last time?'

'You're right, son. You are right. He talked till the clock wis dizzy. It didny know a.m. from p.m. That last time? Wait a minute. He said he had a benefactor. That was the word. Some rich boy. Name of Veitch.'

Laidlaw and Harkness were sharing the same held breath. Laidlaw's voice came out on tiptoe.

'Anything else?'

'Ah'm no' sure. Some woman he talked about.'

'Lynsey Farren?' Harkness said.

'Whit kinna name is that, son?'

They took that as a very definite no. She couldn't remember her name or anything else about her. Harkness's disappointment couldn't understand why Laidlaw stayed so gentle. He couldn't have been more solicitous to his mother. He thanked her and took the dishes back through to the kitchen, was going to wash them. She was offended.

'Ah'm affrontit enough. A man makin' the tea,' she said. 'Ye'll not be doing the dishes in my house.'

Laidlaw surrendered. He respected where she came from too much to argue. She was one of a species he recognised.

They were decency's martyrs, who would treat death itself with an instinctive politeness, the unofficial good, uncalendared. You wouldn't find their names in any book of fame but Laidlaw believed they were the best of us because they gave off their good, quite naturally, in actions. They weren't dedicated to God or high political principles or some idea but to an unforced daily generosity of giving, a making more bearable for others and themselves. And they were legion.

Everybody, Laidlaw thought, must know many of them.

163

He himself was in debt to countless of them, aunties and uncles, strangers chatted to in pubs, small miracles of humanity witnessed, unself-aware. Recently, on a trip back to Ayrshire, he had caught up again with another, Old Jock, an ex-roadman in his seventies who lived uncomplaining with his wife on a pittance of pension, spending more on his budgies than he did on himself. His modest Calvary had been forty years on the roads for barely enough to feed his family and him, coming home on black winter mornings from a night spent spreading grit, his hands bulbous from overuse and skinned with the cold. He had taken it as no concern of anybody but him. It was what he did. Laidlaw remembered him admitting, almost embarrassedly, that he had never clenched a fist against anyone that he could re-member in his life.

Faced with people like Jock, or Jinty Adamson, Laidlaw was reminded that he didn't want the heaven of the holy or the Utopia of the idealists. He wanted the scuffle of living now every day as well as he could manage without the exclusive air-conditioning of creeds and, after it, just the right to lie down with all those others who had settled for the same. It seemed to him the hardest thing to do.

Jinty herself, he thought, was a hard case. How else could she have stayed so innocent? She demonstrated her hard innocence now. In the middle of her grief her head was still sifting details, trying to remember.

'Baker,' she said. 'Not Baker. Brown. That wis the woman's name. Her name was Brown. Alec wis goin' between her an' him. That boy Veitch. She lives in a big house. She knew where the boy was stayin', right enough. But she only kept in touch through Alec. Some problem wi' her man, Ah think.'

They thanked her again and left her alone with her tele-vision, like the Lady of Shalott with a distorting mirror.

164

26

'Friends, I'm not proud of it. But I can admit it now. I neglected my children. I beat my wife. Drink was my God. Until I found Jesus. Let him come into your life, friends. Behold. He knocks at the door. Will you let him in?'

'Behold' was the give-away for Macey. He didn't like words like 'behold'. To him they were people talking in fancy-dress, acting it, playing at who they weren't. Macey knew who the speaker was. He was Ricky Smith from Govan, a man who had been known to knock at a couple of doors himself, usually with a claw-hammer.

There weren't many people in the Buchanan Street pedestrian precinct. A few of them had paused in the vague vicinity of Ricky, the way they might have for a sword-swallower or an amateur Houdini disentangling himself from ropes. Other people's sin was one way to brighten a dull Sunday.

Macey had chosen a bench a bit apart and to the side of Ricky, so that he wouldn't be recognised. Salvation wasn't what he needed just now, at least not Ricky's brand. It interested him to hear a version of a life he knew about.

'Friends, name a sin I haven't committed, a bad thing I haven't done.' Fellatio with an alsatian, Macey thought. 'When I look back on my life, I'm disgusted with myself. I can hardly believe my own sinfulness.'

Ricky was overstating it, Macey thought. He had been bad enough, wouldn't have done too well in the Duke of Edinburgh Award Scheme. He had punched a few faces, treated wee Mary as if marriage was a fight to the death and he was for surviving, finally behaved as if he had hidden something he had to find at the bottom of a bottle and couldn't remember which one. He hadn't been a nice man.

Macey was glad for him now. Ricky looked a lot better, though his face had that slightly dessicated look a lot of reformed bevviers had. They were like people who've had to amputate a part of their own nature to survive and the infected part was where unthinking pleasure was. It was certainly better for Ricky to be battering people's ears than anything else.

But why did found-again Christians all have to claim they'd been Genghis Khan? Macey looked at the three people who were with Ricky, a woman and two men. They were scanning the faces of the bystanders with a fierce attentiveness, like showmen gauging the effect of the performance. For Macey they had a look he recognised among do-gooders, an intensity that never quite connected, an openness like an iron grille. They were reaching out to shake hands with life, but they kept their gloves on. They kept glancing at Ricky in a proprietary way, as if they'd found the authentic wildness of evil and seen it turn to good.

As far as Macey was concerned, Ricky didn't really qualify. If they had got a few others to stand up there, Macey would have converted on the spot. But he didn't expect to see John Rhodes or Cam Colvin or Mickey Ballater or Ernie Milligan taking Ricky's place. And they were who Macey was trying to deal with in his mind.

'We have a choice,' Ricky was saying.

Some choice. If he told Rhodes or Colvin or Ballater, and Milligan got to hear of it, he wouldn't be seeing Jean and the baby for a while. He couldn't face that Peterhead. But if he told Milligan and the others got to hear of that, he might not be seeing Jean and the baby at all. He didn't fancy being the packing for a concrete stanchion. That's what Cam had done with Vince Leighton. Macey had never told anybody he knew that. Some information you kept to the grave or it became one.

Macey had no illusions about his status in this situation. He remembered a nature film on the telly where he had seen a small bird that hopped about an alligator's mouth, getting the pickings from its teeth. Or was it a crocodile? Same difference, if the jaws shut at the wrong time. Macey saw himself as the small bird. The jaws were the criminals and the police.

Macey just wanted to survive. He had nothing against this Tony Veitch but he had nothing particularly in favour of him either. Everybody was at it. If those were the rules, you better be at it yourself. Macey saw himself as a middle-man. He didn't invent the conditions; he just worked out how to survive in them.

'Friends, when will you make your choice?'

Macey stood up and walked away. He had made his. He would have to put it into operation with care. When you were jay-walking among juggernauts, you had to pay attention.

27

Opening on Sunday evenings was an experiment for "The Tea Tray". It wasn't working.

Harkness, who had been here a few times with Mary, could understand why. Its customers weren't exactly night people. It was a place for morning coffee, afternoon tea, for making small rituals out of the boredom of lives which were 'successful' without ever having found the self-doubt to examine the terms of that success. The voices he had heard here seemed to him to go round and round the same pre-occupation—family, friends, possessions—like well-kept poodles being taken for a walk. It always gave him a quiet dose of the creeps, Madame Tussaud's with words.

The place had been Alma Brown's choice. Having eventually contacted her in Pollokshields, they had found her talking as if the phone was bugged. After much devious finagling, she had fixed a time later than they wanted and a place more boring than Harkness imagined anybody could want.

It reminded him mysteriously of a couple of rugby clubs he had been in, places of raucous masculinity measured by the gullet, where the sexual ravings had a distinctly hysterical tone to them. The connection, he decided, was that this place was the female counterpart of those ones, cliché calling to cliché and wanting to mate in mutual unawareness. He thought, not for the first time, that he must be a people's liberationist. (His mind avoided the word 'libber' because where he came from to lib meant 'to geld'.) This was as good a place as any to set up his standard.

It was quiet. Two well-off ladies in late middle-age were massaging each other's egos over the coffees, listing which of the other's dresses each liked best. The only other people were Harkness and Laidlaw. Harkness was leafing through the *Sunday Mail*. Laidlaw, with *The Observer*, had done the sport, the arts and the news skimpily in that order.

'Maybe the fish is articled to the Church,' Laidlaw said.

Harkness looked at him.

'Nine letters.'

'Thought you'd been putting bennies in your coffee.'

Alma Brown came in. They had only seen her before in the context of Veitch's house in Pollokshields, where she had learned to fit. Here she looked slightly vulnerable, a woman who must have been in her late thirties and still looked almost gawky with her own sexuality. She was flushed with haste or nervousness and when she opened her coat as she sat down the front of her black wool dress was distractingly busy. Harkness caught Laidlaw glancing at him and remembered Laidlaw saying once, 'How many times is that you've fallen in love today? It's been a quiet one.' Harkness ordered more coffees.

While they waited for the coffee to come, she went through a protective routine of checking her handbag for cigarettes and gold lighter, putting them on the table, laying the bag on the floor beside her chair, placing her silk scarf over the back of the chair. Harkness and Laidlaw declined one of her cigarettes, which were menthol. Like inhaling cottonwool, Laidlaw felt. He took one of his own.

'Well,' she said to Laidlaw when she was ready. 'What is this about?'

'D'you know Eck Adamson?' Harkness asked.

Something very small happened, no more than a stutter in her coffee-spoon, and a little coffee shipped into the saucer.

'Eck? What's that short for?'

'Alec. Alexander.'

'Alec Adamson. No. Who is he?'

'Was,' Laidlaw said. 'He's dead.'

She made to lift the cup and didn't bother. It was very full and her hand didn't seem too steady. Laidlaw drank from his.

'What's the Eck short for?' he said. 'Some case this. It's more full of liars than the House of Commons. Maybe we'll find out the truth about Tony Veitch in time to put it on the headstone. Drink your coffee, Miss Brown. It's all you came to do.'

The atmosphere at their table belied the place. Harkness was having a familiar feeling. Why was it that sometimes just making contact with Laidlaw was like trying to shake hands with a hedgehog? It was happening again. Laidlaw seemed bent on pursuing his career as a kind of interior desecrator, going about Glasgow laying quite pleasant rooms with wall-to-wall tension. He was doing a good job this time. She stared at her coffee for a while before looking at Laidlaw.

'I think you'd better explain that remark.'

'Certainly. You were in the room when I mentioned Eck yesterday at Pollokshields. And he still comes as a surprise to you. I'm not saying he's the most memorable name in the world, but under the circumstances I would have thought you would remember. Eck Adamson knew you but you didn't know him. How does that come about? Was he watching you through binoculars? You know nothing about Tony since he disappeared but Eck was an intermediary between Tony and you. Miss Brown, you talk such convoluted crap you must have a tongue like a corkscrew.'

After tapping her cigarette ineffectually against the base of the ashtray, she dropped it in, still smoking. The small bit of stage business seemed to give her the time she needed.

'Uh-huh,' she said. 'You can have my coffee as well. It costs too much for me.'

'Maybe we'll meet at the funeral,' Laidlaw said, putting out her cigarette for her.

She had taken the scarf from the back of her chair but she didn't stand up.

'What does that mean?'

'Nothing, I hope. But somebody's looking for Tony. Judging by the way he's going about getting the information, it's not to give him a provident cheque. Tony's been mixing with a lot of rough people. The kind who could kill a man on the way to the cinema. And still enjoy the picture.'

Harkness could see her eyes trying to back off from the implications of what Laidlaw was saying.

'Why?'

'Maybe he did something they didn't like.'

'But what?'

'Or maybe he's got something they want. Like money. Tony does have a lot of money. Doesn't he, Miss Brown?'

She stared at him, nodding.

'Money can get you anything. If you're careless enough with it, it'll get you dead.'

Harkness thought she was going to cry. Her eyelids flickered as if she had a mote. She let the scarf fall into her lap and seemed to be looking for something. He reached down and gave her the handbag. But after she had ferreted there it wasn't a handkerchief she came out with. It was a grubby piece of paper which she handed to Laidlaw. Opening the two folded sheets out, he skimmed them quickly.

'Milton threw it out,' she said. 'But I salvaged it. It feels like a part of Tony to me.'

Laidlaw passed it to Harkness and, while he read it, she was talking a gloss.

'That's what Tony's been through. Only he understates it . . .'

Dear Father,

I'm conscious of how corny it is to be turning against your father so I'll try not to make this too long. But that's what I'm doing all right. I would say I was 'rejecting your values' except that that seems too grandiose since I honestly don't think I've been able to locate a serious value of yours that was ever more than money.

What prompts me to write this just now is that I've packed up university, didn't finish my finals, and I've got a mental picture of you being convinced that I did it to spite you. That's not true. I did it for myself. What I have

171

against you is a lot more than could be expressed by blowing the finals.

I'll clarify that. That was one weird childhood you gave me. I suppose they all are so I won't labour it. But what age was I when my mother died? Eleven. Up till then the things that happened in the house had just been there like furniture. But when my mother went, the loss sent me looking. I used to spend a lot of time then opening up bits of the past and trying to see what was inside then, turning over memories to see if I could understand them. I suppose I was trying to keep some of my mother.

What I think slowly dawned on me was that they were all really memories of you or maybe of her hurt in relation to you. It was as if she couldn't reach me past you, your dominance of her, your dominance of both of us. I began to realise how badly you had treated her, how badly, it seemed to me, you treated everybody. I didn't rush to judgment. But I had my own sense of you now and I waited and watched and, I'm afraid, confirmed.

I apologise for that now. Who needs a witness for the prosecution in the house, taking notes? All I can say to lessen the rottenness of that is that I was also a witness for the defence. A lot of nights I used to lie in bed, unravelling my sense of you, and try to start again the next day. It didn't work too well.

Anyway, the last thing you need is that stuff. Don't misunderstand me. I don't think I've got any right to accuse you. But I think I've got the right to behave towards you according to the sense of you I have—it took me a lot of years to get it. And don't imagine Alma helped to make me lose respect for you. She always tried to defend you. I don't know how quickly I realised that Alma had been involved with you before my mother died. But, funnily enough, that only made me more sympathetic towards her, I suppose because you seemed to me to treat her the same way.

I don't think we should have any contact from now on,

172

at least not for a while. One of the things I'm trying to do is simply work things out for myself. For example, I've just decided what honour is for me: the refusal to relate to other people exclusively on your terms and the refusal to let them relate to you exclusively on theirs. On one of those counts, I think you're a dishonourable man. And the hypocrisy with which you've bought yourself a progress through the world appals me.

I was making a note for myself the other day and it was only when I had finished I realised I was trying to say something I believed about you: an image of authority: the priest talks steadily, dynamoed on unshakeable conviction. His voice is stern but kind, hardened on his understanding of the nature of the enemy, his thoughts rich with past analogies. The girl's head is lowered in the shame of being known. She is too ravelled in the mystery her body has become to notice that his voice goes momentarily blunt. The priest has seen a unique shard of sunlight, never before existent, never again to happen, caught in her hair. Under his cassock, he is masturbating.

Tony.

'They had some terrible quarrels.' She was raving quietly, saying anything that came to mind. Coming from a person of such studied correctness, the passion of it shocked Harkness, as if they had put a coin in a drinks machine and it was dispensing a cataract. 'Terrible quarrels. And Milton was wrong. He wouldn't give Tony room to breathe. Tony hates what Milton stands for. He once told Milton the only way he could make love to a woman was with a dildo made of tenners.'

She stopped suddenly, aghast at what she had said. She thought it over, accepted that she had said it. She looked from one to the other, took a drink of her cooled coffee. She stared at the table.

'I didn't even know what it meant at the time. When I did, I knew it meant something about me as much as Milton. And it does. Oh, it does. I wish it didn't.'

173

'So why do you stay?' Harkness asked.

The expression she turned to Harkness made him feel naive. It was hurt and baffled, like someone looking through bars and resenting the freedom he had to ask such a question.

'Because I can't see how to leave,' she said. 'I've known him for nearly twenty years.'

The vague misgivings Harkness had had about her crystallised. He thought he understood something. He remembered the assurance of Milton Veitch, like something made of marble, and how long it must have been like that. He imagined her young. She must have been very beautiful. She must have thought how lucky she was having someone like Milton Veitch wanting her. He would give her so much, but only so much. And what he wouldn't give her, a sense of her own worth separate from him, was precisely what would nail her to him. Now she still looked good but not as good as she had looked, and somehow incomplete, like someone who had got herself in a correspondence course and couldn't keep up the payments. Harkness knew who were running that course. He expressed it to himself in a simple thought. Men are a bunch of bastards. Laidlaw confirmed it for him as he thought it.

'Miss Brown,' he said quietly. 'I understand how protective you feel towards Tony. But anything you know about him you should tell us. For his own good.'

'I can't.'

Harkness winced for her because her refusal declared her knowledge and he knew that Laidlaw would make her give up her small pride in her loyalty. Harkness thought he did it harshly.

'Well, if you don't, you could be protecting him to death. You could be putting six feet of ground between him and the nasty world. If that's what you want.'

She took the two sheets of paper, put them in her handbag, clicked it shut. Perhaps it was long practice that enabled her to give up her pride so gently.

'Kelvin Drive,' she said. 'Flat 8, 8 Kelvin Drive.'

Harkness lit her cigarette for her and paid the coffees,

buying her another. They thanked her. Harkness would have lingered but Laidlaw was in a hurry. As they left her in a place where she didn't belong, Harkness wondered where she did. While Laidlaw drove, Harkness stared out the passenger window.

'That felt pretty shitty.'

'Yes,' Laidlaw said.

'Very, very shitty.'

'Come on, Brian. It's hard priorities.'

'Is it?'

'Yes, it is. Chivalry has its limits. Better a hurt woman than a dead man. Kelvin Drive. That's right beside those phone-boxes. If only we'd known. I hope we're not too late already.'

Harkness, in his anger, was looking for some way to get back at Laidlaw, no matter how petty.

'Christ, I hope we're not too late,' Laidlaw said again.

'Perchance,' Harkness said.

'Sorry?'

'Nine letters. Perchance.'

28

There was no perchance about it. There is a mildly disturbing sense of activity that surrounds the discovery of a death in a city, like the buzzing of flies. It is a small distraction in normalcy. The longest running show on earth has come to town and that fascination with dangerous tricks that can dilate with a little wonder the most blasé eyes claims its craners for the riskiest feat of all.

What looked like the advance publicity for someone's last performance was waiting for them. They knew the signs. As they crossed Queen Margaret Bridge they could see ahead of them, at the corner beyond the bridge where you turn left into Kelvin Drive, three or four people standing. They had the unselfconsciousness of bystanders, a pre-occupation like people in a painting. They were practitioners of a style that must have had its representatives at the crucifixion. One of them was pointing towards what Laidlaw knew was his destination.

'No. No,' he said in that way we incant against events we fear have already happened.

That the event had by now hardened into itself he saw in the old woman's face looking out from the nearby window of a private house with nebby curiosity, as if misfortune was lowering the tone of the neighbourhood, and in the parked cars he recognised as belonging to the police and in the uniformed constable who let them in.

The house had been impressive, a fact which worked against it now, just as an old fur-coat can look shabbier than second-hand nylon. The balustrade with thin columns that must have been a proud feature in the past was scruffy with lack of paint. The sagging balcony looked like the kind of place the upstairs residents would only avail themselves of to avoid a greater hazard, like a fire.

176

The inside of the building was what had made its outside begin to admit it wasn't what it had thought it was. One house had become eight flats. Laidlaw remembered where Gus Hawkins stayed and wondered about all the cities where the young and the unassimilated aging must be camping out in the compromised convictions of the past, seeding them with unfamiliar dreams, possibilities for which they hadn't been intended. As soon as he came in he had a strong sense of the place, could imagine strange laughters late at night, someone playing music alone.

It was where Tony Veitch had tried to live, a confusion of smells and sounds and eccentricities, a place where curry argued with fried eggs and, he could imagine, strange thoughts grew. Laidlaw wondered if coming here had been for Tony less of a hiding from things than where he had been. It was the kind of place Milton Veitch had perhaps never thought about. It was a houseful of communal loneliness.

They went up the stairs to where Laidlaw now knew they would find yet another demonstration of the final loneliness. The constable at the door had said, 'Aye, that's right, sir. There's a body upstairs. I don't know the name. But he won't be needing it any more.' Detectives were making enquiries of the other residents but apparently not many of them were in. Spending Sunday in a place like this would be like visiting your grave. Tony Veitch wouldn't have to do that again.

He was closer to blonde than his photographs had suggested. Lying on the floor of the room that was both sitting-room and bedroom, he was dressed in jeans and tee-shirt, his feet bare. His head was turned sideways, eyes closed, as if he had suddenly passed out. He was a very good-looking boy. His right arm was stretched out over the record-player on the floor, his hand rigid above the turn-table. He looked like someone who had fallen asleep changing records. But he hadn't been changing records. Around his right wrist was a piece of metal that looked like an identity-bracelet. But it wasn't an identity-bracelet. The skin around it was

177

black. The metal was just wire. He was plugged in to the socket.

'That's not the only thing,' Milligan said. 'He's got flex wrapped round the body. Wired up like a Trafalgar Square Christmas tree. He wasn't kidding. Don't touch. He's got enough electricity in him to light up Sauchiehall Street.'

Milligan was in control. He was enjoying it.

'You've arrived in time for the funeral,' he said and winked at Harkness.

Harkness looked guiltily at Laidlaw and thought he seemed displaced in the busyness of the room where the others were searching, dusting for fingerprints. The body had just been photographed. Laidlaw was staring around as if he could find something here that nobody else had managed to.

What he was finding was a feeling he had experienced before, that death is the end of small things, lets us absorb its enormity through trivial negatives, like infinity measured in inches. Maybe that was why some people were casual about it.

There was an empty cup on the mantelpiece with the crumpled wrapper of a chocolate biscuit beside it. The smallness of that cup, unfillable ever again by Tony Veitch, was big enough to hold his death. Laidlaw remembered finding one glove belonging to his father in a drawer soon after his death. It was one of a pair someone had given him for his Christmas. He had only worn them once since he belonged to a generation of men who seldom wore coats, let alone gloves, not out of any macho impulse but because coats had been a luxury for so long that they never got used to them. The accidental find in the drawer had held the irrevocable pain of his father's dying so that it seemed at the time there couldn't be much that was more poignant than a dead man's empty glove. The cup came close.

He looked again at Tony Veitch lying dead in a small bare room. He wished he could have spoken to him. But if he couldn't speak to him, Laidlaw wanted something.

'Papers,' he said suddenly.

178

Milligan turned towards him from his energetic super-vision of things.

'Newspapers?'

'Paper that you write on.'

'Why? Should there be?'

'The boy was writing all the time. There should be acres of paper here. Did you find any?'

Milligan looked at Harkness as if he was Laidlaw's keeper and should have better control of him.

'You didn't know that about him?' Laidlaw said. 'He's just a corpse to you, isn't he?'

'He's just a corpse to everybody now,' Milligan said. 'But I'll tell you what I do know. I know I *found* him. First. That's more than you did. Cock of the walk.'

'That's something that puzzles me,' Laidlaw said. 'When you know so little about him, how did you manage that?'

Milligan smiled and tapped his nose, pointed at Laidlaw.

'I know this city,' he said. 'Right to its underwear. That's why I'm a winner.' He turned to Harkness. 'Squared things up with the wife today as well. We're getting back together. Everything's coming up roses.'

Harkness cringed, and heard his feeling expressed by Laidlaw.

'You should get them to give you the boy's head for above your mantelpiece. A wee house-warming present for your wife.'

The others in the room were aware of the tension Laidlaw was generating. One of them defused it.

'There *were* papers,' he said.

'Where?'

He led Laidlaw and Harkness through to the bathroom. Small feathers of ash on the floor drifted about with the movement of their coming in. The lavatory-bowl was black with the ashes of burnt paper.

'Looks as if he's been burning the Mitchell Library,' the man said.

Looking into the bowl, Laidlaw noticed that the few

179

words which had survived were worn to meaningless smudges with the water, as accessible as runes.

'There was nothing left?' he asked.

'One sheet. It had fallen under the table.'

They went back through to the living-room and Laidlaw asked Milligan for the sheet. Milligan was glad he had asked.

'Are you kidding?' he said. 'You want it, you wait for it. This is my show. I'll see about letting you have a photocopy when I'm ready. But you'll have to wait for it.'

Laidlaw stood staring ahead. Harkness was embarrassed for him.

'Jack.'

'We'll wait,' Laidlaw said. He was speaking loud enough for everybody to hear. 'When you've got somewhere you have to go, you don't get put off by a dog barking at you.'

Harkness was speaking confidentially.

'It's over, Jack.'

'It's over for him. But not for us. The dead are our responsibility, aren't they? That's what the job says.'

Harkness was looking at him. Laidlaw's face looked as set as a death-mask.

'Jack. You're over-reacting. Just because Big Ernie chewed you over.'

Laidlaw was lighting a cigarette. He lit it, looked at Harkness and smiled.

'Like being savaged by a chihuahua,' he said.

He meant it. Their discomfort didn't matter here. Laidlaw looked again at Tony Veitch. That Laidlaw knew so little about the boy paradoxically made him more hurt. The fussiness of the others moving about the shabby room was mocked by that terrible immobility. The corpse compelled Laidlaw by its inaccessible nature, the way figures talking behind glass can fascinate because they are unheard. He learned that incomprehensible image like a rune he must try to decipher. He stood staring at Tony Veitch, letting the haunting and mysterious stillness of that destroyed youth brand itself painfully on his mind.

29

The cottage was a very self-conscious act—rough white walls with horse tackle hanging from them and a Gudgeon sketch of the inevitable fighting cock. In Gudgeon's world did they ever just peck corn? The wooden furniture was rough enough not just to have been made by hand but possibly by foot. But Jan liked it.

She knew it was Tom and Molly's romantic sense of a country retreat, as relevant to the urban reality of their lives as a Christmas card is to Christmas. But liking them so much, she felt at home here. The place partook of their liberal niceness, meant no harm. Coming here any time she had days off from the Burleigh Hotel, she was grateful again that they gave her the run of the place. She must get them to meet Jack.

But, glancing at him, she wondered how the meeting would go. How badly he fitted in here wasn't a good omen. He was sprawled in front of the log fire, drinking what must have been at least his fifth whisky and reading a copy of *The Great Gatsby* he had picked up. His shoes were off. His shirt was open to the navel, showing the beginning of a paunch. His face was a small fury of concentration as he flicked back and forwards among the pages.

He belonged to the place the way a bird belongs to a roof, an accidental alighting, right at the time but incalculably brief. She wasn't at all sure that he would stay the night. He might get up at any time and go. He had done it before. At least, he had done before what made you know that what he was doing now you couldn't be sure.

He had no image of himself, she realised. That was why he was so out of place here. This was where Tom and Molly had very understandably built an alternative sense of themselves, like a cache of iron rations they could have recourse to if the going got too tough. But Jack had no such fortress. He often seemed still as raw as a cut umbilicus.

It worried her. She had known the way the car pulled up the kind of pressure he was under. Lately, she had seriously doubted how long he could go on. He was walking the edge of himself like a ledge. She remembered him once saying to her in bed, in that wild dispensation sometimes achieved there, 'You know what I believe? There's no centre as such. The sum of the edges is the centre. You have to keep walking the edges.' But that was how you fell off. She sensed him teetering.

Tonight had been like a warning. He came in both bright and hurt. 'How you doin', darlin'? Nice wee place ye've got. Phoo, I could sleep for a year.' He had taken to the whisky as if it was a swimming pool. His eyes had been like bruises, yet he wouldn't just present her with the pain. He had a meticulous sense of what he should cope with himself. She had felt the desperation in the lightness of his touch but had known he wouldn't come to her fully until he was sure he wasn't abusing her. He was determined to come as a gift, not an act of theft.

She thought, he's so complicated. And so was she. She thought of the tests, unconscious at the time, she had put him to. She had been harder on him than any Lady of Courtly Love, dropping her glove in the bear-pit and asking him to fetch it. She remembered how, meeting him at the beginning, she had been inviting him to pay for where she had been. She thought of the men she had known before, most of them leaving her wondering what past painful assignation with what forgotten bitch they were trying to memorialise on her. But that wasn't the way he worked.

It struck her like a secret that the essence of his nature was the desire to be kind. His anger came from the bafflement of that desire, because he hated to think that his kindness might be abused.

Another thing he had once said to her was, 'Most people can't stand kindness. It compromises their sense of

182

themselves. We all spend so much time working out how to be hard, we don't like the rules changed. Makes us feel guilty. As if kind people were cheating.'

She looked at him, assessing how he was now. His preoccupation was as complete as a child's. She tried to read again what he had given her. But it seemed so wild. Jack had tried to get her to read it soon after he came in. But she had managed to put it off by making him some chicken vols-au-vent. He had been insisting on making the food. Fortunately, she had dissuaded him. As a cook he belonged in the same league as the Borgias.

She finished reading it again and put it down. She took a sip of her glass of wine. She knew he was aware that she had finished reading. He looked at *The Great Gatsby* a little longer.

'Some book,' he said, putting it back on the shelf. 'I worry about it now and again. But the man did it. A naivete as hard as bell metal. If you've got to be naive, that's the way to do it.'

He sipped his whisky.

'Well. What do you think?'

She hadn't wanted the question.

'I'm not sure.'

'You must feel something.'

'Who wrote this?'

'I told you. Tony Veitch. The boy they found dead tonight.'

'Well, the circumstances tend to inhibit criticism a bit. I mean, it would be like spitting on the grave.'

'Come on, Jan. You're among friends.'

'It seems a bit crazy to me.'

'How crazy is that?'

'I don't know. It seems like following ideas beyond the point you can follow them. How do you believe all that and go on living?'

'He didn't, right enough. The question is, why? And how?'

She watched him worry about it.

'What is it, Jack?'

'I can't believe it. We have a case where he killed two people and then himself. I don't believe it. I just don't believe it. There's something we've missed.'

'Maybe it's just the energy you've put into it. Maybe you can't believe it's as simple as that.'

'That's right. I don't believe it's as simple as that. You know what? I don't believe anything is. The simplicity of this case offends me. It's so neat, it's like a preconception. One thing you can be sure about any preconception. It's wrong. If there's a God and he tried to preconceive the world, he got it wrong. If you tried to imagine taking a walk down the street you know the best, you couldn't come near the reality of doing it. There's always the bit of paper blowing you couldn't have imagined. The man coming out of his house you didn't account for. That's it. That's what's wrong. It answers all the questions you would ask in court. But when you ask it anything else, it's totally dumb. Who's been sniffing round the edges of this case? We still don't know. Who does the birth-mark belong to? Whose are the other fingerprints on Eck's bottle? We still don't know. We *have* to know. What we're looking at here isn't the truth. It's somebody's *idea* of what we might expect the truth to be. We're all looking at this from inside somebody's head. Who the hell belongs to the head? That's the question.'

She panicked quietly. Laidlaw was so obsessively lost, like a man in a private labyrinth.

'From here to there we go how?' he said.

'Jack. Leave it just now.'

'Okay, darlin'.'

He smiled at her suddenly, his generous mouth a place she would like to explore. They knew they had access to each other at last. The point of their night till now became a strange wooing, a stillness around each other, a waiting for signs, a delicate keeping of balance until they could move. They moved. He found again the sheer openness of her, the preparedness for anything to happen. She found again his gentle aggressiveness, his desire to overwhelm her into

184

herself. They hunted each other remorselessly over their bodies. He conjured her out with his fingers. She sucked him alive with her mouth. They made a fierce meeting. The end of it was like getting lost in each other.

Beached on their mutual exhaustion, they saw their clothes like part of the shipwreck. Her pants were beside the fire. Her skirt hung strange from a chair. Her blouse was crumpled surprisingly small. His trousers and underpants were the one truncated garment, like lined shorts. Her brassiere lay far away in an odd place. They both realised he was still wearing his shirt. The fire was mottling their legs.

He gave them both cigarettes and they smoked, adjusting the heat by moving away from it. They were as natural as cats. His arm around her felt as if she had been born with it there. When he threw the stub of his cigarette in the fire, she knew what would happen. She felt his arm go limp. He was asleep. She put her own stub away, gave him some minutes.

'Jack,' she said. 'Jack darling.'

He didn't move.

'Jack.' Her voice was touching him as softly as her hands had. 'Let's go to bed.'

His eyes opened like a doll's. He stared at the ceiling.

'Jan! You all right, darlin'? What's the problem?'

'No problem. I think we should go to bed.'

He sat up slowly.

'I think we should.'

He stood up not too steadily. His shirt was like farce, a pretence of concealment that hid nothing. She lay back on the floor and laughed, being honestly naked.

'Oh aye,' he said sleepily. 'Nice to furnish amusement.'

He put the meshed fireguard in front of the fire. He stood vaguely doing nothing, threatening to fall asleep on his feet. Then he took Tony Veitch's message she had been reading, folded it lengthwise and put it in the inside pocket of his jacket that was over a chair. He was handcuffing himself to tomorrow, even though he was drunk.

'It's bed then, lovely,' he said.

She lay looking at him. The fierceness of her love for him

185

was more than he could find ways to avoid, she knew. He was going to settle for her, she decided. She understood his grief for the failure of his family. She would give him time to get over it. She stood up, knowing how right she looked naked.

'Right, Jack Laidlaw. We're going to bed.'

He nodded long enough to suggest senility.

'And all your worries can wait till tomorrow.'

'Aye, right enough,' he said as he put out the light. 'They'll be there all right. They get delivered with the milk.'

30

Harkness passed the photocopied sheet across to Bob Lilley. Bob shook his head and retired behind his whisky like a drawbridge.

'No thanks,' he said. 'Not interested. I don't even understand that stuff. The bit I've looked at reads like a cerebral haemorrhage. So the boy's head burst. I don't have to poke among the pieces. I get enough of that.'

They were downstairs in 'The Top Spot'. They were a wake of three but seemed unable to agree on the identity of the corpse. Bob was utterly and finally in dismay with Laidlaw, wondered if he was contemplating a dead friendship. Harkness wasn't sure how much of his respect for Laidlaw could survive this. Laidlaw seemed to be mourning the still-birth of some understanding he had almost achieved.

Even their appearances suggested different events. Bob and Harkness were spruce. Bob looked healthy and dependable in his checked shirt, neat tie and hacking jacket. Harkness wouldn't have been out of place at a disco. Laidlaw looked hellish, his face raw with sleeplessness, his eyes strained, as if he'd spent the night trying to decipher Tony Veitch's garbled message.

Bob fingered his glass and looked pointedly away from their table, seemed trying to associate himself with the normalcy of the others in the bright room. He whistled infinitesimally under his breath. What hurt him most was what he suspected was the motivation for Laidlaw's dissatisfaction. He wished Jack would leave it alone. He dreaded having to discover that Jack had come down with that mean jealousy of colleagues that was familiar to him in some other policemen, something Bob had always been sure he was immune to.

187

'You should read that more carefully, Bob,' Laidlaw said.

With reluctance Bob abandoned his fascinating study of the wall on his left-hand side.

'Why, Jack? Why should I do that?' He pointed at the sheet lying on the table. 'That's just a production. Like a bloodstained knife. Or a button off a jacket. Not even an interesting production. We don't even need it, because the case is as tight as an earwig's arse. That. Is just a piece of addled brains, Jack. That stuff offends me, that's all it does. Nothing else. I'm not interested in his wanky theories about why he did it—just that he did it, the bastard. And I'm just grateful that he didn't get round to people who were slightly less expendable than those two. No offence to auld Eck but he'd had his whack. And made an arse of it. He was just finishing his apprenticeship drinking paraquat, wasn't he? And Paddy Collins was just pollution. They should've given Veitch a civic reception for that one.' He lifted the sheet and let it fall back on the table. 'But don't ask me to take an interest in that shite. Look. If I find somebody disembowelled, I don't have to take the entrails home in a bag to study them. That's not my job. And it's not yours either.'

'That's not the writing of a murderer.'

'Jesus Christ.' Bob looked at Harkness and smiled, as if humour were aloes. 'How the hell would *you* know that?'

'Because I can read.'

'Can you? Very good. Me, I'm still attacking the *Beano* with one finger. Come on. I may not be as clever as you, Jack. And I'm certainly not as clever as you think you are. Who is? But I've glanced at that bit of paper. He was as daft as a brush. And you know it. He could've done *anything*.'

'No. I don't think so. If he was daft, he was daft in the one direction. John-the-Baptist-daft. A wee one-man religion. A do-it-yourself martyr. Poor bastard.'

Bob finished his whisky slowly. The glance he gave Harkness was a small act of collusion, a signal that he was going to say what was in both of their heads.

'Jack. I think everybody but you realises there's something funny happening here.'

188

Laidlaw looked up at him slowly and assessingly.

'Nothing you've said justifies your refusal to see this case as closed.'

'So what does that mean?'

'It means there has to be another reason.'

Laidlaw looked at Harkness, who happened to be studying the table at the time.

'And you're decorating it with a lot of fancy rational-isations.'

'What reason would that be, Bob?'

Their eyes were a steady confrontation.

'I'm not sure. But I'll tell you what I think it is. I know you don't get on too well with Big Ernie. But he's a good polisman. And he did the job. Before you. And I think you better just accept that, Jack. Put your wee hurt pride away. It's getting in the road of your brains.'

'Bob. Come on.' Laidlaw looked again at Harkness. 'Brian?'

Harkness shook his head at him.

'Jack. The case looks clean to me.'

'I think you should watch the area you're moving into, Jack,' Bob said. 'This job would make a saint go sour. And you were never that to begin with. But I've always thought you were at least generous.'

'What makes you think I'm not?'

'The way you are just now. Your head's trying to see round corners. Just to steal the scone off Ernie's plate. What's that about? And another thing. I know you've just been reprimanded by the Commander. Again. And I know why. And you deserved it. You knew about Tony Veitch before Ernie did. You knew about the possible connection and you didn't pass it on. That's a liberty, Jack. That's what that is.'

'It was a decision I made, that's all.'

'Aye, but why? Are you sure why, Jack? That was a dangerous decision. We're dealing in people's lives. It's not a question of who gets the merit badges.'

'Bob. It's exactly *because* we're dealing in lives that I didn't

189

pass it on. It's exactly because I don't care about making pinches for their own sake. Because I don't want any mistakes. And I think that's what happened. You can say I was wrong. But not for those shitty reasons.'

'Maybe not.'

'Anyway. Somebody sure enough passed it on.'

'Thank Christ. It's a good thing Ernie didn't have to rely on you. I'm worried about you. I don't want to think of you as jealous and I don't want to think of you as mean. But it's getting harder.'

'Well, I'll help by getting another drink.'

He collected their glasses.

'Why not buy yourself something decent this time?' Bob said. 'That lime-juice and soda's giving me the blues. Maybe it's just alcohol-starvation that's wrong with you.'

Laidlaw went along to the bar. The attractive waitress, who still hadn't been discovered, looked at him quizzically as he went past but he ignored her. Bob sighed like a pair of bellows, his hands covering his face. The hands came down till they were over his mouth and he looked at Harkness, shaking his head. He smoothed back what was left of his hair, double-handed.

'It's a problem, Brian,' he said. 'I think you should watch him. I wouldn't be surprised if he cracked up. Why can't he leave *anything* alone? Look at him.' Harkness looked up at Laidlaw standing bleak at the bar, like an undertaker at a wedding. 'He's doing the gantry stare.' It was a phrase they shared to describe a recurring moment of bleak stillness that happened in Laidlaw's eyes and appeared to mean some thing like, 'This won't do.' The gantry was probably irrelevant to that mood. It was just that there was frequently one in front of him at the time. 'He's been knocked onto his horse on the road to Damascus again. Oh my Christ! You know that Paul Newman film? "Cool Hand Luke"? Well, I know who Jack is. He's Cool Head Luke. Don't let his anger kid you on. There's always a few of the brain-cells in the deep-freeze. When they bury him, he'll be watching how they do it. He'll have peep-holes in the coffin. Probably shove the lid back and sit up. Say, "Wait a minute! *Your* grief looks a bit suspect. You can piss off. The rest of you, let's try it again. Okay?" He'll lie back down. A dozen times later, he won't get up. And they can all go home.'

Harkness laughed.

'No kidding, though, Brian. He's in a dangerous frame of mind. Try not to let him blow his career. He could, you know. Anytime.'

Laidlaw returned with Bob's whisky and Harkness's lager. He had bought himself a double Antiquary.

'No, Bob,' he said.

'Oh, Jack,' Bob said. 'Let's talk about the weather. You know they're going to alter this place? Call it "The Opera Bar". You know, since the Scottish Opera took it over. How about that for a bit of fascinating chat?'

'No, Bob. You're wrong. I don't grudge Ernie Milligan the case. So long as he got it right. But he didn't. What seems to have happened isn't what actually happened.'

Bob watered his whisky, sampled it and spoke to Laidlaw with an elaborate patience that suggested he was just keeping him humoured until the strait-jacket arrived.

'Is that right, Jack? How do you make that out?'

'Nothing he wrote suggests a murderer.'

'Oh, Jack. Did Christie advertise? What do you want them to do? Leave signatures?'

'On the bottle that killed Eck,' Laidlaw said. 'Two sets of fingerprints. One of them's Eck's. The other lot don't belong to Tony Veitch.'

Bob was momentarily interested.

'You've checked that off?'

Laidlaw nodded.

'He gave a mate a drink,' Bob said. 'Didn't he? They're sharers, winos. Who wants his liver to die alone?'

'They said he didn't share. You remember that, Brian?'

'Aye, that's right,' Harkness said.

'That's what some of them said,' Bob said. 'So maybe he had a special friend. Or somebody made a grab for the bottle. Thinner than a witch's tit, Jack. To establish the

191

value of that, you'd have to fingerprint every rummy in Glasgow.'

'Oh, I think we could make a shorter leet than that. And what actually ties Tony Veitch to the killings?'

'Only the knife that did Paddy Collins and a tin of paraquat.'

'There were no prints on the paraquat tin.'

'So he wiped them off.'

'And kept the tin in his flat. What sense does that make?'

'Enough.'

'No. Not quite enough.'

'His prints were on the knife all right.'

'They could have been put there easily enough. Only *his* prints were found in the flat. But there were plenty of smudges consistent with the wearing of gloves.'

'Pimples, Jack. They don't alter the essential features of the case.' Bob smiled, as if he had suddenly remembered how much he liked Laidlaw. 'Tell us, O wise one, what really happened. Eh?'

Laidlaw neutralised the facetiousness by taking the question seriously.

'It's what didn't happen I think we should start from. Tony Veitch didn't commit suicide. At least, I don't think he did. He was manic to talk to the world. Suicide tends to amputate your larynx. I know how thin that is, Bob. I've done this job long enough to know the kind of somersaults the head can take. I know we often express our most intense feelings by doing the opposite. The more desperate the talker, the more effectively he defines his own silence. The bit he knows he'll never be able to say. So maybe Tony Veitch went in the huff with the world. Because it wouldn't listen. Or killed himself just because of the distance between his ideals and the things he'd done. If he'd done them. It could've been like that. But I don't think so. I think somebody did him and set it up to look like suicide. And I think I know who did it. But I don't expect anybody else to agree with me.'

'That's a relief,' Harkness said. 'Who, though?'

'Unfair to say. But I'm going to do a bit of scuffling myself today, Brian. Nothing too official, like.'

'Jack. I'll come with you.'

'No. I think I'm going to need you later on. If I get what I'm looking for. And I'll be in touch. But I'm going to hassle a few people first. And you shouldn't be involved in that.'

Bob was staring at Laidlaw.

'Jack,' he said. 'Maybe you shouldn't have gone on to the hard stuff. You seem to get pissed very quick. Maybe you're not used to it now.'

Laidlaw smiled and drank the whisky.

'You going to get me another one?' he said to Bob,

'I'll do that,' Harkness said and winked at Bob as he left.

'Not for me, Brian,' Bob said. 'They must be spiking it. Come on, you,' to Laidlaw. 'You've been a mug. But you're trying to graduate to being a loony too quick. What's this you're talking about?'

'It's what I'm going to do.'

'Who you going to see?'

'Some people.'

'Stick the mystery up your arse, Jack. Tell me what you're going to do. I may have to go bail.'

'Forget it. I'll stand by anything I do.'

'Listen, bloody Robin Hood. You've got a career. If you do this, tomorrow you may not have.'

'Naw. You listen. I've got a life. That's more than any career. And I wouldn't be able to spend it sitting beside myself if I let this pass. And this case isn't right. Some bastard's put it together like a meccano-set. And I'm going to take it apart. Three people are dead. And their bodies are buried in lies. Not on! Not for me it's not. That's why I'm here, supposed to be. To arrive at whatever half-arsed version of the truth's available. And that's what I'm going to do. If I have to break in doors to do it.'

Harkness was back at the table. Laidlaw stood up, watered his drink and downed it.

'Thanks, Brian. I'll be in touch.'

'Jack,' Bob said. 'Don't work so hard at getting it wrong. You'll get it wrong anyway. Everybody does.'

Laidlaw went out. Harkness sat down. Bob was staring blankly round the room. Harkness lowered his head, put his hand on his brow and studied the pattern of beads on the surface of his lager.

'You think we should take up a collection for his widow?' he muttered.

'I've worked out the way to beat Jack with words,' Bob said.

Harkness looked at him.

'Batter him unconscious with a copy of the Oxford Dictionary.'

31

Gus Hawkins was alone in his flat. He admitted Laidlaw to an atmosphere he remembered from his own brief time as a student. There was an old armchair near the window, with several books lying round it and on the arm an open paperback of *The Psychopathology of Everyday Life* with heavy underlinings in biro. There was a can of export on the floor beside the chair. Sunlight shone on the open pages of the book, seeming to hackle that delicate fur the surface of cheap paper has.

It was a still life of studenthood, evocative of long hours spent alone, intense head-wrestling matches with the dead, endless arguments on which the world depended, cups of coffee at strange hours, time contracted to a pellet and dissolved to disappearance. Laidlaw remembered his own discovery that his mind was there and knew the poignancy of possibilities felt in this kind of book-lined womb before career or circumstances yank you out. The awareness made his impulsiveness pause, but only briefly.

'You don't have a job in the summer?' Laidlaw asked.

'I've managed to get part-time in a pub. You want a can of beer?'

Laidlaw did. Gus fetched him a can. Sitting back down to sip his own beer, Gus waited. His eyes had lost their abstractedness of when he answered the door. His recovery from that state made it occur to him to explain it.

'I didn't know who you were at first there. If something happens when I'm working, takes me a week to focus. I'm only even money to remember my name.'

'I know what you mean.'

Laidlaw pulled the tag on his can and it made a small geyser of escaping gas.

'I didn't know the polis drank on duty.'

That inflection of aggressiveness in his voice towards the police, something Laidlaw sometimes felt must be taught in the West of Scotland along with 'choo–choo', disturbed the idle pleasure of the moment. Laidlaw's mind put on its working clothes. He took a drink.

'Who's on duty?' Laidlaw said. 'This is a discourtesy call. You've heard about Tony Veitch?'

Gus nodded.

'We found his papers, by the way. Burnt to ash in a lavatory pan. Those papers interest me. He writes to his father, Lynsey Farren, you. But none of you keeps the letter. He writes reams of other stuff. It's all destroyed. Why is that? It's almost as if he was trying to say what nobody wanted to hear. What was it, I wonder?'

'A lot of things, I suppose.'

'You've read some of them, have you?'

'Some.'

'I mean, what were they about?'

'Just trying to understand things, I think. Anyway, surely Tony destroyed them himself.'

'You think so?'

'What else could it be?'

Laidlaw took a drink and seemed nonplussed.

'Anyway, he's dead,' Laidlaw said. 'How does that strike you?'

'As a fact.'

'That's all?'

'That's not enough? I mean, I can think of a couple of other people I wouldn't mind volunteering to take his place. But they probably wouldn't agree. So there we are.'

'I thought you liked him.'

'I did. But now he's dead.'

'God preserve me from you as a friend.'

'Your wish is granted.'

Laidlaw looked at him—so sure, so young. Laidlaw himself seemed to know less every day. If it kept on this way, he would die in the foetal position with his thumb in his mouth, but probably still looking apprehensively around him, his wonderment as strong as it was now.

'How do you do that?' he said. 'Be so unconcerned. So bloody unsad.'

'There are bigger sadnesses about.'

'Like what? You mean the Third World and capitalist oppression and that?'

'Something like that.'

'But pity for one precludes pity for the other, does it? What if I tell you I reckon Tony was murdered?'

Gus Hawkins looked at the open pages of Freud as if consulting his notes, glanced at the window, stared back at Laidlaw. A lot was happening behind his eyes but none of it was for release.

'You think that?' he asked.

'I feel sure he was. If he was, can you think of any contenders?'

Gus shook his head immediately.

'Jesus Christ,' Laidlaw said. He was holding his beercan so tightly it buckled a bit and sent a small splash of beer on to the frayed carpet. He wiped it with a handkerchief as he went on. 'You're a cracker. Brain of Britain. You answer a question like that off the top of your head. It's like talking to a computer. Or a balloon. And I think you're a balloon.'

Gus's shoulders went rigid under the sweater.

'If you've finished your beer, I think you'd better go. In fact, whether you've finished or not. Don't sit and drink my beer and insult me.'

Laidlaw smiled at him slowly.

'It didn't take long for the cosmic objectivity to turn personal,' he said. 'A wee bit of the embourgeoisement there, Gus, eh? Fair enough. I've had enough spunk in my eye for one day, anyway.'

'How do you mean?'

'I mean you're a wanker. I noticed it quick. You offer a man a drink and then, before he can get it to his mouth, you dig him up about drinking on duty. What's that about?' Knowing he had put himself on his way out, Laidlaw saw

197

no point in going quietly. 'But a lot more than that. Tony's supposed to have destroyed his papers. That doesn't give you a tremor. Do you think that's likely? Did you know him? I never met him and I know that's hardly on the cards for him to do. You better lay into old Sigmund there. You're not exactly a great reader of the human heart. I doubt Tony wasn't either. He could've got better friends in a lucky bag. Look at the people near him. You and Lynsey Farren. And his father. But at least those other two practise an honest selfishness. You've got to dress it up in a lot of sanctimonious theories. Why not admit it? You just don't give a shit. I've seen more compassion in a fucking wolverine. How do you manage to make love to your girl-friend, Gus? You put it together like an identikit from what you read in books? Do you? Because there can't be anything in the middle of you but theory.'

Gus looked at him steadily. The word he said was a small one but it seemed to grow as slowly as a glacier and, spoken, it filled the room with chill.

'Cheerio.'

'Oh, don't worry about it. I fancy doing something jollier. Like kissing lepers. Most of that beer's still there, by the way. You could maybe send it to the Third World.'

Laidlaw stood up. The rage he felt frightened him. His hatred for the prevarications people practised was hardly containable. He knew the sensible way to live was to leave this alone. But he couldn't leave it alone. He believed three people had been murdered. And nobody seriously cared who did it. It wouldn't do.

'Your kind of intellectual sickens me,' he said, and had no idea what else to say.

He stood looking at the wall. Like a stag at bay, he was who he was, he was what he was, and nothing else. He saw no hope of proving what he suspected. He had half a vision and nobody else would begin to admit the possibility of the other half. He knew they were lying. It was all he knew. For the moment, it was all he cared about.

'I know you,' he said. 'Where you are. You're protecting

your brother. And your friend can go die as he likes. It's not your business. But it is. It's everybody's business. There's no other business we *have*. How each of us dies matters. Eck Adamson is dead. I'll bury him proper. You better believe it. You'll help me or you won't. But I'll bury him proper. I mean, in my mind. He'll have a proper funeral in meaning. Or I'll cause so much trouble even I won't believe it. I don't want your brother, Gus Hawkins. Unless he did it, I don't want him. But I'll understand what happened. Yes, I will. You better believe it.'

Laidlaw himself couldn't see how until Gus Hawkins rose and put on a parka. He looked round the room, then at Laidlaw. It was a strange moment. Laidlaw felt that at last someone had heard not just the words of his anger but the pain behind them and was admitting that he shared it. They were in contact with each other.

'You got a car?' Gus said.

Laidlaw nodded.

'I'll take you one place. That's all I'll do. It's up to you.'

In the car Gus explained her name was Gina. She was Italian. Tony Veitch had been with her. Gus didn't know her surname but he knew the tenement she lived in. When he got out of the car and said he would walk back home, they smiled at each other like a shared secret.

'I hope you get it right,' Gus said.

'For both our sakes,' Laidlaw said. 'Eh?'

Gus nodded.

32

The name on the door was the first Italian one he had come to. He rang the bell. She was wearing black cords and a black blouse loose at the waist. She looked like a woman you might jump a few lights to get home to.

'Gina?'

She appraised him for a moment and he saw her generous smile bloom on a misunderstanding, like a flower that comes out too early. She had assumed he had been told about her, was chancing his arm. He felt as if he had picked her purse.

'I have little time this now. But—' She looked at her watch. 'You come in for a few minutes. Only a few. All right?'

He came in. She closed the door and walked ahead of him into the sitting-room. She was wearing backless high-heeled shoes. As he gave her a cigarette, lit it and sat down opposite her to light his own, he thought again that such trustingness was a dangerous trade to practise. There was an open travelling-bag on the floor with three freshly ironed shirts lying on top of it.

'I'm not havin' much time,' she said, and smiled again. 'You're nice.'

'That's you and my mammy think that,' Laidlaw said.

He had a brief reluctance to process the moment into practicalities. This was a pleasant hiatus. He liked the decadent innocence of her assumption. But it was unfair to prolong it.

'You are shy?'

He laughed.

'I didn't think you'd notice.'

'You want to talk? You have a problem?'

'Thousands,' Laidlaw said. 'You got a spare year? No. Listen, love. There's something I better explain. I'm a policeman.'

It was farewell to commercial Eden. Suddenly, what had looked like growing into an uncomplicated exchange was a computer job. Complex things were happening in her eyes. Her face had set like concrete. To complete the alienation, he resignedly passed across his card.

'This is unfair,' she said, giving it back. 'I don't like policemen. Some take without payment. You didn't say.'

'I'm saying now. Come on. You would've let me in anyway, love. Look, I just want to ask you some questions. About somebody who's dead.'

'I don't know anybody who's dead.'

'We all do. Some of them still walking about as well. This was a boy called Tony Veitch.'

She hadn't known he was dead, he was sure. Her face showed the first shock of impact and then a series of withdrawals into the implications of the fact. She didn't know how to react. What had looked like being sadness became thoughtfulness, worry and then panic.

'I'm sorry,' she said. 'You have to go. I'm expecting someone.'

She half-rose.

'Wait a minute,' Laidlaw said. 'That was a sudden decision.'

'He is coming,' she said.

She made it sound like a tidal wave, or Grendel at least. She crossed and put the shirts carefully into the travelling-bag, as if that solved everything. She turned vaguely, seeming to look for something she couldn't find. Laidlaw wondered if it might be sandbags. He stood up.

'Gina. Who is it?'

As her head swivelled, Laidlaw appeared again in her vision and her hand gestured him away like a midgie.

'He didn't tell me any of this.' Her hand went to her mouth, sealing it. 'I can't talk to you. He is coming soon.'

She was starting to cry. Laidlaw took her by the shoulders and felt the tremors of her panic, like a small earthquake. He held her firmly, earthing the hysteria. The comfort of his contact, perhaps a gentleness of touch she was starved of, finally released the emotion in her and she lay against him and abandoned herself to crying. With his arms round her, he let her cry. She needed the confession of tears to admit to herself that she could no longer cope with what was happening.

Eventually he said, 'Sit down, Gina.'

She sat down slowly. He gave her a handkerchief and, as she dabbed at her face, he lit a cigarette and gave it to her. He walked through to the small kitchen, filled the kettle, plugged it in. He watched her from the doorway.

'I'll make a cup of tea.'

The realisation that he was staying renewed the panic in her.

'But he's coming.'

'Gina, who the hell is coming? Unless it's Godzilla, you're over-reacting, love. Let him come. I'll wait with you. Who is it?'

'A man.'

'I'm a detective, Gina. I'd worked that out.'

His attempt to make her laugh hadn't succeeded but she did look at him as if she was actually seeing him. She sniffed determinedly and the hiccoughing of her body subsided. A small calm had been achieved.

He rinsed out a couple of mugs, found the necessary things and made the tea. She didn't take sugar. With their cups of tea they looked like a nice couple nicely at home.

'Who is he, Gina?' he asked.

He had given her time to make her decision.

'His name is Mickey Ballater.'

'Tricky Mickey,' Laidlaw said. 'That's what they used to call him. So that's who's turned private detective. The

202

Birmingham snooper. What's the connection with you?'

He could see her wondering about catching amnesia.

'Gina. I'm going to wait here till he comes anyway. It would be better, for me and you, if I knew what I was getting into.'

'He comes to the door last week. And he is staying here since.'

'But why? Why does he come to *your* door?'

She closed her eyes, shaking her head.

'It is a dirty story.'

'Most of them are. Some folk just tell them nice.'

'Paddy Collins?'

Laidlaw nodded.

'I am from Naples. My husband is from Naples. We are married and come here. My husband is cousin with a family with a café. He is to work. But he doesn't work. We quarrel, he leaves me pregnant. I have the baby. I meet Paddy Collins. He is all right. But soon he makes a suggestion. How I should manage to live. I am not going to do it. But I do it.'

Laidlaw wondered how often he had heard the poignancy of whole lives reduced to the compass of a small ad. Was it her problem with the language that made it sound so simple? He imagined a terrible inarticulate pain behind the words, but perhaps he was being fanciful.

'Don't misunderstand. I am not blaming Paddy. Perhaps I do this anyway.' She looked at him defiantly. 'Sometimes I don't dislike it.'

He shrugged, abjuring judgment.

'But then a bad thing. A very bad thing. Paddy takes me to meet someone. He is not to know what I do for living. Then I did not know why. Now I know. His name is Tony Veitch.'

'Let me guess,' Laidlaw said. 'It sounds like an old script. You and Tony get together, right? But after a time you develop a husband. And it's going to take money to buy him off. Because he's found out.'

She looked at Laidlaw, relieved that he had got there without the pain of having to tell him.

'I did not know this. When I do, I am too afraid to get out.'

'So who's the husband?'

'Mickey Ballater.'

'You picked a beauty.'

'I did not pick.'

'No, I know, love. So that's the story. That's why Ballater's been looking for Tony Veitch?'

She nodded.

'Maybe he found him. Trickey Mickey. I wonder. Paddy Collins was demanding money from Tony Veitch? And Ballater was the way of getting it out of him?'

'But Tony disappears. I felt glad. Tony was nice.'

'Do you know if Mickey Ballater found where Tony was?'

'He tells me nothin'.'

'Did he ever mention Eck Adamson to you?'

'No.'

'When was it Ballater came here?'

She thought about it.

'Friday.'

'Did you get the impression he had only just arrived in Glasgow?'

'He comes at night. Next day he says he will get his things from left luggage. He brings this.'

She nodded towards the travelling-bag.

'He's due back for it, is he?'

Her renewed fear was sufficient answer.

'Is he carrying?'

She didn't understand.

'Does he have a weapon on him?'

'He has a knife.' She crossed her arms, trying to remember on which side he wore it. Her left arm gave up first. 'On the left, I think.'

'Think hard. I would like to keep on breathing.'

'It is the left. I think.'

204

'Thank you. If it's the right, my favourite flowers are gladioli. If he's threatened you with it, you should remember. No?'

'Does he need to?'

She pulled up the sleeves of her blouse. Both arms had bruises that obviously dated from different times but were almost in the same place. He wasn't even an inventive sadist. Having begun, she warmed to her rancour. She pulled her blouse up from the waist. There were three of what looked like cigarette-burns on her belly like small, not quite extinct volcanoes. Laidlaw added them to the debit column of his anger.

'I'm sorry to be so personal, Gina. But he must have made his strange kind of love to you.' He waited but she just stared at him. 'So he must have touched you there.' He pointed between her legs. 'Which hand did he use?'

He noticed how she put him down in her estimation, as if he were some kind of voyeur. Prudishness grows in strange places.

'His right hand,' she said.

'So he carries on the left. You have a phone?'

'In the bedroom.'

Laidlaw wrote something on an envelope he took from his pocket, passed it to her. It was a telephone number.

'When you let him in, you go into the bedroom. You phone that number. Ask them to send a couple of men right away.'

'And you?'

'I'll be trying to keep him here.'

'But if he kills you? What do I do?'

'Well, I'll probably have lost interest by then. I think you might say you'll be on your own. You could maybe jump out a window or that.'

'I have a child sleeping.'

'Should be all right. Even Mickey Ballater's shiteyness must have limits. Have it away on your toes with the wean.

Anyway, Gina, I didn't volunteer for God. I'm just trying to work it out as I go along. Maybe—'

The outside door had opened. Of course, Laidlaw thought, he's got a key. As he moved behind the door of the sitting-room he was mentally thanking Gina for keeping him posted. How could she be so stupid as to let him talk about letting Ballater in without mentioning that she wouldn't have to? His stomach went delicately molten. His hands had a familiar divining-rod tremor to them—there's violence here, but where exactly? He shook his head distantly at her pleading expression. He had given what he could give. It was Laidlaws in the boats first. Otherwise nobody would be saved. The outside door had closed and the feet were coming along the hall. Laidlaw made a double-handed, crossed-arm wiping gesture—you're on your own. In a moment of terrified inspiration, Gina lifted the paper from the white-tiled table beside her chair and pretended to be looking at it. As the door opened, Laidlaw realised she was holding the paper upside-down. It seemed a stupendous error at the time.

But Ballater walked into a room he had pre-decided.

'Uh-huh,' he said. 'Ah'm for the off. Everything ready?'

But caution came in after him like a double-take. He stopped unnaturally, not because he had a specific reason for doing so but because he didn't know what was wrong. Laidlaw reckoned it was the cup beside the other chair. He didn't give himself time to refine the thought. He took two strides across the room and battered Ballater in the back, knocking his face against the wall.

'Get out, Gina,' Laidlaw shouted.

Ballater had fallen against the wall and Laidlaw grappled him, trying to reach his left inside pocket. There was a moment of quiescence in Ballater when Laidlaw thought he had done it. Through cloth he felt something hard then he felt something harder. It was Ballater's elbow in his stomach. Laidlaw retched breath and as he subsided Ballater erupted

206

with an elbow in his face. Laidlaw staggered several paces back against the door, slamming it shut.

Fear gave him panoramic vision. He saw that Gina had got out. He saw that the room was a lot smaller than it should be. He saw a bird scudding past the window. He saw a slim white chair against the wall beside him as more than something to sit on. He saw the knife in Ballater's hand, looking as long as Excalibur. He saw the birth-mark as a core of rage that shouldn't have been his problem.

A few swift thoughts went past like the carriages of a train he was too late to catch. This was a crazy job. He hoped the G.P.O. was on form. He had done it wrong again. He had over-rehearsed. If he hadn't been so determined to get the knife he could have knocked Ballater out. Come on, come on. Perhaps they could talk about this.

'Wait, Mickey. Wait a minute! You know who I am?'

His own voice sounded crazy to him, wild and irrelevant, like somebody insisting on introductions before he was murdered.

'You're the wan that's gonny get it.'

'I'm polis, Mickey.' Beyond his own control, his card was thrown on the floor. 'You're tryin' to kill polis.'

The card lay between them in a way that neither understood, seemed to build an invisible fence. While Mickey paused fractionally, as if going back inside himself far enough to make the jump, Laidlaw took the chair in one fluid nervous movement as compulsive as orgasm and fired it at Mickey. Its trajectory, as it happened, was almost enough to make him believe in God, but once completed wasn't quite. One leg of the chair caught Mickey glancingly above the right eye. He went down. The knife went to the wall like an intention. Laidlaw scrabbled across and picked it up.

While Laidlaw stood gasping, holding the knife, Mickey sat gasping, without the knife. Both of them were bewildered.

207

'What's this about?' Mickey said.

'That's what I'd like to know,' Laidlaw said.

He noticed blood seeping through the left-hand side of Mickey Ballater's shirt. The blood puzzled Laidlaw because it wasn't the result of their scuffle.

33

Sometimes you believe them, sometimes you don't. Laidlaw had believed him for the moment. He had only found out where Veitch was when it was too late. Anyway, all he had wanted was the money. The rest would have been up to Cam Colvin. And Ballater was a knife man, subtle as a road accident. Why would he arrange to make it look like suicide? You might as well expect a gorilla to take up origami. Tricky Mickey, maybe, but broad tricks, painful slapstick, not the theatrical cunning Laidlaw thought he saw behind the corpse of Tony Veitch trussed in electricity.

That body haunted him, seemed to mock Laidlaw's private law of gravity, whereby hard truths must be seriously pursued till they surrendered their full meaning. So the fact that Ballater was being held for possession of an offensive weapon and that Gina was safe for the moment to indulge again the normal pains life brought her gave Laidlaw no respite from the feeling in him. That past moment was already like a booster rocket, falling into irrelevance. It had only served to kick him further into the manic orbit he was following, fuelled on his compulsion to find what everybody else said wasn't there.

All other concerns had fused for him, and when his preoccupation found him standing again in the living-room of Lynsey Farren's flat in East Kilbride he wasn't sure he could remember exactly how he got there. He wasn't even entirely sure what he was doing there. Certainly, nobody else seemed to know. He was like yesterday's news nobody was interested in any more.

They had been reluctant to let him in. Now that he was in they contrived barely to notice him. Lynsey Farren was packing. Her face was blotchy with crying and she was abstractedly filling two big leather suitcases on the floor.

Her father, Lord Farren, was waiting to accompany her back to his estate. He looked in his eighties and was hovering about so vaguely it seemed as if he wasn't sure of the century, never mind the day of the week. He still hadn't worked out who Laidlaw was. He was a charming old man who had asked Laidlaw how he got the lump on his cheek. He kept returning to the window, perpetually looking for something he couldn't find, perhaps a hansom cab to take him to an address no longer there.

The Mercedes Laidlaw had recognised outside belonged to Milton Veitch. Mr Veitch was there to run Lynsey and her father home. He had taken control of them. Having manfully overcome his grief, he was helping Lynsey pack and telling Laidlaw that they wanted to be left in peace. He was very solicitous towards Lynsey. To an outsider he would have seemed a nice man, doing the right thing.

Rectitude is a sanctimonious bastard, Laidlaw thought. It would unravel the jumpers from its shivering children's backs to knit gloves for public charity.

'I just need to talk to Miss Farren,' Laidlaw said.

'No, you don't,' Veitch said. 'She's suffered enough. We all have.'

'Not quite as much as Tony.'

Lynsey broke down at the mention of the name, beginning to sob. Veitch put his arm round her.

'What a filthily tasteless remark!' he said. 'How dare you!'

Lord Farren turned from the window and saw Lynsey crying. It must have appeared to him like a tableau he had accidentally stumbled across. He seemed to make no connection with what had gone before.

'Lynsey dear,' he said and crossed towards them. Veitch shepherded them both into the bedroom, waited with them a little, came out and closed the door. He looked at Laidlaw as if he was very small. His contempt was the height of a cliff.

210

'Do you enjoy other people's suffering?' he asked.

'I need to talk to Miss Farren.'

'You won't be doing that.'

'So what's going to happen? You all retire behind your moat of money and leave it at that? I can't do that. This is where I live. I need to know what it's really like.'

'That's your problem. We have the right to cope with this tragedy any way we can.'

'No, you haven't. Not at the expense of the truth you haven't. You don't get monopolising that as well. A share of it's mine. And I'm claiming it. Listen, I think your son was murdered.'

'I think you're off your head. That's what I think. And I think this is harassment. Why are you here alone, for example? That's hardly official procedure. You really don't care about anybody, do you?'

'I must have walked through a looking-glass,' Laidlaw said. 'I don't care? Your son's *dead*. And all you can do is help somebody to pack who knows more about it than she admits. You're going to ferry her silence away for her. You know what you are? You're playing batman to your own son's death. Dressing it up nice. Now why is that? Because you know the truth would be an accusation against you?'

'That's it,' Veitch said. 'I'll be phoning Bob Frederick. Bob can deal with this.'

Laidlaw couldn't believe it. That familiar use of the Commander of the Crime Squad's name was supposed to be the ultimate sanction applied. It felt like living in a different world from everybody else. Did he really think that mattered?

'Phone,' Laidlaw said. 'Phone right now.'

'I'll phone when I choose.'

'No, you won't. Listen. If you can make a phone-call and blow me away, then do it. But don't threaten me with it. You want to pull strings, pull. I'll arrange to have you strangle yourself on them. Or if I can't, I'll be glad to lose. Because this job won't be worth doing. Which actually

211

maybe it's not. But if you're not going to do that, get out of my way and let me speak to that lassie. Make your choice.'

Veitch wilted slightly and sat down. He put his head in his hands briefly, looked up.

'Laidlaw. Do you think my son's death doesn't matter to me?'

'Mr Veitch. I'm not interested. I don't want to talk to you. I've tried that already. Let me speak to the girl.'

'Laidlaw, I *wish* I could believe what you believe. But I *knew* my son. You want to think he wasn't capable of that. But I know he was. God forgive me. But I *know* he was. I've seen him get seduced by every spurious extremist philosophy. Become an intellectual whore. Just to pay me back for some imagined wrong. Since he went to university he developed a mind like a swamp. A breeding-ground for sickness. He was capable of anything. I know he was.'

'Mr Veitch. You know what I think happened to you? You lost the taste for whisky because you owned the pub. Don't tell me what you know. You wouldn't know the truth unless it had Bank of Scotland written on it. I don't want to waste my time with you, Mr Veitch. That's what I really don't want to do. What are you? Some kind of guardian of the golden fleece? Let people talk. If you're so sure you're right, just let me test it. Is that too much to ask?'

Mr Veitch put his head in his hands again. He looked up slowly.

'I'll give you five minutes with Lynsey,' he said.

'Mr Veitch,' Laidlaw said. 'You'll give me as long as I need. Your son's dead and I care more about why and how he died than you do. That gives me rights. Go and get Lynsey, please. And if you really care about people, keep the old man through there. His head doesn't need to try to cope with this.'

When she came through, she was fairly composed. The door had closed on the bedroom and she put down the lid on a suitcase as she passed and then sat down in one of the leather armchairs beside the electric fire. But what she hadn't realised was that she had walked into Laidlaw's obsession. The room was no more than a backdrop for his mood. He sat down across from her.

'Tell me what happened,' he said.

'I beg your pardon?'

'Tell me the truth as far as you understand it.'

'About what?'

'About the national economy. What do you think? About Tony Veitch.'

'I've told you what I know.'

'You've told me nothing. I sat in this room and listened to your cabaret. All right. That was then. But now somebody you're supposed to have cared about is dead. Take the make-up off. I want to know anything you can tell me that might help.'

'I don't know what might help.'

'I'll help you then. Who beat you up?'

'That's my affair.'

'No, no. It's not. You don't understand. I saw Tony Veitch lying dead. Barbecued like a bit of butcher-meat.'

She gasped and covered her eyes.

'You could cry for a week, Miss Farren, and it wouldn't count. That picture's burned into my head. And I'm not carrying that for you. Or anybody. You have to turn up and take your part of it. You're maybe sensitive but you're not sensitive enough. What matters isn't the effect it has on you, but what you *do* with the effect it has on you. You feel it bad, then turn up for the man you feel it for. A boy is dead. I don't think he deserved to die.'

She was crying quietly.

'So tell me now. Who gave you the bad time that night here?'

'It—' Her words were drowning in phlegm. 'Paddy Collins.'

Laidlaw nodded, having established that she wanted to tell the truth.

'You'd been with him before Dave McMaster. Was that why he got vicious? Because you had gone with Dave?'

She shook her head.

'It wasn't that.'

Laidlaw waited. It hurt him to look at her but it would have hurt him more to leave her alone. The way he felt, that other hurt could be terminal.

'I had told him about Tony's money. When Paddy and I were still together. That night he thought I knew where Tony was. He said. He said. If he couldn't get me, he could at least cut his losses. He could make money from it. He wanted to know where Tony was. He was trying to make me tell him. But I didn't know. I didn't know. I'm glad I didn't. He hurt me so badly I think I would have told him. But I didn't know.'

'Who knew about what Paddy did to you?'

'Dave and Tony knew. That's why Tony killed Paddy Collins. I know that's why he killed him. Tony had always said, since we were small, he wouldn't let anybody harm me. Tony could be wild. You've never seen anybody as wild as Tony could be.'

'Maybe I have. Just possibly.'

'No. You didn't know him. No, you see. When you came the last time with the other man. I tried to protect Tony. I told you nothing because I didn't want him hurt. I knew he had done it for me. He still loved me, you know. How could I do anything but protect him when he did it to protect me? He loved like an angel. That was his problem. I think I lost his letter because I was ashamed to keep it. He loved you so much you felt guilty at how much less your own love was. If you'd met him you'd know what I mean. Even when I realised he'd killed that sad old man, I could never have helped to turn him in. I don't know why he did that. Maybe because the old man knew about Paddy Collins. He must have been desperate by that time. I found out from Alma where he was. And we tried to help him. But we were too late. I wish

214

we could have been sooner. I wish we could have been sooner.'

Laidlaw was staring past her at the unconscious support she was giving to his own suspicions.

'Who's we?'

'Dave and I.'

'What did you do to help?'

'We told Macey. So that he could tell the police.'

'Why didn't you tell the police yourselves?'

She hesitated. He found her discretion pathetically touching, as if she thought Laidlaw didn't know.

'Well, some of the people who know Dave wouldn't have liked it.'

Laidlaw knew for sure now. It only remained to confirm it.

'If only we'd been sooner,' she said.

She sat staring into lost possibilities. Laidlaw wondered if there were people who would never get it right, regretting the wrong things, bestowing their compassion like a lead weight thrown to a drowning man. He stood up and crossed to the bedroom door. He knocked and pushed the door open. Mr Veitch was there before the door had opened half-way.

'I think you should take her home now,' Laidlaw said.

'My God, thank you very much. You're sure we have your permission?'

Laidlaw looked at him. Mr Veitch was sneering, his main concern to reinstate himself. The end of his nose was limbo. If he travelled beyond it he'd fall off the edge of the world. Laidlaw thought, not for the first time, that there must be those who, if a dying man told them the secret of all life and swore at them at the same time, would only remember that he swore.

'You're a deeply compassionate man,' Laidlaw said.

'Don't you know that sarcasm is the lowest form of wit?'

'I don't know,' Laidlaw said. 'I think maybe clichés are.'

He crossed towards the door. On the way he touched Lynsey Farren gently on the head.

'Good luck with you,' he said.

He let himself out, thinking that there was more pain ahead for her.

34

"The Crib" was closed. That was a strange fact, about as likely as the sun not turning up. Two men were standing staring at the shut door. One of them looked round bemusedly, then up at the sky, as if checking he had the right universe. As Laidlaw approached, they had started to move off. One of them was saying, 'Mebbe they've drapped the bomb an' we haveny noticed.' Laidlaw let them go round the corner. He thumped on the door. Nothing happened. He did it again.

The door opened slightly, still on its chain. It was Charlie the barman, who used to work in "The Gay Laddie". He knew who Laidlaw was.

'Yes?'

His face was as welcoming as a turned back.

'Charlie. I'm looking for somebody.'

'Yes?'

'Is there anybody in?'

They could both hear the voices from where they were.

'Well.' Charlie was trying lines inside his head. 'There's a wee staff-meeting on.'

Laidlaw wondered what was on the agenda: whose turn it was next week to pick up the bodies?

'That's why we're not open yet. Who is it you're lookin' for?'

Laidlaw smiled, gave Charlie a look that told him not to be naughty.

'I just can't remember his name, Charlie. But I'd know him if I saw him. Any chance I get in?'

Charlie's eyes stared over Laidlaw's head. He looked distant, as if receiving telepathic messages.

'Ye want tae wait a minute?'

'Fair enough.'

Charlie disappeared behind the door to close it. Laidlaw's hand rested casually in the gap of the open door. Charlie's face reappeared, wondering.

'Leave a fella a chink of hope, Charlie.'

Charlie went away. Hearing his feet move out of the corridor, Laidlaw kicked the door in, pulling the chain from the jamb. He stepped inside as Charlie's head volleyed out to look at him. Laidlaw held his hand up.

'I'm sorry,' he said. 'I fell against the door. And your wee chain broke. Now that I'm in . . .'

He closed the door and followed Charlie into the bar. Entering, Laidlaw found himself thinking suddenly that maybe Bob Lilley was right. Maybe he was losing his grip. This was no way to do it. Detective-work was a delicate symbiosis with the criminal world, a balancing of subtle mutual respects. You hoped to give small to get back big. It was a matter of not breaking a fragile web you were both part of, a repeated laying of the senses to different strands of that web to catch what was going, not the axeman cometh.

The craziness of what he was up to ambushed Laidlaw there in the middle of the floor. He felt himself ahead of his own sense of what he was doing; not a place for a policeman to put himself. But he was there already. He couldn't just walk back out. Instead, he rifled the room swiftly, like an expert housebreaker, taking only what he could use.

The room was John Rhodes and Cam Colvin. There were others but those two were what this meeting meant. It had to be very serious business. That's why the pub was shut. That was in his favour. He knew what they hadn't wanted anybody to know. His crassness in breaking in had won him a prize that maybe outpriced their anger. He had perhaps done irreparable damage to his contacts in the long run but, the way he felt about everything, who needed the long run? People were waiting. He addressed himself to John Rhodes because the pub was his responsibility.

'I was saying to Charlie there—'

'Ah heard,' John Rhodes said.

218

Cam Colvin looked at the doorway, looked at Charlie. Charlie shook his head. Cam relaxed.

'You're getting clumsy, Jack,' he said.

'Aye,' Laidlaw said. 'I'm getting pills for it.'

'Ye want tae change yer doctor,' John Rhodes said. 'They don't seem tae be workin'. Polismen breakin' an' enterin'? Dangerous stuff.'

'I fell. Did none of you see me? By the way, don't frighten me, John. I hate to cry in public.'

Laidlaw looked round them innocently. His expression was a parade behind which his mind was crouching, dreading its passing. But a face came into his vision that altered his feeling. Seeing Hook Hawkins, pale as unbaked bread and clearly wounded, whom he remembered from the Bryson case, Laidlaw remembered he was Gus Hawkins' brother. They could have come out of the same placenta. The connection reignited Laidlaw's compulsion to a flame that charred his misgivings about being here. He was going to the bone of this one. This case had come too quick to a corpse. Too many possibilities had been made mute, too many interconnections were unexplained.

'Anyway,' Laidlaw said.

He found himself hoping more words were on the way. The word had declared he wasn't interested in Rhodes' strictures. He had taken over the room. Now he had to work out what to do with it.

'Whit is it ye want?' John Rhodes asked.

He hadn't a clue. But, blessedly, the man he had hoped to see was there. There was Macey, immobile with nerves, trying to act as if his face didn't belong to him.

'Macey,' Laidlaw said. 'I want you to come to the station with me.'

Macey was brilliant. He swallowed his panic in one lump and did the classic accused Glaswegian's act, palms up as if testing for rain. His face went round them like a begging-bowl. He turned it to Laidlaw still empty, an expression of the world's lack of charity.

'Gonny gi'es a brek?' he said. 'Whit's this about?'

Laidlaw understood the danger he had put Macey in. Plucking a tout from the company of other criminals like this could be like asking him to advertise in the paper. But Laidlaw improvised as expertly as Macey had. He stared at Macey with a stern, forensic expression.

'There's been a wee job done. I think it's your M.O.'

'M.O.? Whit's that? A medical orderly?'

Macey had got it right. In taking the mickey out of Laidlaw, he made the others feel him very much part of them. Their appreciation disarmed suspicion. Laidlaw maintained the role Macey had given him.

'M.O. Modus operandi. Your way of working.'

Laidlaw felt a certain aesthetic pleasure in how well they were working together. He thought of something else that must be making this look even more convincing to the others. They would know he had been involved in the Veitch case. His failure there would make them see this as his search for petty compensation.

'No way,' Macey said. 'When did this happen?'

Laidlaw hoped Macey wasn't going to overdo it and make him forget his lines.

'Recently.'

'When's recently.'

'Recently's recently.'

'There ye are then. Ah haveny been workin' fur ages. The boys here'll vouch for me.'

'Uh-huh,' Laidlaw said. 'And then we'll get Bluebeard to alibi for Jack the Ripper. You coming?'

Macey looked at John Rhodes.

'On ye go, Macey. Ye better go.'

As they were going out, John Rhodes said, as a final barb at Laidlaw, 'See you in half-an-hour, Macey.'

In the street, Macey couldn't believe the injustice of the world. As they walked, his words were just articulated froth.

'Mr Laidlaw. You off your head? Does Big Ernie know about this? Ah'm gonny see 'im. What a liberty! Ah mean, ye might as well give me an award on the telly. Tout of the

220

year. Holy Jesus. That's ma life you're playin' games wi'.
These men don't kid. First thing ye know, ye've got yer
head in a poke to play wi'. Oh my. Ma hert's gaun like a
lambeg drum.'

'Macey, I'm sorry.'

'Oh, very good. That's smashin'. Make all the difference
on the headstone, that. No, that isn't on.'

'We got away with it.'

Macey stopped and looked at him.

'We think we did, Mr Laidlaw. But if we're wrong,
who's gonny find out first?'

Laidlaw took the point.

'It was all right, Macey. Come on.'

'Aye, Ah think it was. Ah think we've knocked it off
therr. But two o' that Ah don't need, Mr Laidlaw. Ye
know?'

'Agreed, Macey. Never again. Look. I'm not as daft as
you think. Well, probably not quite. There *has* been a
break-in in Pollokshaws. Quite a big job. That's what I was
quizzing you about. All right? I'll give you the details.'

'So what are we doin' here?' Macey asked. 'Ah mean, Ah
hardly *know* you.'

They were at Laidlaw's car.

'In you get, Macey.'

'What for?'

'In you get. I'm not going to kidnap you. I've got nowhere
to keep you.'

While Laidlaw drove to the entrance to Ruchill Park, he
told Macey about the break-in.

They got out and climbed the hill to the small stone pillars
of different sizes and sat there. Macey had been huffily
quiet. Laidlaw had let him be. Some children were playing
on the swings. Laidlaw gave Macey a cigarette, took one
himself.

'You told Milligan where to find Tony Veitch,' Laidlaw
said.

'Ah didny say that.'

'I'm saying it.'

221

'Look.' Macey threw the cigarette away, hardly smoked. 'What is this? Ah speak to Big Ernie. That's who Ah speak tae. All right? No offence, Mr Laidlaw.'

Laidlaw knew how unacceptable what he was doing was. Trying to hone in on somebody else's tout was a serious breach of the code, something that would get you lionised in the force to roughly the same degree as rabies. But Laidlaw suspected he had perhaps achieved professional ostracism already.

'Who told you where Tony Veitch was, Macey?'

Macey was whistling under his breath, looking away, as if he had just happened to sit beside a loony in the park.

'What's that going on in "The Crib"? That's a weird get-together.'

'Some kinna bother.'

'About Paddy Collins?'

'Don't know. Ah wisny listenin'.'

'There's going to be more serious bother, Macey. And you could be right in the middle of it.'

'Well. It's a way of life, intit? You know it's trouble when trouble comes, don't ye?' Macey was smiling, looking away. Laidlaw's left hand grabbed his lapel like a grappling iron, hooking him off his seat.

'Listen, fuckin' bawheid,' Laidlaw said. 'I'm on serious business. I don't need the Chic Murray kit. You want to be a comedian, practise somewhere else.'

Laidlaw slammed Macey back on to his concrete seat so hard he felt his coccyx might be a lump on his head.

'You're overheads in the shite, Macey,' Laidlaw said. 'You're an accessory to a murder. That's what you are. Clever tout. It's up to you. You answer a coupla questions. Or I'm going to huckle you into the station right now. And get you charged. That's the message.'

Macey couldn't help being interested. He had the tout's bug-eyed sense of survival, as if the thyroid had gone berserk.

'How do you mean?'

222

'You know what I mean,' Laidlaw said.

The two of them watched a small red-haired boy argue with his black-haired friend about whose turn it was to push the swing. The black-haired boy won.

'What are the questions?' Macey said.

'Actually, they're more than a couple,' Laidlaw said. 'What's going on in "The Crib"?'

Macey watched the boy swinging as if his attention could put him back there.

'Mickey Ballater,' he said, and Laidlaw understood Ballater's wound. 'He claimed Hook. Thought Hook had been arsin' him about. Cam and John are havin' a council of war. But nothin's been decided.'

Laidlaw listened to the black-haired boy complain about the way his friend was pushing him, decided he didn't like him.

'Macey,' Laidlaw said. 'Were Dave McMaster and Lynsey Farren the first to tell you about Tony Veitch?'

'Naw,' Macey said. 'Cam talked about him first.'

'But only Cam?'

Macey shifted a little, as if his conscience had piles.

'Macey!' Laidlaw said.

'Big Ernie knew. He showed me a phota.'

'What phota?'

'Tony Veitch. He was readin'.'

Laidlaw was briefly aware that Harkness had given Milligan the photograph and decided it didn't matter much. There were more important things to find out about.

'Who told you where he was?'

'You know that.'

'That's right. I do. So here's the real question, Macey. Who did you tell?'

Macey underwent a small indulgence of retraction. He had said enough. It was finished. But he knew it wasn't. Laidlaw waited.

'I told everybody.'

Laidlaw clicked his tongue impatiently.

'Of course, Macey. It's what you would do. But don't

waste my time. The crucial thing is. In what order did you tell them?'

Macey didn't know what had happened but he knew from the clarity of Laidlaw's sense of it that he was about to explain what had happened. He felt himself no more than a part of Laidlaw's understanding and he surrendered to it.

'I told Big Ernie first,' he said.

Laidlaw understood. Of course, he did. He had his small vision of what had taken place. He had sought it so determinedly and now it was his. It wasn't much but it was his. He had argued with the supposed reality of circumstances so heatedly that they had acknowledged he had a case. For the moment, he was only the second one who knew, not exactly, never exactly, but roughly what had happened.

He let an approximation of the truth unravel in his head. Tony Veitch went into hiding from Paddy Collins. Paddy Collins beat up Lynsey Farren to find where Tony was. Dave McMaster killed Paddy Collins because he beat up Lynsey Farren. Dave McMaster killed Eck Adamson because he knew about Paddy Collins. Dave McMaster killed Tony Veitch because he needed a scapegoat. Mickey Ballater was a makeweight, although he didn't know it. So were Cam and John, although they didn't know it. As always, it was meaner than you would imagine. Private purposes, outside of wars, were the most lethal things in the world.

And Tony Veitch had, in a way, died of his own innocence. He hadn't known what was going on, the complexity of it. Those must have been some papers, a terrible attempt at uninhabitable compassion. Perhaps he had died of those papers, of the inadmissible evidence they represented, how we truly know nothing more than the need to connect but can't find how to admit it.

From his vantage point in Ruchill Park, Laidlaw looked out over the city. He could see so much of it from here and still it baffled him. 'What is this place?' he thought.

A small and great city, his mind answered. A city with its face against the wind. That made it grimace. But did it have to be so hard? Sometimes it felt so hard. Well, that was some

224

wind and it had never stopped blowing. Even when this place was the second city of the British Empire, affluence had never softened it because the wealth of the few had become the poverty of the many. The many had survived, however harshly, and made the spirit of the place theirs. Having survived affluence, they could survive anything. Now that the money was tight, they hardly noticed the difference. If you had it, all you did was spend it. The money had always been tight. Tell us something we don't know. That was Glasgow. It was a place so kind it would batter cruelty into the ground. And what circumstances kept giving it was cruelty. No wonder he loved it. It danced among its own debris. When Glasgow gave up, the world could call it a day.

Standing so high, Laidlaw felt the bleakness of summer on his face and understood a small truth. Even the climate here offered no favours. Standing at a bus-stop, you talked out the side of your mouth, in case your lips got chapped. Maybe that was why the West of Scotland was where people put the head on one another—it was too cold to take your hands out your pockets. But it did have compensations.

Laidlaw had a happy image of the first man out after the nuclear holocaust being a Glaswegian. He would straighten up and look around. He would dust himself down with that flicking gesture of the hands and, once he had got the strontium off the good suit, he would look up. The palms would be open.

'Hey,' he would say. 'Gonny gi'es a wee brek here? What was that about? Ye fell oot wi' us or what? That was a liberty. Just you behave.'

Then he would walk off with that Glaswegian walk, in which the shoulders don't move separately but the whole torso is carried as one, as stiff as a shield. And he would be muttering to himself, 'Must be a coupla bottles of something still intact.'

Laidlaw turned back from the city to Macey.

'One last question,' he said.

Macey dredged his eyes up from the ground.

225

'Where do I find Dave McMaster?'

Macey considered the possibility of not knowing and knew it wasn't one.

'Glasgow Airport,' he said. 'He's covering that in case Mickey Ballater tries it.'

'Macey.' Laidlaw was looking at him very carefully. 'You know I wouldn't have done that. What I said. Taking you in. You know that. Don't you?'

'Do Ah?'

'Sometimes you don't like yourself,' Laidlaw said. 'You want a lift?'

'Naw,' Macey said, sitting where he was and rubbing the base of his back. 'The last lift you gave me was enough for me.'

Laidlaw felt small.

'It's a hard job,' he said.

'Oh, Ah know,' Macey said. 'Ah'm sorry for you.'

Laidlaw was walking away. He paused, turned back towards Macey.

'There's always a price,' he said. 'Imagine having to be felt sorry for. By somebody who's forgotten what morality *was*.'

35

'Come on, come on,' Harkness was saying. 'Some people have their work to go to.'

The elderly woman on the crossing smiled and nodded and mouthed 'Thank you,' and Harkness felt guilty. It occurred to him that the small shopping-trolley she was pulling, which had crossed his vision like a mote, was full of her way of life. Why should he object to the time it took her age to trail it across the road? He blamed Laidlaw, as he waved to her and drove on as if he was pulling out of the pits.

Lifting the phone had been like Frankenstein plugging into a generator. A dead day was suddenly crackling into life. The urgency in Laidlaw's voice seemed to assume that his were the elemental concerns that nobody could deny. He had said, 'Glasgow Airport' like the loudspeaker in an old war film saying 'Scramble!'

Harkness was scrambling, was being a bit subjective with the traffic-lights. He found himself also v–signing a couple of people who were inconsiderate enough to object. The Laidlaw syndrome, he reflected. When he was in the mood, that man could galvanise a cemetery. Harkness prayed that Laidlaw knew what he was doing because nobody else was likely to.

Dave McMaster? Harkness couldn't work it out. They had seen him that once at Lynsey Farren's. Maybe it was a joke. Getting out of his car in the car-park, Harkness thought it probably was. The glass frontage of the terminal building reflected a bland evening. As he crossed the walkway over the shallow water, he saw the thrown pennies in their coats of verdigris. Life was small change.

Then Laidlaw appeared towards him at the front of

the building, sounding taut as a violin tuned for a hard one.

'You ready?' Laidlaw was saying. 'There's bound to be two of them. That's guaranteed. They're here for Ballater. So they're carrying. All right?'

'Wait a minute,' Harkness said. 'My stomach's still on the motorway. Who's Ballater?'

'Mickey Ballater. He's done Hook Hawkins. They're looking for him. Dave McMaster's one. We're going to get him.'

Laidlaw was starting to walk.

'Jack! I don't understand this.'

Laidlaw turned.

'What do you want? A geneological table? Arse in top gear, Brian. And let's go. Trust me.'

'Jack!'

Harkness was still standing. He pointed at Laidlaw.

'Are you sure?'

Laidlaw grimaced.

'Brian. Who's sure? God must be having second thoughts. But if I had to bet, I wouldn't be asking for change of a million. Come on!'

Harkness followed him through the automatic glass doors that Laidlaw almost put the head on. Inside was normalcy and Harkness's misgivings grew.

They were in Glasgow Airport on a summer evening. They looked around downstairs, where the check-in counters were. They checked all around upstairs, where the cafeteria was like Chekhov done by MGM, redundant man in panavision. They studied the upstairs lounge, a busy place.

They heard the rattle of the departure boards, as if all human destinations had a stutter. They saw a couple of groups of teenagers caught in their aggressive uncertainty, here to go nowhere but a Monday night. They saw a young family, parents and two daughters, who looked as if they were waiting to go on holiday and as if the father was wondering how he got here. They saw a woman staringly drinking a clear drink. They saw five men with travelling

228

bags making more noise than a revolution and being harmless. They didn't see Dave McMaster.

They came back downstairs. Harkness was getting fidgety when Laidlaw touched his arm. He nodded towards the toilets at the end of the downstairs area. A man with carefully waved hair had emerged. Instead of going anywhere, he hung about, looking around. That was the first suspicious thing about him. The second was that Harkness slowly realised he recognised him. He had seen him with John Rhodes, during the Bryson case. Harkness followed Laidlaw across to the man.

'Hullo there,' Laidlaw said.

The man had been pretending he didn't see them coming. They became a casual fence around him, pinning him to the wall.

'Where is he?' Laidlaw said.

'Ah beg yer pardon?'

'Dave McMaster.'

'Sorry?'

'We're looking for Dave McMaster,' Laidlaw said patiently.

'Ah don't know what ye're talkin' about,' the man said.

'I'll tell you,' Laidlaw said. 'You're here with Dave McMaster. Waiting in case Mickey Ballater shows up. We're looking for Dave McMaster.'

'Sorry?'

Harkness was beginning to be convinced. The man looked utterly baffled. Harkness took out his police-card and showed it to the man, smiling reassuringly.

'Ah'm sorry,' the man said. 'Ah don't know what ye're talkin' about. Ah'm waitin' for the wife to get back fae Majorca.'

'I know,' Laidlaw said. 'I'm waiting for Partick Thistle to win the European Cup. In the meantime. Where's Dave McMaster?'

The man shrugged and smiled.

'Sorry?'

'And due to be sorrier,' Laidlaw said.

Harkness was about to restrain Laidlaw's anger when he noticed the man's eyes move subtly between them, seeing something. Harkness knew what it was before he turned. Before he turned, he felt Laidlaw start to run. Turning, he was surprised by the arc of Laidlaw's run. Then he understood. Dave McMaster was whirling, caught between Harkness and Laidlaw, with Laidlaw blocking off the outside doors. McMaster had two cans of lager in his right hand. With a mouth as wide as a cannon he fired one at Harkness. Harkness fended it with his left arm and thought his elbow was broken. Instinctively, he knew something. He turned in one predetermined movement and butted the man with the wavy hair straight in the mouth, where his smile had been. The man stopped in mid-rush and his head bulleted back against the wall and he slid, as if he weighed two times himself, to the floor. It was a lucky hit but it would do.

Noise was what Harkness was aware of, cacophony. Screams, they were. He turned back. One scream was from a woman. Outside the moment, she might have been pretty. Her black hair was bouncing and her arms were outstretched. She was ready to spring. A tall man had dropped his case. It was falling over. He was reaching for her, to hold her back. He made it, pinned her to him. Another scream was from a boy. He looked about five, dark-haired. His legs were kicking. He was held in Dave McMaster's left arm. A knife was at his throat. Other screams were from other people somewhere. One was from Laidlaw, backing off like a tiger behind a chair.

'You bastard!' Laidlaw was screaming. 'That's how you live. Fucking time up!'

In a moment Harkness would never forget, because he could never have imagined it, a small, balding man, who looked as if he wouldn't have the gall to argue about wrong change, came in the doors behind Dave McMaster and grabbed the arm that held the knife. The small man was pulled up off the ground, swung kicking like a monkey that has lost its balance. But he stayed where he was, as if the arm was a lifeline. He didn't know how to give up his hold. He was cut on the cheek and he fell, but the knife came with him. Dave McMaster threw the boy away like an empty wrapper.

He ran, with instinctive skill, up the upward escalator. But Laidlaw was tight as a shadow. Breasting the top of the escalator behind them, as if his lungs had the yieldingness of stone, Harkness understood, with a kind of compassion, how crazy panic had made Dave. He had run into the lounge-bar, the entrance of which was the exit. It was over.

Like watching a match on television when you already know the score, Harkness was still fascinated to find out how it would happen. He watched it as calmly as a replay, knowing now there was only one way to bet.

McMaster threaded the tables expertly and Laidlaw knocked over two. The beer from one went up like a small tidal wave. It was the table where the five noisy men had been sitting.

'Jesus fuck!' one of them said, and Harkness, in the doorway, smiled.

He saw the woman with the clear drink stand up, staring. McMaster went to the far wall and turned. He knew, Harkness knew, Laidlaw knew it was the end of something. McMaster lifted an empty pint-dish from a table and threw it at Laidlaw. Laidlaw ducked. The pint-mug bounced off the bar. And Laidlaw moved in. It wasn't a fair fight.

McMaster had decided he was beaten. He knew he was trapped. He needed somebody to help him out of the impasse. Laidlaw obliged. He hit McMaster twice, with the left from fear, with the right from courtesy. McMaster went down. Harkness arrived in time to help to pull him up. All three became a conspiracy against the place they had found themselves in. McMaster needed assistance to get out of the pretence he had lived with for so long, and this room was full of it. Laidlaw and Harkness needed as little hassle as possible. The three of them thought they might make it.

But the five jolly drinkers didn't agree. They blocked their way.

'What's this about?' one of them said.

'You spilled ma beer,' another said to Laidlaw.

Laidlaw looked at him. Glancing at the look, Harkness realised that Laidlaw was still high on his own excitement. He felt as if he was going to have to get two heavies out of the bar.

'We're from the Salvation Army,' Laidlaw said. 'It's part of a drive to make people drink less.'

The aggression of it made Harkness grit his teeth.

'Two tae wan's no' fair,' another said.

His face was on fire with drink but the eyes were calm. He was like a Guy Fawkes who hasn't yet noticed he's on fire.

'You don't understand,' Laidlaw said.

'Well, make me understand.'

'I don't have the time to give you a head-transplant.'

Harkness understood what Laidlaw was feeling. You didn't have to understand specialisation. But you had to understand that it was there.

'Listen,' Laidlaw said. 'I think the five of you should all go away and do something more sensible. Like putting the head on a wall. In unison. Okay?'

Laidlaw looked round the five of them. Harkness flipped out his card and showed them it. Among mutterings, they let them pass. Harkness was glad.

At the top of the stairs, they found the mother and her son and the man who had saved him. They were the centre of a fair crowd. The mother was threatening to kill Dave McMaster. Laidlaw tried to calm her. He found out the small man's name and address. While he was talking, the woman with the clear drink had come out, still holding it. Her expression hadn't changed throughout the whole sequence of events. She just stood, staring at Laidlaw. At last he looked towards her.

'What's that you're drinking, love?' he said. 'Gin and catatonic?'

The puzzlement saw them out of the building. The wavy-haired man was nowhere. They took Laidlaw's car. Harkness heard Laidlaw ask a strange question.

'Were you in the lavvy?'

232

Harkness moved the rear mirror so that he could see Dave McMaster's face.

'Uh?'

'Did you go into the lavatory when you were up to buy those cans of lager?'

Dave nodded. Harkness turned the mirror so that he could see Laidlaw's face. Laidlaw was nodding. He seemed satisfied. Harkness was amazed. Laidlaw had a mania to know as much as he could. Even when he had achieved what he set out to achieve, he still wanted to know how. Bob Lilley had described him accurately in the "Top Spot". He would die trying to get it right. He was still trying.

'Tony Veitch didn't know what Paddy Collins had done to Lynsey Farren, did he? You told her you had told Tony, didn't you? That way, you could make her believe Tony had killed Paddy. Is that how it was?'

'How what was?'

Laidlaw was looking at Dave, not without sympathy.

'The jig's up, son,' he said. 'You're going to have to admit more than you did that night in East Kilbride. You're not going out for a fancy meal now. Not for a long time. Like a lot of people who've done bad things, I think you wanted to get caught. Know why?'

Dave was staring carefully ahead.

'That lounge-bar. I caught you just outside the lavvy door. There's another exit from that lavvy into the rest of the building. Why didn't you use it?'

In his mirror Harkness saw Dave's eyes thinking about that.

'You don't have to say anything,' Laidlaw said. 'We can save you the trouble. We've got a bottle of vintage paraquat with your prints on it.'

Dave's eyes softened for the first time into doubt.

36

Hanging about the main office, Bob Lilley was glad that he saw Harkness first. Harkness sent his eyes to the ceiling in admission of what they both knew would have to be acknowledged. Bob looked at his left lapel and took in enough breath to launch a zeppelin.

'It's what they say, is it?' he said.

Harkness nodded.

'Has he burst yet?'

'Aye,' Harkness said. 'He's burst. His fingerprints were on the bottle. That's what did it. He's writing his memoirs now.'

'Jesus,' Bob said. 'Old Jack gets it right now and again, though. Doesn't he? Sometimes I wish he didn't.'

'No,' Harkness said. 'I'm glad he does. Sometimes I don't like him. But people like that deserve to get it right.'

Laidlaw came in with a paper cup of coffee, looking for sugar. He had no problem finding it, being popular for the moment. He stirred his coffee and looked at Bob.

'Ernie Milligan's not around, is he?' Laidlaw said.

The room winced. Laidlaw smiled at Bob.

'Naw,' he said. 'I'm only kidding. He did it according to his lights. Which are about two-kilowatt.'

Harkness was about to defend Milligan when Laidlaw looked at him. It was a hard look, as sore as your father finding you out in a lie at the age of seven. Harkness knew what was coming.

'Brian. There's something I better say. I'm disappointed in you. I like you but you're a slow learner. So you gave Big Ernie the photo. Fair enough. But you should've said. That's all. It was fair enough giving it to him, if that's what you felt. But you should've said. I felt a bit betrayed. When

234

Macey let that slip. He didn't know what he was saying. But I did. Aw, Brian.'

'I was going to tell you.'

'Going to's what they put on the headstone. Be quicker next time. Friends should share.'

'Come on, Jack,' Bob said. 'Maybe friends should share. But did you share with Ernie?'

'Friends? I don't see Ernie Milligan as a friend. "A thing devised by the enemy." That's what he is.'

Laidlaw was testing his coffee, put in more sugar. He lit a cigarette.

'Jack,' Bob said. 'You've done well. Don't crow.'

'I'm not crowing. Because I didn't do well enough. Tony Veitch is dead. This case was a failure. But it could've been a bigger one. That's all. I want to admit the failure but I don't want to flagellate myself with it. You know?'

Bob was pushing back his shoulders and putting on his the-world's-my-junior face.

'I still say you should've told Big Er—'

'Bob. Don't say. You've had your say. I sat in the "Top Spot" and listened to you a long time. And apart from the Fenwick Fury here, you're the closest thing to a friend I've got in this place. And I took it because I couldn't prove otherwise. But now I can. I've just proved it. So don't tell me again. That I should've told Big Ernie. Because I shouldn't. You accused me of careerism. Bob. I'm still here because I think it's where it really matters. But only if you do it right. This time I haven't done that. I just came closer than some. That doesn't mean much. But *maybe* it could exempt me from your advice for a wee while. Eh? As auld Eck used to say.'

Bob sculpted his face into impassiveness.

'Okay, Jack. I was maybe out of order—'

'Bob. I think you were definitely out of order.'

'I was *maybe* out of order. But I don't see any need to dig up Brian. He did what he thought was the right thing.'

'Nobody's digging up Brian. Brian. Am I digging you up?'

'Well. I feel as if my second name was Pompeii.'

'Ya bastard,' Laidlaw said.

'See what I mean, Jack?' Bob said complacently. 'You dig people up even when you don't know you're doing it.'

'But I should've said,' Harkness said.

'Why?' Bob said. 'Jack would probably've needed tranquillizers if you had. I mean, what was wrong with telling Ernie?'

'I'll tell you,' Laidlaw said. 'Because this thing isn't finished yet. I'm sorry, Brian. But it's what wee Frankie Millers sings: "You mighta brung brains to the show". You know what you've done? Just by giving a photograph to Big Ernie. You've extended the problem.'

'Oh Christ,' Bob said. 'Here we go again. Jack and his amazing crystal ball. Tell me, Jack. Why was that a problem?'

'Because people like Ernie Milligan are dangerous. He knows this city, he says. Brian. You have to learn where to put your trust. He's like a lot of policemen here. He knows the names of streets. He doesn't know the city. Who does? Walk down a side-street on your own, you're finding out again. Who ever knew a city? It's a crazy claim. And those who make impossible claims are always going to cause more trouble than they solve.'

'Aye, all right, Jack.' Bob was trying to be patient. 'But could you be more exact.'

'Certainly. Somebody else is going to die. Like tomorrow or the next day.'

'That's a safe bet,' Bob said. 'In China, you mean?'

'Brian. I'll talk to you. Bob's head's on holiday. Milligan doesn't solve bother. He manufactures it. Because he *is* a careerist. If trouble wasn't there, he would invent it. He feeds on it, he needs it. You listened to Dave McMaster there. But did you hear him? He was telling us two things. He killed three people. And. There was Ballater. Hook Hawkins. John Rhodes. Cam Colvin. And Macey. You know what "volatile" means? That's what that mixture is. I mean, Cam and John. They don't await the fullness of time. They're looking for someone. Because they know this deal

236

was gerrymandered. They may not know how. But they're going to decide they do. Because they're angry. And their kind of violence is just anger declaring independence from reason. That's what Ernie Milligan's helped to do. He puts his X into the equation and doesn't give a shit how it affects the final calculation. Knows this city? He couldn't get a bargain at the Barras.'

'That's nonsense, Jack,' Bob said. 'All that seeing into the future. You using Tarot cards?'

'We'll wait and see,' Laidlaw said. 'Anyway'—he was staring into Harkness's quietness—'what about more normal things? The stuff of life and that. How's the women situation, Brian?'

Harkness looked up at him, winked.

'I'm getting engaged.'

'Congratulations,' Laidlaw said.

'Same from me. I think,' Bob said. He looked at Laidlaw's face. 'Some bruise that. It's a good thing Mickey Ballater was half-dead when you fought him.'

'I know.' Laidlaw was finishing his coffee, gruing at how sweet the dregs were. 'My hands are lethal weapons. They could get me killed.'

37

Laidlaw's usual problem with funerals was complicated this time. Always unable to bear the reduction of the dead individual's complexity to a paint-by-numbers icon, his method was to clench as hard as he could on the sense of the person he remembered, like a rag for his mind to chew on. But all he had of Tony Veitch were the image of that grotesquely barbecued body and a few fragments of his writings like crazy paving that led nowhere.

He wasn't the only one who didn't know what he was paying respect to. The minister seemed to be reading from the Book of Profound Platitudes. About as much as a stranger might have deduced about Tony Veitch was that he had eyes ('a student not just of books but of life's lessons'), a mouth ('always anxious to discuss the world with his friends') and that it had stopped breathing: 'God took him to his bosom'—some bosom, an embrace like kissing a shark.

Laidlaw sympathised with the minister. How do you say the unsayable, especially when you're talking about someone you never knew to people most of whom probably don't want to know? It made it tricky. Added to that, the ceremony he was trying to perform had its origins in something for which people were prepared to walk into the mouths of lions but which had since often been processed into spiritual Valium that reduced God to the role of a celestial chemist. Why blame the minister? People got the religion the honesty of their confrontation with death entitled them to.

Laidlaw compensated for the anonymity of the service by including Eck Adamson in the minister's words as well as Tony. It wasn't hard. Both of them could be seen as orphans of the same society, one disowned because he couldn't pass the test of its ideals, the other because he took those ideals too seriously. Both their lives were not easily acceptable. Laidlaw felt the event not as an admission about someone's life but as an attempted conspiracy against admitting it. What was going on in him and what was happening outside only converged at the end, when the frozen ritual thawed again into a painful humanity.

He was waiting near the end of the line that was filing past Milton Veitch. There was someone Laidlaw assumed was a family friend with him. Passing in front of Mr Veitch was a group of young people, presumably students who had known Tony. They were casually dressed but in subdued colours. Inconspicuous among them was Lynsey Farren.

As each shook hands with him, Mr Veitch was checking the faces as if he were looking for something. Whatever it was, he obviously wasn't finding it. In the bewilderment that made an accident of his face the way weather can erode sculpture, Laidlaw recognised a kinship with Eck dying. He seemed looking for lost reassurance. He wouldn't find it in the small, passing parade that must have been to him like a celebration of the fact that there comes a point in our lives when the world seems younger than we are and determined to unlearn what it has taught us.

In that moment he could be seen to be lost, his money just so much paper, his status a terrible irony. With luck, he wouldn't be able to buy himself more illusion. Laidlaw felt a brute gladness in observing him, a weird gaiety in sadness. The feeling had nothing of revenge in it, didn't happen because Laidlaw had felt contempt for his spurious self-assurance. It was about hope, the way Milton Veitch seemed almost capable of trying to begin again because he had no option.

It was like the possibility of growth from wild Tony's death, from Eck's bleak living. The odds were such growth would never happen, but the renewed affirmation of belief in its possibility was the best you could hope for from life. Laidlaw was moved. He was also glad to see Alma Brown beside him, like a wife.

He remembered Dave bursting like a haemorrhaging tumour in the police-station, spilling the pus of his guilt, his compulsive need to share himself with someone, anyone. Once started, he couldn't stop.

'Ah liked Tony, though. Ah liked him. But Ah couldn't have respect. Ah jist couldny. He was a mug. Ye know whit Ah mean? He didny know the way it was. He didny know. He was livin' in Disneyland. He had no right to be so stupid. Nobody has. Collins was a shite-head. He thought the world was his piss-house. He's healthier dead. When he did that to Lynsey, I knew it was time. Ah mean, who did he think he was? He was out of touch. So Ah put him in touch. An' Eck knows Ah've done it. So he has to go. Jesus, he wisny a bad auld man. But he wisny a great loss, either. Not even to himself. Ah thought at the time maybe Ah done him a favour. Then Ah knew Ah wis in bother. But Tony. Ah shouldn't have done that. But he was askin' for it. He was, ye know. Tony wanted to pay for everybody. Ah needed somebody to pay for me. Ah cashed the lot in on him. Oh Jesus, Ah did. That was the bad one. Collins, Ah was angry. Ah'd do it again tomorrow. Eck Ah didn't even see. But Tony was slow and sore. We talked a bit. Ah knocked him out, ye know. Jesus, killin' him was hard. But Ah did it. An' faked it up. Nobody else knew. Ah liked Tony. But Ah liked me more. But Ah liked Tony.'

Laidlaw reached Mr Veitch and shook hands with him. They both said, 'I'm sorry' simultaneously. It seemed to Laidlaw like the most authentic communication they had had with each other, perhaps the most authentic communication two temporarily honest men could have.

Outside, the sunlight didn't know Tony was dead. Some groups of people stood on the steps of the crematorium. Gus Hawkins detached himself from one of the groups and came across.

'Hullo,' he said. 'How does it feel to be right?'

'I wouldn't know,' Laidlaw said.

'I mean about Tony.'

'I wasn't right. I just didn't believe anybody else was.'

'I didn't know policemen came to the funerals of people who were murdered.'

'I don't know if they do. I just came to this one.'

'Why?'

'It felt like something I should do. Your girl-friend. What's her name?'

'Marie.'

'She didn't come?'

'She couldn't face it. She went through to see her folks today. She'll be back tonight.'

'Where are you going now?'

'Straight into a depression.'

'You want to share it?'

'You not working?'

'Day off. I'll stand you lunch.'

Gus looked at him, looked back at the students he had been talking to. His next remark seemed inspired by his identification with them.

'This business? You get it on expenses?'

'Okay. I'll eat on my own.'

'I'm sorry. It's just habit. Fair enough. But I want mine mainly liquid.'

'Don't worry. I'll be going to the bottom of a bottle or two myself. I just want some food as a lifeline. The car's over there.'

They ate in the Lanterna—*Sole Goujon* and Frascati, mainly Frascati. They were a strange conjunction and they knew it. At first about the only thing they seemed to have in common was their separateness from the others in the room. There was a large group of businessmen at a table near them, full of expense-account bonhomie and the kind of laughter that sounds like the death-rattle of sincerity. One of them, a man about thirty whose smug abstention from proceedings had been suggesting that everything was a joke and he had heard the punch-line, began to talk about how boring travel was. His remarks developed into an account of all the places he had been.

'He's made his point well, that fella,' Laidlaw said.

Gus was looking round a lot as he ate, frequently shaking his head at what he saw.

'Look at that,' he said.

Laidlaw saw a middle-aged fat man eating with a young woman. He wondered what Gus was seeing.

'Jesus Christ,' Gus said. 'No wonder old Tony got angry.'

'How?'

'Look at him.'

'It's a fat man eating his dinner. What's he supposed to do? Shove the food in his ears?'

'You don't see it?'

'But I'm keen to learn. Tell me what you see, visionary.'

'He's just a bag of appetites, isn't he? He's lookin' at her as if she's next for eating. If he could pickle the world, he would swallow it.'

Laidlaw had to admit to himself he knew what Gus meant. The man had achieved that physical grossness you sometimes see, not just a matter of size. It was as if whatever alchemy it is that transmutes our hungers into an identity had broken down and he was left like a bulk container for all he had taken in. Laidlaw could understand how one of the idealistic young might see him as a slander on the species.

'You're not so far from Tony yourself, young Gus.'

'In what way?'

'You're down with the galloping idealism. Your dreams are so pure, reality has no chance. You've got a kind of graffiti of the eyes. Most things you look at, you vandalise.'

'Don't compare me to Tony. I'm a Marxist.'

'Is that why you have to sauce your meal with contempt for all the capitalists in the room? To make it edible?'

'I want to stay true to my ideals.'

'So did Tony. He was gang-banged by ideals, poor bastard. Mind you, no wonder he fell into their arms. It's raining shite here every day. Everywhere he looked, he saw lavvies posing as temples. So he tried to idealise them out of existence. But that's a bad mistake.'

'So what's that got to do with me?'

'Well, I think you're eventually on the same side. I think

242

there are two main badnesses where we live. One's a kind of total cynicism. Using other people. Reducing them to objects because you can find nothing to believe in but yourself. That's crime in all its multifarious forms, most of them legal. The other's the determined ideal that won't learn from experience. The need to be God's relative. I think they're twins. Bastard twins. The only legitimate thing we have is *human* experience. The possibility of the difference of tomorrow. The unimaginable difference. Unpreconceived. That requires the ability to entertain real doubt. I think Tony wanted certainty. I think maybe he died of the want of it. I hope to go on living. I think the key to that is knowing you don't know.'

Gus sipped some Frascati.

'All right,' he said. 'But maybe you're making my point. You quoted Marx there. Or didn't you know? The reduction of people to objects. That's capitalism.'

'That's true. It's also Marxism. It's a wee bit disingenuous of Marx to restrict that definition to capitalism. It's what he was on about as well. Or didn't you know? What's Marxism but ideological capitalism? He's middle-class, of course. As far as wanting experience goes, more balls on a bumbee.'

'Come on, polisman. Marx is middle-class?'

'So was Lenin. Handed the revolution over to a caucus of intellectuals. Freedom involves the right to envision itself.'

Gus sneered over a forkful of fish, dismissing him. Laidlaw was smiling.

But the issues raised gave them a cubicle of preoccupation within the room. Another bottle of Frascati and a lot of argument later, they had achieved that heightened mutual awareness some discussions generate, a sense of the never-to-be repeated specialness of the collision they were having. Without either mentioning it specifically, it seemed natural to go on.

243

38

A laughing baby boy
One evening in his play
Disturbed the household with his noisy glee.
Well, I told him to keep quiet
But he soon would disobey.
He needed just a gentle word from me.

'How often is he gonny play that Hank Snow record?'
Tich asked. 'Ma gums are bleedin'.'

'I like it,' Sandra said.

'We know that,' Malkie said. 'It's the record we're talkin'
about. Where's Simpsy?'

'Phonin' again.'

'Again?' Malkie was amazed. 'He holds that phone to
his gub like one o' them oxygen-masks. Whit's the
gemme?'

'Some bird in Possil. Must be love. He canny play it
much more often. How long till his train?'

'Just over fifty minutes,' Sandra said.

'Come on, come on,' Tich said. 'Ye think he's still going
to Sammy Dow's for a drink before he catches it?'

'He said he is,' Malkie said. 'Crazy-cuts, though.'

'Well. It's his life.'

'Might be ours as well, though,' Malkie said. 'If any o'
those teams catch up with him in there.'

'Maybe we should tell 'im tae get a gildy on.'

Having said it, Tich looked at Malkie and Sandra. Nobody
was volunteering to act on his suggestion. The music was
like a locked door.

Well, I called him to my side
And said, "Son, you must go to bed
For your conduct has been very, very poor."
With trembling lips and tears inside
He pleaded there with me,
"Don't make me go to bed, papa,
And I'll be good."

Mickey Ballater was lamenting through the music his lack of a son, nobody to take over what he had achieved. Music was for him a way of disposing of the feelings the terms of his life had no use for, like an emotional colostomy. He accepted the relief with gratitude. He was sorry they didn't have any Hank Williams' records.

Hank Williams was the man. He just pulled his heart out his chest and laid it on the table and let it pump the blood all over the carpet. You were wading out the room when he was finished. He was a brave singer.

Still, Hank Snow was penicillin on a record, doing the diminishing pain in Mickey's side no harm and leaving his head clear to work out where he was. At least the police had got a good job done on the wound. But the best ointment for it was remembering how much worse Hook Hawkins must be feeling, if he was feeling anything. Mickey hoped not. He only regretted that he hadn't found the time to attend to the young brother. That Laidlaw had complicated things.

But Mickey had made it to Eddie Simpson's on the South Side. It was a safe house. Eddie remembered the old days. They were all he had since he took ill. The doctors hadn't decided what it was yet, Eddie said, but Mickey had. If Eddie didn't have cancer, it was coming up in the lift. There would be no remission for good behaviour this time. That was why Mickey had told him to stay away from the house as much as possible while Mickey was there. The last thing Eddie needed was any other kind of trouble.

Anyway, Eddie had put together a scratch team for him.

245

They weren't much, so busy looking for trouble that if the real stuff found them they would probably come in their drawers. The only one Mickey thought might give him a run for his money was Sandra. He fancied that. When the others were there, she was always giving him secret looks, like envelopes not to be opened till later. He might arrange a later for her.

Eddie's son Simpsy was a measure of the others, a plastic imitation of his old man, not the same class. He might as well have 'Made in Hong Kong' stamped on his bum. They didn't breed them like before but they still bred them all right. He smiled at the thought of those who believed in improving things. No matter what progress they made in the future, one thing he was sure of was there would still be supersonic robberies, a black market in laser beams.

But he had to get to Birmingham before that. If he had to come back up here for trial, he would have his own team with him. Then they would see.

> Well, it broke my heart to hear him saying
> Just before he died,
> "Don't make me go to bed, papa,
> And I'll be good."

'Thank Christ, he's finished.' Malkie was listening to the silence. 'Maybe the record's worn out.'

They all waited a moment longer.

'Sandra,' Tich said. 'Go and tell him we better make a move.'

She looked to Simpsy, who had come off the phone. He nodded. She went out into the hall and knocked at the door of the room, opened it and went in. Mickey Ballater was still sitting in the armchair. He smiled at her. She crossed self-consciously towards him, aware of the movement of her own body.

'Mickey,' she said. 'The boys think you should go now.'

He put his hand up her skirt and she gasped. He left it there, gripping her. She didn't move.

'Ah think up there's still a kennel for you, Sandra. Ah know a couple of ways tae let the animal out. You phone that number Ah gave you. When Ah get down.'

She nodded. He released her.

'Tell Simpsy to bring the car to Skirving Street. The rest of us are walkin' round tae Dow's.'

As she went back out, he stood up and flexed, testing his side. It would do. He felt for the knife they'd got him, practised taking it out. He replaced it and smiled to think that the only other thing beside it in his pocket was his banker's card, like a repeating egg being endlessly hatched out into money by its mother. He went through and told Malkie to carry his case.

It had stopped raining. The dark wetness of the street was like a whetstone for his memory, sharpening his sense of himself. Out of such moments of windy bleakness his hardness had been honed, a defiant sense of style that gave fear a dramatic form. He felt now he had been right not to settle for a hired car out of here. He didn't drive, and being chauffeured away would have been too much of a come-down, as if he couldn't look after himself. He could. He would leave here as he had lived here, on his own terms.

"Samuel Dow's" reinforced his mood, bringing back the feeling he had had so often as a boy learning to drink in Glasgow pubs, of taking part in your own western. The big bar was busy. Mickey enjoyed standing there knowing he was the man, buying drinks for awe-struck attendants and unafraid of anybody. But he was checking it just the same.

It didn't take him long to notice a face he knew. He was sure the man had seen him because the impression that he hadn't was being given off too strongly. The lifting of a pint didn't need so much concentration. He was reading the beer as he drank it. It was Macey. With him was the one who had got the beer shampoo from Panda

Paterson. Mickey sent Tich to tell Macey he wanted to see him.

Macey came across reluctantly.

'Mickey,' he said, nodding. 'How's it goin'?'

'What time is it?' Mickey asked.

Puzzled, Macey looked at his wrist and told him. Mickey consulted his own watch.

'Some of his information's accurate anyway,' Mickey said to the others.

They were laughing.

'Look, Mickey. Ah told you as soon as Ah knew. Ah canny help it if he's topped himself. Ye know?'

'What you doing here?'

'Ah have a drink here about once a week. Wi' ma wee mate. Sammy.'

'Oh aye. Sammy. That's the one that wears the McEwan's brylcreem.'

He described the incident in "The Crib" briefly to the others. They all looked across at Sammy, whipping him with their laughter. Sammy nailed his eyes to the bar in front of him, his hand too shaky to risk lifting his drink. Macey was fidgeting as if he wanted to get away, but he made no move.

'What about yer train, Mickey?' Simpsy asked.

'It's a five-minute job in the car tae get there, isn't it?' Mickey said.

'Ah'll go across an' get it started,' Simpsy said. 'It sometimes takes the huff.'

He went out.

'Mickey.' Macey seemed poised between the desire to ingratiate himself and the fear of offending. 'You gettin' a train at Central?'

'Why?'

'Mickey. Don't tell them Ah told ye. But they're after you. They're out lookin'.'

'Who are?'

'Baith Cam Colvin an' John Rhodes.'

A taxi-driver had come into the bar. He was shouting that

there was a taxi for Mr Olliphant. He crushed past them to consult with one of the barmen.

'Ah thought they might be,' Mickey said.

'Ah know there's some o' them at Central an' some at the airport.'

Mickey was thoughtful.

'Jesus, Mickey,' Malkie said.

'This is a bloody liberty,' the taxi-driver was saying. 'He definitely said Sammy Dow's.'

'This isny the only Sammy Dow's,' the barman said. 'Maybe the one at Queen Street Station.'

'Two minutes from a taxi-rank?' the driver said. 'Why would they phone a taxi from there? Give us a break.'

'But they're not everywhere,' Mickey said and went across to the taxi-driver.

The others watched him in discussion with the driver. The driver didn't seem keen. But he accepted some notes and was pacified. He came over and picked up Mickey's case.

'Always do the unexpected,' Mickey said and winked at Malkie.

He was already on his way out when Macey spoke.

'Be seein' you, Mickey,' he said.

'Aye.' Mickey didn't look back. 'If you've got the Jodrell Bank telescope, ye might.'

The driver put Mickey's case in the luggage compartment and Mickey got in the back. Before they could pull away, Simpsy had run across to them and tried to open the offside door of the cab. It wouldn't open.

'That door's buggered, pal,' the driver said.

Simpsy contented himself with waving and mouthing something and Mickey didn't bother to wave back.

'Edinburgh road,' the driver said through the opened glass panel. 'We better take the Kingston Bridge.'

In the back, Mickey was taking an unemotional farewell of Glasgow as they came off the sliproad and headed up to the Kingston Bridge. The lights of the city around him evoked no nostalgia. He was neutrally picking out areas that

249

he knew when the driver braked suddenly. A car, which had overtaken them, was pulled up at the parapet of the Bridge, hazard lights flashing.

'The mug canny stop there,' the driver said.

'Neither can we,' Mickey said. 'Shift!'

'Ah'll just see whit the problem is,' the driver was saying and jumped out.

In that moment Mickey knew. In the pretence of the taxi-driver the whole treachery crystallised. His own past violence was like a prompter in his head. His life might have been a rehearsal for this moment, he saw it so clearly, how the other car would pull up behind them. When it did, he tried to open the offside door of the cab to give himself space. It wouldn't budge. In here he had no chance.

He kicked open the other door and dived out, pulling out the knife as he emerged. The open door was less a shield than a weapon against him. He shut it with his body, backing against it.

In the whipping wind above the bleak lights of the city he found the small space he was left with. The cars were parked tight, the taxi further out into the motorway than the others. To his right, Cam Colvin was waiting with two others. To the left there was John Rhodes with one hander.

Mickey dived to his left. He feinted at Rhodes' companion and, as the man moved back, swung at Rhodes who had started to come in. He struck Rhodes' left arm, but with his right hand Rhodes caught the back of Mickey's head and rammed his face against the concrete of the parapet. Mickey tried to struggle through the blood but already knew himself beaten. In an instant his long-nurtured sense of himself dissipated like a dream.

Knowing himself about to die and, fighting against the nausea of unconsciousness, his thoughts weren't of regret or fears for family but of the bitter images of his failure to be harder, of Macey looking innocent, the taxi-driver jumping out, Simpsy mouthing through the glass of the window,

'Cheerio, Big Man.' He had a flash of Cam's face, cold as a talking statue, saying, 'You didn't take this place serious enough,' before he was hoisted on to the parapet and fell.

The sound of the body striking ground was so faint as to seem imagined. The banker's card, fallen from his pocket when he pulled the knife, spun in the exhausts of the leaving cars like a plastic leaf.

39

It was half-past one in the morning and it was raining. Gus and Laidlaw were standing near the end of the queue for taxis outside Central Station. It seemed a suitable ending to an evening that had turned into a belated wake for Tony Veitch.

They had improvised their way from pub to pub, disgorging opinions, feelings, odd confessions as they went. In "The Wee Mann's" Laidlaw had worked out that the answer to one of Tony's riddles was the pyramids. In "The Virginian" Gus had explained that the answer to the other was Tony himself. In "Charlie Parker's", chosen by Gus in the mood of a belligerent fifth-columnist, Laidlaw claimed to see the point of the riddles.

'Eats an egg and tastes feathers,' he said. 'Is everybody else's pupil,' he said. 'The bones of the many housing the bones of the few,' he said. 'Individual sensitivity,' he said, 'and the need for ordinary lives to be seen as the most important things in society. Maybe that's what the papers were trying to say. Maybe the papers are what we should be trying to live with our lives.'

In the "Corn Exchange" Gus cried a little, quietly, and Laidlaw struggled not to join him. They had attacked the city as if they meant to drink it dry, finishing up in "Ad Lib" after one in the morning, toying with hamburgers and slaughtering the house red. Now in that complicated drunken way, they had worked out that Gus was going to take a taxi to his flat, where Marie presumably thought he had emigrated, and Laidlaw would share it with him as far as the Burleigh Hotel.

'Well,' Gus said, wrapping the thought round him like

the coat neither of them had. 'Not be long now. There's no place like home.'

'That's right,' Laidlaw said. 'Not even home.'

He didn't bother explaining his cryptic wisdom.

He couldn't have faced articulating the irony against which his marriage had finally foundered, how Gina had kept the envelope on which he had written the phone-number for her, containing his address, had looked up his number and phoned the house several times, asking for him. Ena's misunderstanding was nevertheless an accurate measurement of what had happened to them and they both knew it. They had agreed he had better move out. The thought of the possible effects on the children was like a future of endless guilt. The memory of the family he had come from made him feel he had betrayed his own past. The decision proliferated into a warren of problems in his mind. Tonight had been like an unsuccessful attempt to postpone them.

But bleak as his moment was, the city wouldn't leave him alone. Looking around him, he felt that maybe this was as near to home as he was going to get, the streets of this place. The queue was about the size of a small football crowd and in the smirring rain it should have been a formula for misery. But the place was jumping joyously.

A small man was passing along the line, playing a mouth-organ and collecting money. He appeared to have found the instrument because he didn't once deviate into a tune. He just made watery clusters of sound. When somebody asked for a request, he said, 'Away tae hell. Ah don't play tunes.'

Reaching into his pocket to reward impertinence, Laidlaw took out a handful of coins, selected a couple and remarked philosophically to Gus, 'Notice that, when you're on the batter? Finish up with pockets like a street-bookie. See, you always buy with notes. Coins are beneath you. You become a whisky-millionaire.'

The man was earning his money. His jaunty noise was the drunken pulse of the group. People were laughing and shouting, vivid rain-streaked faces and loud voices, a queue

253

by Hogarth. A group of women had emerged to dance like maenads around the small man. The whole line was a weird, dynamic unity, like a centipede on LSD.

A small, old woman standing behind Laidlaw tapped him on the shoulder. He turned round.

'Son,' she said. 'This is the best queue I've ever been in in my life.'

Laidlaw was laughing and he elaborately gestured her out of the queue to dance. Watching them jig sedately up and down the pavement, Gus drunkenly thought he was seeing something marvellous, a spirit so determined to enjoy life that it had an aesthetic of queues.